"Is the outlaw the reason you haven't tried to kiss me?"

Bethany asked. "Have you decided that since I enjoyed his kisses, I might not enjoy yours, as well?"

Kane's smile was quick. "Are you asking to be kissed, Bethany?"

She had such a hunger to be kissed by him. A hunger laced with frustration. She hoped, the moment his lips met hers, that she would be able to forget the passion that had been uncovered by the highwayman. She wanted, needed, to put that part of her life behind her, and feel the same desperate desire for this man.

"Kiss me, Kane." She lifted her face to him. "Or are you afraid?"

"You're a witch, you know. A witch who knows me well enough to realize that I can never resist a challenge." His fingers tightened, and he drew her fractionally closer.

"I was hoping as much."

Dear Reader,

With the passing of the true millennium, Harlequin Historicals is putting on a fresh face! We hope you enjoyed our special inside front cover art from recent months. We plan to bring this wonderful "extra" to you every month! You may also have noticed our new branding—a maroon stripe that runs along the right side of the front cover. Hopefully, this will help you find our books more easily in the crowded marketplace. And thanks to those of you who participated in our reader survey. We truly appreciate the feedback you provided, which enables us to bring you more of the stories and authors that you like!

We have four terrific books for you this month. The talented Carolyn Davidson returns with a new Western, *Maggie's Beau,* a tender tale of love between experienced rancher Beau Jackson—whom you might recognize from *The Wedding Promise*—and the young woman he finds hiding in his barn. Catherine Archer brings us her third medieval SEASONS' BRIDES story, *Summer's Bride,* an engaging romance about two willful nobles who finally succumb to a love they've long denied.

The Sea Nymph by bestselling author Ruth Langan marks the second book in the SIRENS OF THE SEA series. Here, a proper English lady, who is secretly a privateer, falls in love with a highwayman—only to learn he is really an earl *and* the richest man in Cornwall! And don't miss *Bride on the Run,* an awesome new Western by Elizabeth Lane. True to the title, a woman fleeing from crooked lawmen becomes the mail-order bride of a sexy widower with two kids.

Enjoy! And come back again next month for four more choices of the best in historical romance.

Sincerely,

Tracy Farrell
Senior Editor

Ruth Langan

The Sea Nymph

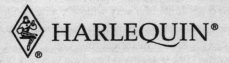

HARLEQUIN®

TORONTO • NEW YORK • LONDON
AMSTERDAM • PARIS • SYDNEY • HAMBURG
STOCKHOLM • ATHENS • TOKYO • MILAN • MADRID
PRAGUE • WARSAW • BUDAPEST • AUCKLAND

ISBN 0-373-29145-0

THE SEA NYMPH

Copyright © 2001 by Ruth Ryan Langan

Please address questions and book requests to:
Harlequin Reader Service
U.S.: 3010 Walden Ave., P.O. Box 1325, Buffalo, NY 14269
Canadian: P.O. Box 609, Fort Erie, Ont. L2A 5X3

To my sisters, Pat and Marg,
Though they neither sail nor swashbuckle
I'd want them on my side in a battle.

And of course to Tom, my dragonslayer

Prologue

Cornwall, 1657

"Winnie. Winnie." Three of the four Lambert children came racing up the sloping lawns of their home MaryCastle, shouting for their prissy nursemaid, Miss Winifred Mellon.

"What is it?" Winnie looked up from her tea. It was the first break she'd had since early that morning, when the children had awakened the entire household with a raucous sword fight, using wooden swords they'd carved themselves.

"Bethany's taken a fall." James, the eldest, was a rough-and-tumble lad. The only trouble was his three younger sisters thought of themselves as his equals. They refused to learn needlework, or flower arranging, or any of the things young ladies needed, preferring to engage in duels with wooden weapons, and sailing the bay in their little skiff.

"Where was she climbing this time?" Winnie abandoned her tea and started after the children.

"The cliffs."

"Oh, sweet heaven." She lifted her skirts and started running. By the time she reached the cliffs, she could see, far below, the flutter of flame-colored hair. It was the only movement of that still, small figure.

"Oh, what are we to do?" She wrung her hands and paced back and forth before turning to nine-year-old Ambrosia. "Run as fast as you can and fetch Newton Findlay."

"Aye, Winnie." The girl ran off, leaving the nursemaid to pace and fret until the old sailor hobbled up.

Newton had lost a leg to a shark, ending his days aboard their father's ship, the *Undaunted*. Now he worked for the Lambert family, doing odd jobs, and generally annoying their housekeeper, Mistress Coffey.

"Look, Newt." Winnie pointed at the little figure far below. "It's Bethany."

"Aye. I can see." He squinted against the sun, before tying a rope to a nearby tree. Then he began the perilous climb down the cliffs, made all the more dangerous with the wooden peg he used as a leg.

When he reached the bottom he bent over the still figure, then looked up and shouted, "She's alive. Just had the wind knocked out of her."

"Oh, praise heaven." Poor Miss Mellon dropped to the ground and began weeping, while the children danced around her, hooting with joy.

It seemed an hour or more before the child got to her feet and began climbing the rope hand over hand, with old Newt following behind her.

"Winnie." As she reached the top, Bethany glanced at her nursemaid. "Are you crying?"

"Crying?" The woman pressed a lace handkerchief to her eyes. "Nay, but you soon will be. Tell me how you happened to fall."

"I wanted to fly."

"Fly?" The nursemaid glanced at the old sailor, who simply rolled his eyes.

"I was watching the seabirds wheeling and diving among the cliffs, and I decided to see if I could join them."

"Join them." Now that her fear had vanished, it was replaced by a much stronger emotion. Miss Winifred Mellon rarely grew angry. But when she did, two bright pink spots appeared on her pale cheeks. And little sparks flashed in those normally placid blue eyes.

"This time you have gone too far, Bethany. You will march to your room. And you will write down all the reasons why humans cannot fly. And when you are finished, you will present it to me, and I will tell you what further punishment you may expect."

"I'm to be punished for trying to fly?"

"Nay. For that wild streak, young lady. Unless it is curbed in your youth, it could become a serious impediment to your development as a proper young woman."

Bethany glanced at Newton, but he showed absolutely no emotion as he coiled the rope around his arm and sauntered away.

She ran after him, her voice high-pitched with childish outrage. "It isn't fair, Newt. I didn't do anything wrong, did I?"

The old man chose his words carefully. "Seems to me Miss Mellon has a point. Ye don't have wings, lass."

"Nay. But I could fashion wings from...tree branches," she said, glancing up at a lovely tree beside the house.

"Ye could. And ye'd likely fall again. Ye must be hurting a bit. That was a nasty fall."

''I do hurt. But Papa says when we get hurt, we simply pick ourselves up and try again.''

''Aye. But the body's a fragile thing, lass. It weren't meant to be bounced off rocks from high cliffs. Ye could have been killed.''

''Then I'd be in heaven with Mama. Papa says heaven's a wonderful place to be.''

''Aye. So I've heard. But not too many of us are eager to get there.''

''Why is that, Newt?''

He grinned. ''Maybe some of us have found our heaven here on earth. Now, lass.'' He hung the rope on a hook in the shed, then closed the door. ''Ye're putting off yer punishment. If ye want to be grown-up like yer papa, go upstairs and do what Miss Mellon said.''

''And then what?''

He winked. ''Tell her ye won't try to fly again.''

''But I will, Newt.''

He sighed. ''Go on now, lass. Take yer punishment like a…'' He'd almost said a man. For the truth was, these girl-children were unlike any females he'd ever known. Wild and free, they were, and every bit as tough as their brother, James.

They were a handful.

And he doted on them all.

Chapter One

The Atlantic—Off the coast of Cornwall, 1665

"A ship with no flag dead ahead." Bethany Lambert, high above the rigging of her family's ship, the *Undaunted,* shouted to the crew below. "I recognize it. It's the pirate ship, the *Shark.* Gaining fast on a small vessel flying English colors."

Every sailor aboard the *Undaunted* knew what the fate of the smaller boat would be. Of late, pirates had begun attacking small pleasure craft, usually owned by titled gentlemen, in the hope of lining their pockets with gold and jewelry, before sinking the craft and sending its unfortunate occupants to a watery grave.

The *Undaunted* was pledged to the safety of all English vessels. After the deaths of their father and brother, Bethany and her sisters had boldly vowed to carry on their father's legacy as privateers in the employ of King Charles II of England.

At her shouted warning, Bethany's grandfather, Geoffrey Lambert, called for more sails, and soon was able to gain enough speed to place their vessel between the pirate ship and the smaller boat. While the small craft retreated to safety, the sailors aboard the *Undaunted* engaged the pirates in a fierce battle.

"Brace yourself, lass," Geoffrey shouted as the first cannonball slammed into the bow of the *Undaunted*, sending up a shower of flame and a cloud of billowing black smoke.

Within minutes the pirates came streaking across the rail, swords and knives flashing in the sunlight, their voices screeching obscenities guaranteed to put fear in the hearts of all who faced them.

"Behind you, Grandpapa." Bethany calmly aimed her pistol, and before her grandfather could turn and lift his sword, the man who had been about to attack him fell to the deck, mortally wounded.

"Newt." She shouted a warning at the old sailor. It was he, along with their grandfather, who had taught Bethany and her sisters all that they knew of the sea.

The old sailor turned in time to save himself from an attack by a pirate, then waved his sword. "I thank ye, lass."

There was no time to respond as Bethany found herself surrounded by three menacing pirates. She stopped the first with her pistol, then, unable to reload, was forced to use her sword and knife on the other two.

"Fine fighting, lass." Her grandfather stepped up beside her. The two stood back to back and battled several more pirates to the railing, where they fell to the foaming sea below.

In the hours that followed, the decks of both ships ran red with blood. And when it was finally over, the pirates had been conquered. Though none of the crew of the *Undaunted* sustained any serious wounds, the same couldn't be said for their ship. She'd taken a cannonball to the prow, causing water to seep into the hold. The *Undaunted* was listing badly, and the wood of the deck was badly charred. But like a noble warrior, she limped, slowly and painfully toward the safety of shore. As she sailed away, the crew aboard the small craft cheered and remained where they were until the pirate ship sank beneath the waves.

In his private cabin a man standing by the porthole lowered his spyglass. The battle alone would have been enough to hold him spellbound. But when he'd noted that one of the *Undaunted*'s sailors was actually female, he'd been unable to believe his eyes. She'd been dressed like all the others. Tight breeches tucked into tall boots. A colorful shirt with billowing sleeves. A scarf tightly wound around the head, to hide her hair. What had been impossible to hide was the lush body beneath the sailor's garb.

During the course of battle her scarf had been dislodged, revealing a cloud of fiery curls. It was a potent, unforgettable combination. A lush body and flaming tresses.

She'd wielded her pistol like a man. And like the others, had leapt into the thick of battle without hesitation. She had been, quite simply, magnificent to watch.

One of his crew rapped sharply on the cabin door. At once the big dog lying at its master's feet issued a warning growl.

From outside came the call, ''We're coming into Land's End, your lordship.''

''Aye.'' He put a hand on the dog's head as a signal that there was no threat. ''What is the name of the ship that came to our rescue?''

''I know not, your lordship. Shall I inquire at port?''

''Nay.'' It would be useless to ask. It was whispered

that there were several ships masquerading as cargo ships, while keeping the waters safe for English vessels. Their identities were known only to the king. They guarded their privacy as fiercely as they fought their enemies. But he had his own methods of learning the name of the ship.

As he prepared to go ashore, the titled gentleman cast a last glance at the ship that had saved him and his men, before it rounded a finger of land and disappeared from view. What he wouldn't give to have the freedom to join them in their quest to rid the sea of villains.

Aye. And what he wouldn't give to meet the female who lived so freely and had battled so fiercely.

"Rocks and shallows on the port side." Though the voice from high above the rigging was decidedly feminine, the figure that came shimmying down toward the deck was dressed like any other sailor.

"Aye, Bethany. I see them. Praise heaven we're almost home." Geoffrey Lambert kept a steady hand on the wheel while the crew began preparing to drop anchor.

The run from the little town of Port Hellick to Land's End should have taken less than half a day. But that was before they'd encountered the pirates.

"Would you like me to take the wheel, Grandpapa?"

"Aye." He was grateful for his granddaughter's help. The lass, like her sisters Ambrosia and Darcy, was an excellent sailor. She knew these waters around the coast of Cornwall better than most men.

"Look, Grandpapa. There's Darcy. And Winnie and Mistress Coffey are with her." She waved to her younger sister, and the old nursemaid and housekeeper standing on the widow's walk of a house that stood alone on a spit of land, facing the Atlantic. Her father, Captain John

Lambert, had named it MaryCastle, in honor of their mother. Many in Land's End referred to it as Lambert's Folly, and predicted that any house built that close to the sea would eventually be swallowed up by it. But it continued to stand all these years like a fortress, buffeted by wind and waves.

When the ship entered the protective cove, the crew worked quickly, securing the lines, and running the little skiff back and forth until all the crew had been deposited on shore.

"Our cargo's ruined, Grandpapa." Bethany climbed the ladder from the flooded hold. "There'll be no payment for soggy tea and spices."

"Aye, lass. And if that's not enough, we'll need to start repairs at once." Geoffrey Lambert stared around at the damage. "Though I know not how we'll pay for it."

Looking weary and defeated, he descended the rope ladder to the waiting skiff.

"I'll find a way." Bethany saw his shoulders sag, and knew that they were perilously close to losing everything they'd worked for. Without a ship, they had no way to keep up their home and the aging servants who depended on them. But without payment for this latest cargo, they had no way to pay for needed repairs to the *Undaunted.*

If Ambrosia and her new husband, Riordan Spencer, were here, it wouldn't be a problem. Riordan was a wealthy man who would be only too happy to loan them the money. But he and his bride were aboard his ship, the *Warrior,* and wouldn't return for a month or more.

Bethany knew that the burden must be borne on her slender shoulders.

She gave a last look around, then followed her grandfather down the rope ladder to the waiting skiff.

By the time they reached the shore, the crew, under

old Newton's direction, was already climbing aboard wagons that would haul them to town. Also waiting on shore was Bethany's younger sister Darcy, who couldn't help but notice the weariness etched on their faces. "From the looks of the *Undaunted,* I'd say you had a bit of a fight on your hands."

"Aye."

"Then you must tell me everything."

"I will. But not until you've given me a chance to catch my breath. Where are Winnie and Mistress Coffey?"

"Waiting in the parlor. You'd best hurry. They've been pacing for hours."

"Aye." Bethany caught her sister's hand and looped her arm with her grandfather's. "Come on, Grandpapa. The others are waiting."

Though she had fought like a man, and worked like a seaman, she was now just a young woman. A woman eager to share the news of their sea battle with the rest of their family.

"Oh, look at you." Winifred Mellon glanced up as they entered. Though her labors as nursemaid to the three sisters had long ago ended, they had insisted that she remain with them when they had discovered that she had no place to go. "You're wounded, Bethany."

"Just a scratch, Winnie." Bethany touched a hand to her arm and seemed surprised to see blood staining her sleeve.

Geoffrey Lambert paused in the doorway. "If it hadn't been for Bethany's skill with a pistol, I wouldn't be here."

The young woman blushed. "I did no more than the others, Grandpapa."

"You think not?" The old man shook his head. "Praise heaven for your quick thinking, lass."

Their nursemaid sat on the edge of her chair. "You must tell us everything."

"Aye." Mistress Coffey passed around goblets of ale and tea before settling herself on a chaise before the fire. Like Winnie, she had been with the family for more than twenty years. A widow, she wore only black, and walked straight and tall, refusing to bend with age. But more and more the burden of running the household was falling to the three sisters. "We desire every little detail. Was it as exciting as our...last adventure?"

Bethany exchanged a smile with her sister. What had started out as a promise to carry on their father's legacy, had become a family adventure, shared not only by their grandfather and old Newt, but these two sweet old women, as well. The adventure had transformed all of them, adding confidence to the sisters, and restoring a taste of youth and vitality to these old people. It was another strand in the threads that bound them together.

"It wasn't nearly as dangerous as the one we all shared, Mistress Coffey. In fact, it was most uneventful until we spotted a rogue ship about to attack a gentleman's vessel. We merely engaged the pirates, and soon dispatched them to a watery grave."

"And the gentleman's ship?" Winnie looked from one to the other. "Do you know it?"

Bethany shook her head. "I've not seen it in these waters before. But it matters not. It is now safely in port, I wager." She drained her tea and set the cup aside.

As she headed toward the door the housekeeper called, "Where do you think you're going?"

"To my room. To enjoy a hot bath, a leisurely dinner,

and then to my bed, where I'd like to stay for the next week.''

"Not tonight, young lady." The old housekeeper exchanged a smile with their nurse. "Did you not agree that your duties aboard ship would not interfere with your duties here at home?"

"Aye." Bethany glanced toward her sister, but Darcy evaded her look.

"There's a Bible reading tonight at the vicarage. With Ambrosia off on her honeymoon, that leaves only you and Darcy."

"Why can't Darcy attend in my place?"

"Because she already agreed to fill my place with Miss Mellon at the ladies' sewing circle."

The two sisters rolled their eyes. Two more hated events they couldn't imagine than the Bible reading and the ladies' sewing circle.

"I'll expect you to attend, Bethany," Mistress Coffey said firmly. "And I, of course, will go along as your chaperon."

Bethany turned to her grandfather with a look of horror. "Grandpapa, I return from an adventure at sea, and I'm expected to attend a Bible reading?"

"Feeding?" The old man grinned. "Of course we'll be feeding you, lass."

"Reading, Grandpapa. A Bible reading." She nearly stomped her foot, knowing he only heard what he chose to hear. Many years earlier a cannon had misfired aboard deck of the *Undaunted,* leaving him stone deaf. The accident had forced him to give up his life at sea. But through the years they all believed that his hearing had gradually returned. Still, he used the infirmity to his advantage, whenever he chose. "It isn't fair."

"Fair?" The old man nodded vigorously. "Aye.

There'll soon be a fair in the village. We'll go together, lass. And bring Newt along. He does love the village fair.''

Seeing that Newton had just returned from the village, she turned to him, hoping he would take her side.

But he merely winked. "Ye must be pleased to see that nothin's changed at home while ye were gone, lass.''

"Aye.'' She gave him a mournful look before turning away and heading toward her room. "Nothing at all.''

"Bethany, have you heard?'' Edwina Cannon, the village gossip, caught Bethany Lambert's arm as they headed toward the waiting carriage. The two had just emerged from the vicarage where they had spent the past hour hearing the handsome young deacon, Ian Welland, reading from the Book of Psalms.

Beside them, Mistress Coffey looked pleased with herself. Bethany understood why. For some strange reason, Mistress Coffey had decided that one of the Lambert sisters ought to consider marrying a man of the cloth. And since Ambrosia had already wed her dashing sea captain, Riordan Spencer, and Darcy was soft on a sailor named Gray Barton, that left only Bethany. Though many young ladies in the village of Land's End sighed at the look of him, and hung on his every word from the pulpit, he was simply too bland for Bethany's taste.

As the housekeeper and Edwina's mother, Mistress Cannon, climbed into the carriage behind them, Bethany turned to Edwina. "Have I heard what?''

"The earl of Alsmeeth has completed his tour of Cornwall and has settled into his family's estate.''

Bethany sighed. "I was hoping for something a bit more exciting. A pirate ship spotted near shore, perhaps. Or another sighting of the infamous highwayman calling himself the Lord of the Night.'' All of Cornwall had been speculating on his identity. ''I thought the old earl was dead.''

''Not the old earl, you silly goose. His son Kane.'' Edwina sat back, with that hungry, self-satisfied look she always got when she had a man in her sights. ''No one has yet seen him, but I just know he'll be sinfully handsome.''

''What is known is that he's reclusive and arrogant.'' Mistress Coffey took the seat across from the two young women. ''One of his housemaids told one of our maids that he spoke not a word when he arrived. The entire household staff, as well as his tenant farmers and their families, had assembled to welcome him. Instead of greeting them, he simply strode inside and told his houseman to order them back to work.''

''Oh, Mistress Coffey.'' Edwina pursed her lips. ''As one of the wealthiest men in England, that's his right.''

''His right?'' Annoyed at Edwina's reasoning, Bethany glared at her. ''Papa used to call it the curse of the rich. Instead of feeling obligated to care for those less fortunate, they think the world should bow to their wishes.''

''And who can blame them?'' Edwina sighed. ''I hope someday to be as rich as a queen. And I will expect everyone to bow to me.''

''Now there's a noble goal.'' Bethany gritted her teeth at the knowledge that she would have to share a ride home with this frivolous young woman. ''I wonder why the earl of Alsmeeth returned to Cornwall if he doesn't wish to be civil?''

''Because he's hiding out here. He's no longer welcome in London circles.'' Edwina gave a mysterious smile.

''Why would a man of great wealth have to hide?''

"Perhaps he has gambling debts," Mistress Coffey muttered.

"Nay. It's much worse than gambling." Edwina's voice lowered conspiratorially. "His father was brutally murdered, and the son was sent to Fleet Prison for the crime."

The others gasped and covered their mouths.

"Now he's been set free, but no one else has been charged. Think about it. Who stood to gain the most from the old man's death?"

"Are you saying he'd kill his own father for wealth?"

"Can you think of a better motive? But that isn't all," Edwina said with a shudder. "It's said his bride killed herself on their wedding night." She could see that she had their undivided attention now. "There are those who speculate on what sort of brute would cause a beautiful titled Englishwoman to plunge a dagger into her heart rather than submit to her husband."

Mistress Coffey and Mistress Cannon exchanged horrified looks.

"Who told you this?" Bethany demanded.

"People who have friends in London." Edwina's voice lowered to a whisper.

"In other words," Bethany took no pains to mask her impatience with Edwina Cannon. "You don't know that a word of what you've just told me is true."

Edwina's face paled. Leave it to Bethany Lambert to question everything.

Now she crossed her arms over her chest and pouted. "Very well, Bethany. Reject my word if you will. There are dozens more who will tell you the same. But you have to admit the earl of Alsmeeth is an intriguing figure."

"Not nearly as intriguing as the Lord of the Night."

At the mention of the notorious highwayman, Edwina shivered. "Lord of the Night indeed. He's a disgusting thief. A cruel, violent monster. It's said he targets wealthy men and violates their women." She tied the ribbons of her bonnet a little tighter as the team trotted smartly, hauling the carriage through a stand of trees at a fast clip. "I still say having a nobleman in our midst should make for an enjoyable summer. Even a nobleman as sullen and mysterious as the Earl of Alsmeeth. Admit it, Bethany. Aren't you just a little curious about him?"

Bethany shrugged. "Not in the least. And it's a good thing, since I doubt he and I will ever have the occasion to…"

Her voice trailed off as she looked over the heads of the two older woman facing her. A horse and rider materialized out of the woods and pulled alongside their carriage. No wonder he hadn't been spotted until he was completely upon them. His mount was black. He was dressed all in black. Black breeches tucked into tall black boots. A black waistcoat. Over the lower half of his face was a black scarf. Pulled low on his head was a black hat. And in his hand was a very dangerous-looking black dueling pistol which he lifted into the air.

At the sound of the single gunshot, their driver struggled to pull the frightened team to a halt. When he finally succeeded, it sent the passengers into a panic as they were tossed about like rag dolls.

The horseman pulled his mount alongside the carriage and aimed his pistol at the driver. His voice was little more than an ominous whisper. "Stay where you are, old man, and you won't be harmed. Do you understand?"

The driver nodded and kept a firm grip on the reins.

The horseman dismounted, then strode to the carriage. Edwina and her mother began weeping. Mistress Cof-

fey caught hold of Bethany's hand and was squeezing it
so tightly, it began to go numb.

"What do you want of us?" Bethany demanded.

For a moment the man merely stared at her. Her bold
question had caught him by surprise. Usually the women
were the first to collapse at the sight of a highwayman.
The men soon followed. Especially the wealthy, titled
ones, who had the most to lose. But this young beauty
showed no sign of fear. In fact, if the fire in those green
eyes was any indication, she was more angry than afraid.

His gaze swept her, from the top of her fiery head to
her sturdy, boot-tipped toes. "You will step from the carriage."

"Oh, sweet heaven." Edwina rocked from side to side
as she began moaning. "He's going to kill us all."

"Be quiet, Edwina." Bethany gritted her teeth, wishing she had her pistol. But who would have thought it
necessary on a simple journey to the vicarage? She patted
her housekeeper's shoulder, offering courage, before getting to her feet.

The highwayman held out his hand. "Allow me to
assist you."

When he tried to take her hand, she gave a huff of
anger and pointedly ignored his help as she stepped to
the ground. Then she turned. "Come along, Edwina. Mistress Cannon. Mistress Coffey."

At her urging, the other three stepped from the carriage. While the housekeeper stood beside her, Edwina
and her mother fell into each other's arms, clinging together for courage.

Bethany faced the highwayman. "Take what you came
for and let us be on our way."

"In a hurry, are you?"

"Aye. Eager to be rid of the likes of you."

''Please don't anger him.'' Edwina's voice trembled, as the tears fell harder. ''Or he'll surely kill us all, Bethany.''

''Bethany?'' Cool eyes appraised her. ''You'd best heed your friend's warning. You wouldn't want to anger me.''

''And why shouldn't I? You anger me.''

At that he threw back his head and chuckled.

Suddenly his gaze frosted over as he caught sight of the diamond-and-ruby ring on Edwina's finger. ''Hand over your valuables.''

''Oh, no.'' Edwina began to back up as tears flowed down her cheeks. ''Not my ring. It was a gift from my beloved Silas. He had once promised me all the Fenwick jewels. Had he lived, I would have been a titled lady.''

''Silas Fenwick? All the more reason.'' He reached out and slipped it from her finger. He tucked it into his pocket, then turned to her mother. ''I'll have yours, as well, madam.''

The older woman was trembling as she removed her ring.

''And the necklace and ear bobs,'' he said in that same fierce whisper.

When Mistress Cannon had given him her jewelry, he pointed his pistol at the bag dangling from her wrist. ''I'll take your gold now, if you please.''

With a whimper she handed it over and watched as he shook the contents into his palm. After slipping the gold into his pocket, he returned the bag to her trembling hands.

Then he turned to Mistress Coffey. ''Your valuables, madam.''

''I...have only this.'' Her voice nearly caught in her

throat as she unpinned the brooch that adorned the bodice of her gown.

Before she could hand it over, Bethany closed a hand over hers, stilling her movements. "Wait, Mistress Coffey." She turned to the outlaw. "This was a gift from her late husband. It's all she has. You have no right to take it from her."

"No right?" His eyes darkened as he snatched the brooch from the old woman's hand.

"Aye. No right. She's worked all her life in the service of others. No one, least of all a thief, has the right to take what little comfort she has in her old age."

For long minutes he stared at her. Then he gave a cursory glance at the brooch. "You're right. It's of little value except to its owner." He surprised all of them by handing it back.

Tears filled the old woman's eyes as her fingers closed around the treasured gift from her long-dead husband. A treasure she'd feared would be lost forever.

The highwayman turned to Bethany. "Now that you've persuaded me to return the old woman's trinket, it will be up to you to make up the difference. What will you contribute to my estate, dear lady?"

She lifted her chin. Her eyes flashed fire. "I am not your dear lady. And I have nothing of value."

"Nothing of value, you say?" He looked her up and down in such a brazen manner that all four women gasped at his meaning. "I should demand double, simply because the gods have bestowed more upon you than upon most women."

"How dare you?" With her cheeks burning Bethany started to turn away.

He caught her arm. A mistake, he realized. The mere touch of her had him burning. But it was too late. Without thinking of the consequences, he muttered, "Very well. If you won't offer, I shall simply have to take. I am, after all, an accomplished thief."

Before she could stop him, he cupped a hand to the back of her head and drew her close. With a quick tug he lowered his scarf and covered her mouth with his.

At his boldness, the other women began weeping in absolute terror of what was to come. It would seem the horrible tales they'd heard of this man's cruelty toward women was true. While Mistress Coffey watched in horror, both Edwina and her mother dropped to the ground in a dead faint.

For Bethany, it was the most shocking encounter of her young life. In that instant, time seemed to stop. She had been kissed before. But never like this. Always it had been a hurried kiss attempted by an awestruck village youth. But this was no youth. This was a man. A man who kissed her with a thoroughness that left her dazed and breathless. His lips were full and sensuous, and moved over hers with slow, deliberate skill. When she tried to pull back, his fingers tightened at her scalp, sending strange waves of fire and ice spiraling through her veins. As he lingered over the kiss, she felt her entire body growing hot. So hot that her blood seemed to flow like molten lava. Her flesh felt on fire. She feared, if he didn't soon stop, her bones would melt.

He lifted his head and she dragged precious air into her lungs.

"I'll consider that more than enough payment, my lady." With a smile, he lifted his scarf in place and took a step back, breaking contact.

For a moment Bethany had to struggle to keep her balance. It felt as if the earth beneath her feet were still moving, shifting, tilting. Her head was spinning wildly.

She would die before she'd let this rogue see what effect his kiss had on her. "You are—" her voice trembled, and she stiffened her spine, determined to get through this without faltering "—the vilest of all creatures. How dare you prey on helpless women?" She couldn't control herself. She swung her hand, determined to slap that arrogant face.

"Helpless?" With seemingly little effort his fingers closed around her wrist, stopping her movement. He threw back his head and laughed. Then his voice returned to that intriguing whisper. "I have an idea that if you were given a weapon other than those dangerous eyes of yours, my lady, I would be lying dead in the road by now."

"Aye." She hated the fact that she was unable to fight his strength. All she could do was endure another wave of heat as those strong fingers pressed against her flesh. "It's no more than you deserve."

"In the end, my lady, we all get what we deserve."

"Then you shall surely burn in the fires of hell for all eternity."

"Of that I have no doubt." He released her and took a step back, bowing grandly. "I thank you all for sharing your...treasures with the Lord of the Night. And now, I fear, I must leave your fascinating company." He pulled himself into the saddle and nudged his horse into a trot. In the blink of an eye horse and rider blended into the forest.

Edwina and her mother fell into a fit of weeping and trembling. It took all of Bethany's strength to coax them to stand and return to the carriage. As soon as the four were settled inside, the driver took off with all haste.

As they crested a hill, the horseman watched their progress through narrowed eyes. Then he let loose with a string of vicious oaths, calling himself every vile name he could think of. What in the world had happened, to make him violate his principles, such as they were? He'd never before taken such liberties with any of his victims. In truth, he'd never even been tempted. But there was just something about that arrogant, fiery female that had him breaking every rule he'd ever set for himself. Maybe it was that cloud of hair, spilling in rich red waves down her back, almost to her waist. Or perhaps it was the lush young body which even the simple frock couldn't disguise. But most of all it was the look of defiance in those eyes. Eyes in which a man would gladly drown.

What a magnificent creature. All fire and flash and fury. Now there was a woman who would challenge a man.

He leaned down to run a hand over his horse's neck, and realized that he was still trembling slightly. He'd never had a woman affect him like this before. He was going to have to see her again. If only to satisfy his curiosity.

Bethany. Her name was Bethany. It was a beginning.

He wheeled his mount, and disappeared into the gathering darkness.

Chapter Two

"Oh, it was so dreadful. So horrible."

The minute they stepped into MaryCastle, Mistress Coffey dissolved into a puddle of tears and was quickly surrounded by the rest of the family.

"What is it, Mistress Coffey?" Winnie and Darcy clutched her hands and stared from her to Bethany, with matching looks of concern.

"We were—" the old woman's lips quivered, and she drew in a shuddering breath "—attacked by that highwayman."

"The Lord of the Night?" Darcy drew the old housekeeper into the circle of her arms to offer comfort. "Did he harm you?"

"Nay. Not me. But he—" she began weeping again, and Darcy had to hold her at arm's length and nearly shake her before she finished "—violated our poor Bethany."

"Nay! I'll murder the bastard." Geoffrey Lambert, just coming down the stairs, stopped dead in his tracks and clutched the banister. And though he'd been a good distance away, it was clear he'd heard every word.

At once their old nurse hurried forward and caught his

arm, fearing he might fall. "You mustn't alarm yourself, Geoffrey. You know it isn't good for..."

"Not now, Winnie." He shook off her hand and stared at his beloved granddaughter. "This monster violated you, Bethany?"

"Mistress Coffey is hysterical. She doesn't mean what she's saying. He...merely kissed me, Grandpapa."

"He kissed you? That's all?"

"Aye, Grandpapa."

The old man waited until his thundering heartbeat began to slow. Then he descended the rest of the stairs and wrapped his arms around her. "But you're all right, lass? Truly all right?"

"Aye, Grandpapa." Bethany leaned into him for a moment, loving the familiar smells of sea and salt and tobacco that had always been a part of her life. Then she pushed herself free and took a deep breath, preparing herself for the questions to come.

"What did he look like?" This from Darcy, who had both hands on her hips and looked as though she'd enjoy engaging this outlaw with her knife. No one in Land's End, man or woman, was better with a knife than she.

"Like any monster would," the housekeeper said quickly. "A big man. All in black he was. His face covered. All I could see were his eyes. Cruel they were. Like him. A bully. I could tell that much about him." She began to weep again, softer this time.

"You need some tea." Miss Mellon turned to Darcy. "Perhaps you'd fetch a plate of those biscuits we had with our dinner. And a pot of fruit conserve."

"Aye." The young woman exchanged a look with her sister. "Don't tell any more until I return."

Within minutes the family had gathered around the fire in the parlor. They were joined by old Newton.

"What did this highwayman steal?" Geoffrey Lambert refused the tea and helped himself to a tumbler of ale to steady his nerves.

"Edwina's ring and her mother's jewelry and gold."

"That's all?" Darcy nibbled a biscuit.

"He almost took my brooch." Mistress Coffey lay a hand over it, still unable to believe her good fortune. "But Bethany told him he had no right to it, since it was all I had left of my Ned."

"And he allowed you to keep it?" Darcy looked from her grandfather, who was listening in silence, to old Newt.

The housekeeper nodded. "He said it had no value. But I'm inclined to believe that our Bethany's appeal to his heart may have been the real reason he changed his mind."

"So." Darcy helped herself to a second biscuit. "It would seem this Lord of the Night isn't a complete monster?"

"I didn't say that." The housekeeper shook her head. "When I think how brutal he was to our Bethany..." She held a napkin to her trembling lips.

Darcy turned to her sister, who had fallen strangely silent. "And what say you, Bethany? Does this highwayman have a heart? Or is he as cruel as all his victims claim?"

Bethany shrugged. "I suppose you really ought to ask Edwina and her mother. When they weren't fainting, they were weeping uncontrollably over the loss of their valuables."

"Don't tell me they fainted again?" Darcy grinned. "Don't they realize they miss all the excitement?"

"Perhaps that's their plan," Geoffrey said dryly.

"Now about this outlaw, Bethany. Is there anything that might identify him?"

She shook her head. "As Mistress Coffey said, he was dressed all in black, and had his face covered."

"His voice?" old Newton added. "Did you recognize it?"

"He spoke in a whisper."

"His eyes?" her grandfather demanded.

"It was growing too dark to see them."

Around the room there was a collective sigh of frustration.

"At least—" Geoffrey helped himself to a second tumbler of ale, wishing he'd been there "—he had no occasion to use that pistol he's said to carry."

Bethany nodded. "He fired but a single shot. And that was to force Edwina's driver to bring the team to a halt. After that, he merely brandished it." She looked up. "Has he ever used it to kill?"

"Not that we've heard. But then, so far at least, no one's been foolhardy enough to go against his orders."

"Nobody except our Bethany." The housekeeper began to wring her hands. "When I think of the dangerous risk you took, I still can't believe it."

"He had no right to your brooch, Mistress Coffey. I couldn't let him take it. At least not without putting up a fight."

Old Newton met her grandfather's glance with a knowing look. He'd learned, since his first encounter with the Lambert women when they were no more than wee lasses, that they were incapable of yielding, no matter how dangerous the circumstances. The three Lambert sisters were absolutely fearless.

Bethany stifled a yawn and set aside her tea. "I really

must get some sleep. Then I'll have a look at the *Undaunted* on the morrow.''

''Will you be able to transport that cargo bound for the Netherlands?'' Darcy asked.

Geoffrey set aside his ale. ''There'll be no more voyages aboard the *Undaunted* until we make some repairs. We'll have to allow another ship to handle the run to the Netherlands. I've asked for a meeting with the earl of Alsmeeth on the morrow. Since he owns all the forested property here in Cornwall, we'll need his permission to harvest a few trees needed for wood.''

Bethany's interest was sparked. ''Edwina Cannon told me a little about the young earl.''

Geoffrey held up a hand. ''Spare me Edwina's comments, lass. But if the rest of you agree, I'd like to dispatch Newt to meet with the earl on the morrow.''

Bethany nodded absently. As she kissed the others good-night, she found herself thinking, not about the earl of Alsmeeth, but of another. A dark, mysterious stranger whose kiss had left her more unnerved than she cared to admit.

''What are you doing?'' Bethany looked up from the dressing table where she'd been seated, to watch as her sister stepped inside her room. Darcy closed the door, then leaned against it, staring intently at her. ''You ought to be asleep by now.''

''And so should you.'' Darcy stood very still. ''But there you are, studying your reflection in the looking glass.''

''I was not—''

''Don't deny it.'' Darcy skipped closer and caught her sister's hand. ''Tell me what really happened tonight, Bethany. Please.''

She looked at her younger sister, then gave a sigh. "Nothing happened. The Lord of the Night kissed me. Then he pulled himself onto his horse and disappeared into the darkness."

"What was the kiss like?" Darcy studied her from beneath her fringe of lashes.

Bethany gave a careless shrug. "It was merely a kiss."

Sensing otherwise, Darcy decided to press. "Did he seem nervous?"

Bethany shook her head, sending red curls tumbling. "As though he had all the time in the world."

"Did you sense anger in the kiss?"

"Anger?" Bethany sank down on the chaise. "Nay. It wasn't anger so much as…impatience."

"With himself?" Darcy smiled.

"Aye. And with…the situation. As though he regretted what he'd done, but couldn't seem to end it."

"Did you think him cruel?" Darcy asked softly.

"Vexed, perhaps. But not cruel. Especially when he returned Mistress Coffey's brooch. That was so unexpectedly kind." She shook her head. "I must sleep now." She glanced at Darcy. "As must you. Your eyes are nearly closed."

"Aye. I must take myself to bed. The ladies in Winnie's sewing circle nearly put me to sleep." Darcy leaned close to kiss her sister's cheek. "What an extraordinary evening you've had. Why is it that my sisters seem to have all the excitement, while I merely spend my days and nights listening to Grandpapa and Newt tell the same old stories of their seagoing adventures?"

"Because someone must listen," Bethany whispered as she returned the good-night kiss. "Besides, your day will come."

"Aye. I certainly hope so."

When she was alone, Bethany pulled back the bedcovers and settled herself comfortably for the night. But she found it impossible to sleep. Thoughts of the dangerous highwayman kept playing through her mind. The way he'd looked in that instant when their mouths met, as stunned as she. And the way he'd tasted. Dark as the night. Mysterious. There'd been a moment when his touch had gentled. Just a moment. But it had been enough to convince her that he regretted his action. And then he'd lingered, as though reluctant to end it.

She turned away, annoyed at the direction of her thoughts. He was an outlaw. A man who preyed on the weaknesses of others. She was wasting far too much time on him. Time he ill deserved. But if she were to be honest with herself, she had to admit that he'd made her feel things she'd never felt before. All hot and cold at the same time. And dizzy with need. A need that she couldn't put a name to. A need she'd never even known she possessed.

As she drifted into the first hazy stages of sleep, she couldn't erase his image from her mind. The strength she'd felt in those hands. The press of hard muscled flesh against hers. And those eyes. Dark as the night. And gleaming with secrets.

The others had barely finished breakfast when they heard the sound of carriage wheels, followed by the slamming of the door.

Newton paused in the doorway to the dining room. On his face was a puzzled expression.

"What is it, Newt?" Bethany set aside her tea.

"I've just returned from the estate of the earl of Alsmeeth."

"Did he give us permission to harvest the timber we need?"

"He refused to meet with me, lass. He sent word through his manservant that he had no interest in selling any of his timber at any price. In fact, I was told that he refuses to see anyone. I'm sorry. I've failed ye."

Bethany gritted her teeth. "The blame isn't yours, Newt."

Mistress Coffey paused while pouring tea. "It would seem that Edwina's account of the earl could be true, after all."

Darcy led the old sailor to the table and coaxed him to soothe his distress with some of Mistress Coffey's freshly baked bread. "What did that silly twit say about him?"

"That he'd come to Cornwall to hide out."

"Hide from what?" Darcy's interest sharpened, as did that of everyone around the table.

"He spent time in Fleet Prison for the murder of his father, though he was later set free. On top of that, it seems his bride took her own life." The housekeeper passed around a tray of biscuits before adding, "On their wedding night."

"How dreadful." Darcy pushed aside her plate. "What do you suppose would bring a woman to do such a thing?"

"Perhaps she loved another," the dreamy Miss Mellon said. That thought appealed to her romantic nature. After pursuing Geoffrey Lambert for a lifetime, she'd recently given up wearing all white, her symbol of maidenhood, in favor of pale pinks and lavender, giving rise to speculation by his granddaughters that the two old sweethearts may have caught a spark. "Perhaps she was forced to marry against her wishes."

"It happens all the time," the housekeeper muttered as she circled the table filling their cups. "But women don't kill themselves over it."

"Some might." Darcy sipped her tea. "Especially if the man they are forced to wed is cruel."

There was silence around the table.

Bethany glanced at her grandfather. "We'll just have to make plans to find someone beyond Land's End who will sell us the timber we need to make our repairs."

Geoffrey nodded. "Newt and I will make some inquiries in town. Perhaps someone will know of a landowner who has what we need in a distant village." As he pushed away from the table he muttered, "It's a shame that this happy place must now be plagued with not one, but two miserable men. One an earl, the other a lord." At their questioning looks he added, "A lord of the night."

That brought a chorus of laughter, relieving the tension that had begun to take hold of the entire family.

But for Bethany it rekindled the thoughts she'd tried to bury throughout the night. Thoughts of a dark, mysterious lover whose mere touch had her trembling with unnamed needs.

Kane Preston stood on the balcony of his room and stared at the landscape below without really seeing it. He'd thought he could find escape in the place where he'd spent so many happy childhood summers. But there was no solace. Not in the lovely rolling green hills. Nor in the cool forest. Nor the rocky coast. This house, which used to ring with laughter, now mocked him with its silence. He realized that he carried the misery with him. It lay like a stone around his heart. Wherever he went, he felt the pain and saw the faces of those who had inflicted it.

He should have known there would be no relief from it. Even the outrageous things he did that once brought him comfort, seemed merely foolish, empty gestures now.

At a knock on his door he sighed and turned away. The dog at his feet growled a warning. He touched a hand to the animal's head.

"Come."

The door opened and his houseman entered, carrying a small missive on a silver tray. "An invitation, your lordship. To tea at the estate of a Miss Edwina Cannon. I informed her maid that you do not accept social invitations of any sort. But the young lady, having already surmised as much, thought you might be more amenable if you knew that she was once betrothed to a Lord Silas Fenwick of London, before his unfortunate death. She also wanted you to know that your cousin, Oswald Preston, would be attending her tea." He cleared his throat. "The young lady seems to think such facts will somehow open doors to her that might otherwise be closed. Shall I send the usual response?"

Kane muttered an obscenity. "Aye. Send my usual refusal, Huntley."

"Very good, your lordship."

As his manservant turned away, a sudden thought struck. "When is this tea, Huntley?"

"This very evening, your lordship."

When he made no further comment, the butler let himself out.

Kane returned to the balcony and stared at the sleepy little village in the distance. He absolutely loathed teas. And he hated being fawned over by people who were impressed by his title. The same people who whispered and pointed fingers of blame behind his back. It wasn't people he craved. What he wanted, more than anything else right now, was some relief from this pain that lay like a stone around his heart.

A smile touched the corners of his mouth as a plan began to take shape. Perhaps Miss Edwina Cannon had just offered him the perfect solution.

Bethany stormed up the stairs and nearly bumped into old Newton as she rounded a corner.

"Hold." Newt put a hand on her shoulder to keep her from colliding with him. "Ye'r racing like a ship in a hurricane. Is a nest of hornets after ye, lass?"

"If I had a choice, I'd prefer the hornets," she said between clenched teeth.

"Sounds serious." The old sailor smiled. "Whenever ye look like this, lass, it usually has something to do with Edwina Cannon."

"That silly twit is having a tea this very day, and Mistress Coffey told her I'd attend."

"What about Darcy?"

"She claims to have the sniffles. So she's excused."

"And ye're jealous that ye didn't think of it first, are ye?" His eyes twinkled.

"Aye. Now I'm stuck, with Grandpapa as my chaperon."

"At least ye'll have someone to talk to," he said with a laugh.

"If the repairs had been made to the *Undaunted,* I'd have the perfect excuse." Bethany frowned. "It's just one more reason to resent the haughty earl of Alsmeeth."

"Amazing, lass." Newt couldn't help shaking his head

at the look on her face. "The earl even gets blamed for Edwina's tea."

"If the *Undaunted* were rendered seaworthy, I'd be halfway to the Netherlands right now, hopefully encountering a few pirates along the way."

The old man turned away. Over his shoulder he called, "If poor Edwina Cannon only knew. Ye'd actually rather do battle with pirates than be in her company."

"Aye. It's true." For the first time since hearing about her obligation to attend, Bethany found herself chuckling as she stalked toward her room to dress.

On the carriage ride to the village, she sat beside her grandfather and consoled herself that she could get through this. It was only for a few hours. All she need do was smile and nod occasionally, and let silly Edwina carry on as she always did. In no time they'd be able to leave. And she would have the whole evening to challenge her grandfather to a game of chess, or perhaps ride her frisky mare Lacey along the beach.

"You're quiet, Bethany." Her grandfather smiled indulgently. He knew how she hated these fussy occasions when she was forced to behave like a lady.

"Aye, Grandpapa. I'm practicing for the tea. I'm sure Edwina is capable of filling every silence with the sound of her own voice. Like the screeching of barn owls."

"An apt description, Bethany."

The two were still laughing as the carriage came to a halt in the courtyard of the Cannon estate. Old Newton leapt from the driver's seat and offered a hand to them.

As she stepped down Bethany leaned close. "You're the lucky one, Newt. You get to stay out here and gamble with the other drivers."

"Aye, lass." He winked. "And sip a bit of ale. No one to impress out here."

"Nor in there." She glanced toward the windows of the estate, glowing with candlelight. "I'll leave that to Edwina, who is so impressed with her own importance, she probably believes the entire village of Land's End is longing to be in her company. In truth, the only reason they've come is to get a glimpse of the earl's cousin, since the earl himself refuses to ever leave his estate and mingle with common folk."

Bethany lay a hand on her grandfather's arm as she headed up the stairs, looking for all the world as if she were going to her own hanging. Beside her, the old man couldn't help chuckling.

When they stepped inside, they heard the sound of voices raised in laughter. Above the sound was Edwina's voice, high and shrill, regaling her guests with her latest bit of gossip.

Bethany straightened her shoulders and marched in. Behind her trailed her grandfather. At the far side of the parlor Edwina was holding court. While maids passed among the assorted guests with trays of ale and tea and pastries, she was engaged in a most animated tale, guaranteed to keep their attention riveted on her.

"He was a fearsome monster. Dressed all in black. A black dueling pistol, which he pressed to our heads. While the others began to cower in fear, I alone had the courage to order him to let us go at once."

That brought a collective gasp from the rapt crowd.

"How very brave, Edwina," one of the young men called.

She brightened. "Aye. But such outspokenness was to cost me dearly. To retaliate, he stole the ring given me by my beloved Silas. And he relieved Mama of a fortune in gold and jewels." She managed a moment of pained silence, broken only by a sigh.

"Are you certain you haven't forgotten a few things, Edwina?"

At the sound of Bethany's voice, made even more husky by anger, Edwina's head came up sharply. "I didn't see you come in, Bethany."

"Nay. I guessed as much." She was nearly shaking with anger. This silly little fool had just embroidered her tale with so many falsehoods, it was barely recognizable.

"I haven't forgotten, Bethany. I was just getting to the most important thing of all." Edwina turned to the others with a look of triumph. "The Lord of the Night stole a kiss from Bethany. Can you imagine her lips being pressed to those of such a beast?"

The entire crowd went silent, staring at Bethany with looks that ranged from shock to horror to revulsion. Several of the men were seeing her in a whole new light. The looks in their eyes made her feel sullied.

Stung with embarrassment, Bethany started to turn away, but Edwina's voice stopped her.

"Wait. You haven't yet met our guest of honor." Edwina wrapped her hands possessively around the arm of an impeccably dressed young man whose satin breeches and fine ruffled shirt were the rage in London. Her voice rang with importance. "Oswald Preston, I'd like you to meet Captain Geoffrey Lambert."

"Captain." He offered his hand, which Geoffrey accepted.

"Your lordship."

The younger man smiled. "I'm afraid that title is reserved for my cousin, Kane. He's the wealthy, titled one." Oswald smiled at the others. "I'm merely the poor relation."

"Hardly poor." Edwina looked adoringly into his

eyes. "I'm told you have one of the loveliest estates in all of London."

Oswald stared directly into her eyes. An affectation he had perfected with the ladies. Then he lay a hand on hers and squeezed ever so gently before turning to Geoffrey Lambert. "I believe we were speaking of my cousin, Kane."

"Eh?" Geoffrey cupped a hand to his ear. "You think it'll rain?"

"Kane, sir. My cousin Kane."

"Never use one myself." The old man pointed to his toes. "Still got two good legs. But my hearing's not so good anymore."

"Oh, you didn't have to tell me that."

Oswald and Edwina shared a knowing smile, which only had Bethany gritting her teeth when Edwina turned to her. "This is Captain Lambert's granddaughter, Bethany."

"Miss Lambert." Oswald bowed over Bethany's hand, then lifted it to his lips. "Do you live here in Land's End?"

Before she could reply, Edwina's shrill voice interrupted. "They don't live in the village, but rather in a quaint house they call MaryCastle."

Oswald was watching her in a way that made her extremely uncomfortable. "Would you care for some sweets, Miss Lambert?"

"Nay. Thank you." Her tone hardened a fraction. "If you'll excuse me, I believe I'd like some air."

She deliberately turned her back on the others and crossed the room, stepping through a doorway into the garden.

Bethany took several deep breaths, then made her way along a path until she came to a stone bench. She didn't know who annoyed her more. Foolish Edwina Cannon or Oswald Preston, cousin to the earl of Alsmeeth, with his oh-so-smooth demeanor. Men like that always made her feel uneasy. As though they were secretly laughing at the very people who were so eager to be in their company.

She breathed in the fragrance of roses and felt herself beginning to relax. It mattered not to her. She gave not a care about Edwina or her silly guests. If she could remain here just a little longer, she would go and find her grandfather and persuade him it was time to go. There would still be a chance to ride. And if she couldn't be at sea, feeling the wind in her hair and the taste of salt spray on her lips, then she would make do with a wild gallop along the beach.

She was so deep in thought, she didn't even see the darkened figure until she felt a hand at her shoulder. She leapt to her feet and found herself staring into the dark, penetrating eyes of the Lord of the Night. He was dressed as before, all in black, with a black scarf pulled over the lower half of his face, and a black hat pulled rakishly low.

"Forgive me, Bethany. I see I've startled you once again." As before, his voice was a low whisper, that did strange things to her nerves.

"Why...are you here?" Her eyes narrowed with sudden understanding. "You've come to rob Edwina's guests."

She could see the smile in those eyes. "They make it so easy. Especially when they're so eager to flaunt their wealth. But tell me. What are you doing here in the garden? You're not enjoying Miss Cannon's tea?"

"Not particularly."

"And why is that?"

She turned away. "It's none of your concern."

His hand closed over her upper arm, holding her still. She could feel the strength in those fingers. Could hear the thread of passion in his voice. "I choose to make it my concern."

She felt a little thrill along her spine. And though she knew she ought to fight or scream or shout a warning, she merely stood very still. She kept her face averted. "I don't...fit in. I suppose I never will."

She heard his chuckle, soft and low, and wondered at the heat that spiraled through her veins. "Is that all? You should be pleased to know you don't fit in with those peacocks."

"Why do you hate them so?"

At her bold question, he found himself smiling. "I don't hate them, Bethany. I merely wish to teach them a lesson."

"A lesson?"

"That their gold and jewels are of no consequence. Without such things, they are simply people. Some good. Some evil. But without wealth, their lives go on. Unfortunately, they rarely learn. They have a desperate need to amass more of what they have in such abundance."

She turned to face him. "And you think you are more deserving of their wealth than they are?"

"Is that what you think?"

"I don't..." She swallowed, and wondered about these strange feelings she was experiencing. She ought to be afraid. And completely repulsed by this thief. But his touch was neither repulsive nor threatening. It was, in fact, causing her a great deal of anguish of another sort. She turned away from him. "I don't know what to think."

"Then don't think at all." He closed his hands over

her shoulders and drew her back against the length of him.

She knew that he'd removed his scarf, for she could feel the warmth of his breath against her ear. A warmth that had her shivering with delight as he whispered, "The other night, when I kissed you, Bethany, I knew that you were different from every woman I'd ever known. Your courage, your spirit, your strength of will, set you apart from all the others."

"Stop. You mustn't say these things." She tried to pull away, but his hands tightened, holding her against her will.

"I must admit, Bethany, that I've never before encountered a woman who took offense at such a compliment."

"A compliment?" She shook her head, sending that rich cloud of hair dancing at her shoulders. "I'd call it empty flattery, coming from you."

"Even a thief can discern a diamond in a handful of glass. And you, Bethany, are a jewel worthy of a king's ransom."

"You wield words as you do your pistol, I see."

He chuckled. "You refuse to believe you are special? How can I prove it to you?"

"You can release me at once."

She was startled when he lowered his arms to his sides and took a step back, breaking contact. At once she felt strangely chilled as she turned to face him.

His face was in shadow. "I am, as you can see, your humble servant, Bethany."

"If that be true, then leave this place without accosting the guests inside."

"That I cannot do, even for you, lovely lady."

He leaned down and brushed his lips over hers. She

felt the quick jolt to her heart and had to reach out to steady herself. As she did, her hand encountered his muscled wall of chest beneath the black waistcoat. It left her fingers tingling.

He'd intended only a quick kiss. But the moment his mouth found hers, he couldn't resist taking more. She was as sweet and fresh as a summer garden. And a complete innocent, of that he was certain. It only added to her allure as he moved his mouth over hers, tasting, feasting. And then, with a sigh, he dragged her roughly into his arms and covered her mouth with his.

Bethany's immediate instinct was to resist. She brought her hands, balled into fists, against his chest. But then the heat spiraled upward, and she was caught in the most amazing whirlpool of sensations. Without realizing it, her hands opened. Her fingers curled into the front of his shirt and she held on as though her very life depended on it.

Her mind was suddenly wiped clean of all thought. His lips were warm and firm, moving over hers with slow deliberation, as though savoring every taste. She heard the sound of a sigh, and wasn't certain if it was hers or his. She knew only that his hands, those big, clever hands, moving along her back, were lighting fires wherever they touched. And though she could have pulled back, she didn't. She was frozen to this spot, as surely as though she'd been imprisoned, while a dozen different sensations assaulted her.

She was hot. So hot she felt as though her flesh were burning. And cold. Icy needles danced along her spine, sending delicious shivers slicing through her veins. She was so confused, she couldn't hold a single coherent thought. Her eyes were closed. But slowly, they opened, and she saw him watching her as he pressed moist kisses to her temple, her cheek, the corner of her mouth. Then his lips were on hers again, and all she could do was cling to him as heat poured through her.

She was delightful to watch. Everything she was feeling was there in those expressive eyes. Eyes as green as deep pools of cool water. He could read her surprise, and her first inclination to resist. And then the gradual awakening of desire. It was the most incredible thing to experience.

He knew he was taking her too high, too fast. But there was a devil inside him that made him want to go on kissing her until they were both beyond reason. It took all his willpower to finally stop.

When at last he lifted his head, she took in deep draughts of air, filling her lungs. She felt light-headed. Disoriented. But she was determined to retain her dignity. "You had no right."

He confounded her by agreeing. "No right at all."

Though her heart was thundering, she managed to push herself free of his arms.

He saw the anger dancing in those green eyes. And something else, as well. Though she would deny it, he could see the beginnings of passion. A passion that had been slumbering until his kiss awakened it.

He knew, in that instant, that he would have to kiss her again. For he wanted to be the one to take that passion to its ultimate conclusion.

"Though I'm not willing to leave before relieving the guests of their valuables, I can assure you that you'll be safe, Bethany. Simply remain here in the garden until I'm gone."

Before she could respond he was striding through the darkness toward the lights and the laughter.

It took her several seconds before she could regain her

composure. Then, realizing that her grandfather was inside, she began running after him.

By the time she reached the open doors, it was too late. A shot from his pistol had everyone in a panic. The women were weeping. Some, Edwina and her mother included, had already fainted. The men were cowering in one corner, as the highwayman circled the room, accepting their gold and jewels.

As he stepped in front of Geoffrey Lambert, the old man picked up a candlestick, brandishing it like a sword.

Seeing him, Bethany shouted from the doorway, "No, Grandpapa. It isn't worth the risk."

The highwayman turned, then turned back just in time to see the old man swing out wildly. He ducked, then stepped back out of range.

"I bow to your courage, sir," he said that fierce whisper. "What is your name?"

"Captain Geoffrey Lambert."

"Lambert. And the young wildcat is your granddaughter?"

Geoffrey smiled in spite of himself. "Aye. That she is."

"You two are cut from the same cloth, sir."

He bowed grandly, then turned and walked to the doorway, where he said to the assembled, "The Lord of the Night thanks you for your generosity."

While the others stared in surprise, he lifted Bethany's hand to his lips, then disappeared into the darkness.

Chapter Three

"All of Land's End is talking about Edwina's tea last night." Mistress Coffey circled the table pouring tea.

"If I were a younger man..." Geoffrey muttered.

"You were splendid, Grandpapa." Bethany turned to the others. "Grandpapa was the only one in the entire company who tried to stop the thief. And if you recall, Grandpapa, he complimented you for your courage."

Winnie beamed. "How fine of you, Geoffrey."

The old man smiled and closed a hand over hers.

Mistress Coffey said, "Edwina's maid told our Libby that he even kissed your hand, Bethany."

Bethany blushed. If they knew what had transpired in the garden beforehand, they'd all be shocked. In truth, she was still a little dismayed at her own behavior. Long after the others had fallen asleep, she'd lain awake, going over every word, every moment in her mind. And she'd come to the conclusion that she'd had a momentary lapse of common sense. What else could explain her behavior? She'd forgotten everything she'd ever learned at the knee of her prim nursemaid. She'd allowed a common highwayman to touch her. To kiss her. And if truth be told, she'd actually enjoyed it.

"You're awfully quiet this morrow, Bethany." Darcy glanced at her sister. "Is it because that outlaw humiliated you in front of your friends?"

Before she could reply there was a knock on the door. Minutes later Libby, their little maid, hurried in, completely out of breath, carrying a scroll. "There's a messenger here from the earl of Alsmeeth, Captain Lambert. He's been told to await your reply."

Geoffrey unrolled the missive and read, then looked at the others. "It's a request from the earl that Bethany come to his estate this very day to discuss buying his timber."

The others turned to Bethany, who appeared thunderstruck. "Are you certain it's me he wants to see, Grandpapa?"

He handed her the scroll. When she'd read it, he asked, "I wonder what happened to change the earl's mind?"

She pushed away from the table and walked over to kiss his cheek. "I know not, Grandpapa. But this much I know. We dare not pass up this opportunity."

"Aye, lass. I quite agree."

Winifred Mellon looked scandalized. "It isn't proper for a young lady to spend time alone with a titled gentleman."

"You can be assured, Winnie, that the earl of Alsmeeth doesn't want to seduce me. He wants to discuss timber."

"How do you know?"

Bethany laughed as she headed toward the doorway to speak with the messenger. "From the things I've heard about the earl, the only thing he wants is to be left alone. A wish I'll surely grant him, as soon as he agrees to sell us his timber."

A short time later Bethany heard the knock on her door and looked up to see Darcy in the doorway.

Darcy's smile disappeared as she studied her sister. "You're not planning on wearing that to the earl's estate, are you?"

Bethany glanced down at her simple white shirtwaist and navy skirt. "What's wrong with this?"

"Nothing. If you're hoping to work as a housemaid. But if you intend to charm him into allowing us to buy his timber, I suggest something a bit more exotic."

"Are you suggesting that I ought to flaunt myself?"

Darcy burst into laughter at the look of horror on her sister's face. "Oh, Bethany." She draped an arm around her shoulder. "Of course not. But I do think you can do better than this old shirtwaist."

"I'm not going there to impress the earl of Alsmeeth. I'm going there to conduct business."

Darcy smiled. "But it wouldn't hurt to soften the business with a pretty gown, would it?"

Bethany turned to study her reflection in the looking glass. She'd taken great pains to tie her mass of red curls back into a neat knot. The prim shirtwaist was buttoned clear to her throat. The plain dark skirt brushed the tops of black kid boots. "This suits my purpose. I'll not change. Especially not for a man who wouldn't even give Newt the courtesy of a proper greeting."

Darcy stifled her laughter as her sister snatched up her shawl and headed toward the stairs.

Behind her Darcy called, "Winnie is still horrified that you're going to the earl's estate alone. She said it simply isn't proper, and fears the earl is an evil lecher."

"I'll wager the lecher is less handsome than a toad, and not nearly as dangerous."

That had both sisters giggling.

"Now." Darcy smoothly changed the subject as she descended the stairs behind her sister. "Try to see as much of the earl's estate as you can, so you can tell us all about it when you return."

"Aye. I'll do my best. Though I expect it will reflect the man who lives there. Dark and brooding, and more than a little dull."

Outside, Newton stood waiting with the carriage. "'Morning, lass."

"Good morning, Newt." She accepted his help as she climbed aboard and settled herself.

He pulled himself to the driver's seat and flicked the reins. As the carriage jolted forward he called, "Ye're right on time, lass. In a hurry to see the earl's estate, are ye?"

"I'm in a hurry to acquire his timber."

"Well, while ye're there, ye should take a look around ye, lass. Penhollow Abbey is one of the finest estates in all of Cornwall. And ye may never have the opportunity to see it again."

"Aye." She leaned back, willing herself to relax. "Especially if I should forget my manners and tell the earl exactly what I think of him."

"Ye'd be wise to hold ye'r tongue, lass, until after ye've heard what he has to say."

She nodded, and actually began to smile. Old Newt was right, of course. This was a rare opportunity to see how the wealthy lived. All her young life she'd heard stories of Penhollow Abbey. Now she was about to see for herself if all those things she'd heard could possibly be true.

The forest seemed to go on for miles. Cool and dark and damp. It had more than enough timber needed to repair the *Undaunted*. Bethany sighed, hoping she could persuade this reclusive man to change his mind. After all, what were a few trees to a man who owned so many?

Suddenly, as the carriage rounded a curve and started up the long, winding road, everything changed. Bethany stared around in amazement. Instead of tangled weeds and dense forests, there were lovely formal gardens and great expanses of sweeping lawns, embellished with ornate fountains. There was even a pond on which glided a pair of elegant swans.

Everywhere she looked, she saw workmen trimming hedges, polishing the stonework of the fountains. And as the house came into view, her jaw dropped.

It wasn't so much a house as a palace that would rival that of the king. Built of light-buff stone, glistening in the morning sunlight, it rose to three stories. On the roof were ancient stone turrets, used in defense against enemy attack. An army could have taken refuge inside the top floor alone, with room to spare.

There was a lovely cobbled courtyard which led to huge double wooden doors. The minute their carriage halted, the doors were thrown wide and a tiny, silver-haired woman stepped outside. "You'd be Miss Lambert?"

"Aye." As Newton assisted her from the carriage, Bethany crossed the courtyard.

"His lordship is expecting you." The woman was frowning, and wringing her hands nervously. "I'm Mistress Dove, housekeeper here at Penhollow Abbey." She turned as a tall, imposing man in a spotless dark suit stepped outside. "This is Huntley, his lordship's butler. He'll take you inside."

"Miss Lambert." The man flicked a haughty glance over her, then turned as though he'd smelled something unpleasant. "If you'll follow me."

Bethany paused and said to the housekeeper, "I don't know how long I'll be. Perhaps you could see to the comfort of my friend and driver, Newton Findlay. For it's a long drive here and back."

"See to his comfort?" She saw the surprise on the face of the old woman before she composed herself and nodded. Her features softened slightly. "Aye, Miss." She turned to Newton. "Come along, then. I'll fix you some tea and a bit to eat while a servant sees to your horse and carriage."

"I thank ye." Newton winked at Bethany.

Satisfied, she turned and followed the houseman inside. Though she managed to keep up with his brisk pace, she couldn't help swiveling her head from side to side as she climbed the stairs.

If the gardens and fountains were impressive, the interior of Penhollow Abbey was magnificent. The stairs were carved from ancient timbers, and polished to a high shine. Overhead was a chandelier hung with hundreds of crystals, and at least that many candles, all aglow. Elegant tapestries adorned the walls. The hallway on the upper level was hung with portraits of the titled men and women who had once lived here. As she passed them, Bethany could see the haughty stance, the brooding look, that had no doubt shaped the man who now lived here.

The butler paused before closed doors and knocked once, then opened the doors and announced, "Miss Lambert is here to see you, your lordship."

"Thank you, Huntley. Show her in."

The older man stepped aside and Bethany entered.

For a long moment there was a chilling growl, that had the hair at the back of her neck lifting. Then there was only silence.

The room was so dark, it took her eyes a moment to

adjust. Heavy draperies had been drawn over the windows. No candles glowed on the mantel, or along the walls. Except for the fire on the grate, and a single candle set before him, there was no light.

She was finally able to discern a dog that greatly resembled a wolf, standing at rigid attention and watching her with avid interest.

Kane Preston was seated behind a desk. At first glance he looked sad. Or perhaps deeply troubled. But in the blink of an eye the look was gone as he flicked a cool glance over her.

"Welcome to Penhollow Abbey, Miss Lambert." The voice was deep and rich, and slightly bored.

"Thank you, your lordship."

He looked past her to the butler. "Have Mistress Snow send up some tea, Huntley."

"Very good, your lordship."

When the doors closed, Kane indicated a high-backed chair across the room. "Please, Miss Lambert. Be seated."

She took a seat and wondered at the fact that he neither rose to welcome her, nor offered a handshake. Edwina had called him the young earl. Since his age wouldn't deter him, could it be that he was infirm?

"I was surprised to receive your missive, your lordship."

"Why is that?"

"Because you refused to even meet with Newt."

"Newt?"

"Newton Findlay."

"Of course. The sailor."

"That sailor is an old and dear friend who sailed with my father and grandfather until a shark took his leg. He now works for us at MaryCastle."

"MaryCastle?"

"That's what my father called the house he built for my mother. Just yesterday my family dispatched Newt to Penhollow Abbey to ask if we could purchase some of your timber to repair our ship, the *Undaunted*. But you refused to even meet with him."

"So I did. But of course, I had no way of knowing that the sailor worked for your family."

"You would have known, had you shown him the courtesy of meeting him."

His eyes narrowed. "Are you scolding me, Miss Lambert?"

She bit her lip, remembering Newt's warning to hold her tongue. Too late. The words had already spilled out. Now there was nothing to do but muddle through. "I…suppose I am. It shouldn't matter whether your visitor is someone grand or the humblest citizen in all of Cornwall, he is worthy of a moment of your kindness, your lordship."

He studied her in total silence for a full minute before lowering his gaze to the open page of the ledger before him. While Bethany waited nervously for whatever was to come, he began to write in the margins.

She studied his face in the flickering light of the candle. He had a haughty, aristocratic bearing, with perfect, even features, and full, sensuous lips. Dark hair spilled over a wide forehead. His face might have been considered handsome, were it not for the frown that tugged at the corners of his mouth. But it was his eyes that held hers, whenever he looked up and pinned her. Eyes as hard as flint.

The only sounds in the room were the occasional hiss and snap of the log on the fire. And the heavy panting of the dog, who continued to study her with avid interest.

The longer the earl wrote in his ledger in silence, the more uncomfortable she became. Was he testing her? Hoping to stretch her nerves to the breaking point before launching into a tirade? Or was she so insignificant that he had forgotten about her?

It was almost a relief when there was a knock on the door. Huntley carried a silver tray across the room and placed it on a table beside the desk. "Shall I pour, your lordship?"

"Nay. Leave it, Huntley." Kane seemed mildly annoyed at the interruption. "We'll see to it shortly."

"Aye, your lordship." The man let himself out, closing the door softly behind him.

When he was gone Kane returned his attention to his ledgers.

After perhaps ten minutes, he glanced up. "Tea, Miss Lambert?"

"Aye. Please."

He indicated the tray. "Would you mind pouring?"

She leapt at the chance to do something. Anything was better than being forced to sit here in total silence. She crossed to the table and filled two cups, then offered one to him. The moment she reached toward him, the dog growled a warning. She froze.

"It's all right, Storm." At the earl's voice, the dog relaxed and lay down.

"Is Storm a wolf?"

"His parentage is unknown. He's a mongrel. But from the looks of him, I suspect there's a good bit of wolf in him."

She handed him his tea. As their fingers brushed, she felt an unexpected rush of heat and prayed she wouldn't spill hers.

"Perhaps..." She turned away, feeling the need to put

some distance between them. She settled herself in a chair across from his desk. "We should discuss the business that brought me here."

"Perhaps we should."

She found herself wondering at the look in his eyes. Like a cat playing with a mouse.

He set aside his cup and steepled his hands as he studied her. "You came here to arrange to buy some of my timber. I've given it considerable thought. I believe it can be arranged. But I will exact a price for what I offer."

Her heart started to race. Whatever price he set, she would find a way to pay it. For the sake of her family. "What do you require, your lordship?"

"These are my terms, Miss Lambert. First, for as long as it takes to harvest the timber, I will expect you to accompany the men to my estate."

"To the forest?"

"To my home here at Penhollow Abbey."

She blinked. "For what reason?"

He remained stone-faced. "I don't need a reason, Miss Lambert. I am the earl of Alsmeeth."

She felt a bolt of anger at his words. Such arrogance. Her own tone hardened. "What will I do at your estate?"

"You will keep me company here in my library. At times you may explore the house and grounds. Second, I wish to sail aboard the *Undaunted* when the repairs are completed. And I desire that you accompany me on my voyage."

His requests were so unexpected, she couldn't frame a single thought. "That's...not possible."

"Why? Are you telling me that you don't sail, Miss Lambert?"

"Of course I sail. I come from a family of sailors."

She took a deep breath. "I must remind you that the *Undaunted* is a cargo ship, not a pleasure ship."

"If I wanted a pleasure ship, I'd commission one. What I want is to sail aboard your ship."

Her eyes narrowed. "Why?"

"Again, I remind you, I need no reason other than that I desire it."

She looked down, staring into her cup. "I'm not prepared for this. I merely came here to buy timber."

His voice, low and deep, sent shivers along her spine. "And I'm prepared to sell you that timber, Miss Lambert. If you consider my price excessive, then you must also consider the fact that I am the only one in Cornwall who can supply you with what you need."

Her head came up, and she turned, meeting his dark gaze. "You ask too much."

"Too much? I thought I was asking far too little. The timber you wish to cut has taken years to grow. It will take many more to replace." A hint of a smile tugged at the corner of his mouth. "Do we have a bargain, Miss Lambert?"

For the space of a heartbeat, she paused, trying to sort out his motives. Reluctantly, she nodded. "Aye, your lordship. You are well aware that I have no choice but to agree to your terms."

His dark gaze roamed her face, then centered on her lips. And though he didn't move, she could almost feel the press of his mouth on hers. It sent the most incredible rush of heat racing through her veins.

The moment stretched out, and Bethany felt her throat go dry. Felt her heartbeat speed up. And felt a strange yearning, before she found the courage to get to her feet. Thoroughly shaken, she turned away and set down her empty cup on a small table. "I must leave. I'll say good day, your lordship."

"Until the morrow, Miss Lambert. I'll expect you at first light."

She tore open the door. Waiting in the hallway was his butler, who accompanied her down the stairs and out the door. In the courtyard, old Newton was waiting beside the carriage. "Are ye all right, lass?" he asked as he helped her inside.

"Aye, Newt."

He studied her, wondering about her high color. Knowing Bethany, she probably lost her temper and said things she'd soon regret. "Did he refuse to sell the timber, then?"

"Nay, Newt. He has agreed to sell."

The old man gave her a curious look before climbing to the driver's seat and flicking the reins. As they pulled away, Bethany glanced up at the balcony. It was empty. But she thought she could see, standing just beyond the curtains, the shadow of someone watching her departure. She felt a shiver along her spine, and realized that she'd just been manipulated into agreeing to a most unusual bargain. A bargain with a man who could turn out to be the devil himself.

Chapter Four

"**W**ell?" The family gathered around Bethany in the parlor the minute she arrived back at MaryCastle. "What did he say?"

"That he'd be willing to sell us the timber we need."

"Such grand news," Miss Mellon clapped her hands in delight.

"Aye." Geoffrey Lambert lifted a decanter and began to fill several tumblers. "This calls for a celebration."

"Wait." Bethany sighed. "You haven't heard the terms I agreed to."

"The terms?" Darcy glanced at the others, then at Bethany.

"I must accompany the men to the earl's estate each day while they harvest the timber."

"And remain with them in the forest?" Darcy arched a brow.

"Nay. The earl has said I shall visit with him at Penhollow Abbey until the men have finished their labors each day."

"Strange." Geoffrey glanced around at the others, and saw the way Winnie's lips pursed. "Did he say why?"

"Nay. And there's more, Grandpapa. He wants to sail aboard the *Undaunted* when the repairs are completed."

"For what reason?" Geoffrey demanded.

Bethany shrugged. "To sail. It seems he enjoys sailing, and wants to use our ship."

"I don't understand." Darcy glanced from Bethany to her grandfather. "The earl of Alsmeeth owns some of the finest properties in England. He could afford to buy a fleet of ships if he so desired. What does he want with the *Undaunted?*"

"What does it matter?" Geoffrey Lambert looked around at the others. "Isn't this what we wanted? The earl is making his timber available. And if he proves to be an eccentric who simply desires to sail aboard a cargo ship, what is the harm in that?"

"Don't you see?" Bethany lowered her voice. "What if he should learn that the *Undaunted* is more than a mere cargo ship?"

"How could he learn that?" her grandfather asked.

Bethany shrugged. "I know not. Do you think he could prove to be a danger to us, Grandpapa?"

The old man considered for several moments before replying, "I would think, if we're careful, and keep our weapons out of sight, he would accept the *Undaunted* as just another cargo ship. We could take him on a quick sail along the coast, then bring him back before dark. What's the harm?"

"He strikes me as no fool. Still..." Bethany gave a shrug of her shoulders. "I don't see that we have a choice."

"Then there's but one question left to resolve." Geoffrey paused a moment. "Do you object to being in his company while the timber is being harvested? After all, lass, it could take the crew several days to complete their task.''

Bethany thought of the strange feelings he'd elicited. Feelings she hadn't yet been able to sort through. Not so much fear as…fascination. Aye. A horrible fascination. No doubt caused by Edwina's gossip. And then she thought about her family, and the fact that they depended upon the *Undaunted* to survive. ''I shall find a way to tolerate his rather unpleasant company.''

''Then Newt and I had best ride to the village and hire a crew to start cutting timber at first light.'' Her grandfather clapped a hand on her shoulder. ''Well done, Bethany. The *Undaunted* will be ready to sail in no time, thanks to you.''

When the two old men left, Bethany hurried to her room where she changed into comfortable clothes. A hard fast ride along the beach on her mare Lacey was just what she needed to clear her head. And dispel the lingering unease at the terms meted out by a certain arrogant nobleman.

Dawn seemed to arrive much too soon. Downstairs, the others had already assembled to break their fast.

Darcy studied her sister with a critical eye. ''Another simple shirtwaist? What happened to all your pretty gowns?''

''I'm not going to one of Edwina's fancy teas. I'm simply accompanying the villagers to cut timber.''

Darcy laughed. ''You talk as if you're going to be handling the axes yourself.''

''Maybe not. But I'm aware that I'm nothing more than part of the terms of the earl's contract. I intend to fulfill my part of the bargain. But since he said nothing about how I must dress, I'll dress as I please.''

Darcy stifled a laugh. "Is this to be his punishment?"

"If you wish to call it that."

"Tell me." Darcy grew thoughtful. "Does the earl of Alsmeeth seem as eccentric as we've been told?"

Bethany nodded. "Aye. He seems…almost sad at times. Angry at others. And too arrogant for my taste. But his is some of the loveliest property I've ever seen." She turned to the others. "Everything we've ever heard about his estate is true. It's as fine as any palace, with lovely gardens and fountains and servants everywhere. The earl lives a life of such luxury we can't even begin to imagine it."

"And you got to see it." Darcy leaned close. "Tell us more, Bethany. What was it like inside?"

"Finer even than the king's palace at Hampton Court. Hung with rich tapestries, and the most elegant crystal chandeliers. And he shares all of that with no one but his servants."

"What are the servants like?"

Bethany smiled. "His butler, Huntley, frightens me. He never smiles."

"Does the earl smile?"

"Nay. And his housekeeper seems terrified of him."

"Huh." Mistress Coffey sniffed her displeasure. "Perhaps she has a right to be afraid. Perhaps she's afraid he'll have her beaten if she doesn't please him."

"Now, now, Mistress Coffey." Geoffrey Lambert placed a hand over his granddaughter's. "Let's not frighten poor Bethany any more than she already is."

"I'm not afraid, Grandpapa." Despite her pounding heart, Bethany lifted her head and even managed a smile.

Newton drained his tea and shoved away from the table. "It's time we were on our way to Penhollow Abbey. I hear the rumble of wagons outside."

Bethany set aside her napkin and followed him from the room. Outside, morning light was just beginning to color the sky. Newton helped her up to the hard seat of the heavy wagon they would use to haul the logs. Then he climbed up beside her and flicked the reins. As they started off, a long line of wagons and carts followed, filled with villagers who would labor in the forest.

On their way, Bethany found herself thinking again about the notorious outlaw who had accosted them in this very woods. Thoughts of his bold kiss still rankled. Now, to add to her discomfort, she found thoughts of the earl of Alsmeeth equally disturbing. Why had he set these strange terms? Did he think his wealth and title gave him the right to use her as he would a tavern wench? She reminded herself that he had behaved in a perfectly civilized manner. And if he was lacking in warmth, at least he had been respectful. She would do the same. Today she would be cool, aloof and maintain a certain distance. And she would do whatever necessary to fill the hours until she could return to the solace of her own home.

Their procession was met at the forest by the arrogant Huntley, who led Newton to the stand of trees tall enough for harvest.

"Each tree was personally inspected by the earl himself," Huntley explained. "And marked by a servant's axe. Only those bearing such a mark are to be cut and hauled away."

Newton nodded before calling to the village men, who began stripping off their tunics in anticipation of the work that lay ahead.

Huntley turned to Bethany, who was standing beside the wagon. "His lordship has sent a carriage for you, Miss Lambert. He awaits you at Penhollow Abbey." He led the way and Bethany followed him to the waiting carriage. As he assisted her inside, she sank back against the softest cushions she'd ever encountered. A team of matched white horses moved smartly through the forest and up the winding path that led to Penhollow Abbey. With such comfort, why was she feeling like a lamb being led to slaughter?

She swallowed back her fears, determined to get through this day with as little difficulty as possible. "Tell me, Huntley. How long has the earl been in poor health?"

"Poor health, miss?"

"He isn't...infirm?"

"Nay, Miss Lambert. The earl is quite robust."

"But he...spends so much time at his desk."

"Aye. The earl has many properties he must see to. He keeps meticulous ledgers."

As they rolled into the courtyard, and Huntley helped her from the carriage, she gave him a quick smile.

"Ah, Miss Lambert." The housekeeper stood in the doorway, a bundle of nerves. "His lordship awaits you in the library."

Huntley led the way up the stairs, where, as he had the previous day, he knocked, entered and announced her arrival in that same stuffy tone.

As before, the dog growled a warning, then relaxed at a word from its master.

"Thank you, Huntley." Kane was seated at his desk. Through a part in the heavy draperies sunlight spilled across his face, leaving it half in light, half in shadow, giving it a satanic appearance. Dancing sunlight turned his dark hair to blue-black and accentuated his handsome, arrogant features. Though he showed no emotion, she had the feeling that he was fighting a smug smile of triumph.

"Good morrow, Miss Lambert."

"Good morrow, your lordship."

"Have you had time to break your fast?"

"Aye."

He nodded. "Fine, then. Make yourself comfortable while I attend to some work."

He bent his head to the ledgers on his desk, effectively dismissing her.

For the space of several minutes she stood watching him. Then, realizing that she was to be left on her own, she began to prowl the room, pausing to touch a hand to the ancient, jewel-encrusted hilt of a sword over the fireplace.

He looked up. "Six generations have carried that sword into battle."

"And you are the seventh earl of Alsmeeth." She paused at the row of books and ledgers that lined the shelves. "Do you know what's in each of these?"

"Aye. They're part of my legacy."

Her tone softened. "I would know a bit about legacy."

"Sailing?"

She nodded and turned to him. "For as far back as we can recall, the Lamberts have always been sailors."

"But now there is just your grandfather to carry on the legacy."

Her chin came up defiantly. "Why must everyone assume that only sons can carry on tradition?"

She thought she detected a hint of a smile on his lips. But almost at once it disappeared as he leaned back in his chair and regarded her. "Because that's the way it's always been done, Miss Lambert."

"Aye. It's always been done by men, who insist upon making the rules to protect their own interests and to preserve their authority. If I ruled England..." She stopped, appalled at what she'd just done. She'd been lecturing the earl of Alsmeeth. She turned away to hide the flush that crept over her cheeks. "Would you mind if I went outside and explored a bit?"

"Not at all, Miss Lambert." He watched until she'd opened the door and stepped out into the hall. Then he got to his feet and moved to a window overlooking the gardens.

Minutes later he saw her moving along the grassy path of the rose garden, where she paused now and then to stop and cup a flower, before bending to breathe in its perfume.

As he watched, she stopped one of the gardeners and began an animated conversation. In no time the old man was leading her toward a fountain, where the two of them stood admiring the view.

At a knock on the door Kane called, "Come."

"Your lordship." His butler stood in the doorway. "Mistress Dove wishes to know if the midday meal will include your guest."

"Aye, Huntley. Miss Lambert will be with us until possibly sundown."

"Very good, your lordship."

"Huntley?"

The butler paused and turned.

"Did she say anything to you on her way from the forest?"

"Nay, your lordship. Except to ask if you were infirm."

"Infirm?"

"The young lady seems to think you...frail, your lordship, since you never leave your desk."

"Frail." He turned away with a thoughtful look.

"Will there be anything else, your lordship?"

"Nay. Thank you."

When the door closed he returned his attention to the gardens below. At first he couldn't see anything except the carefully manicured hedges and stone benches. Then he spotted her, moving along beside the old gardener, her arms now filled with brightly colored flowers.

Minutes later, when he heard the sound of footsteps outside his door, he quickly settled himself behind his desk. There was a knock on the door, and it was thrust inward as Bethany hurried inside.

"Look what Quinlan gave me." She crossed the room and deposited an armload of roses on the table beside his desk.

"Quinlan?"

"Your gardener. What a sweet old man. His father was a sailor from Ireland. He met a lovely Cornish beauty, and never returned to his homeland. Quinlan is the youngest of twelve children. His father brought him here to Penhollow Abbey when he was eight years old. He's been here ever since. And just look at the roses he manages to grow in your gardens. He says they're cuttings from your mother's original roses, which she brought all the way from London. Your father teased her about them, saying they'd never survive. But just look. Not only have they survived, but they are still thriving."

She paused for a breath just as a servant hurried in, carrying several silver vases. The little serving girl took one glance at the master's frown and stared hard at the floor.

"Oh, thank you, Petula." As soon as Bethany took the vases from her hands, the servant fled the room. "Poor Petula. She's only ten and one, and extremely shy. Especially of you. I think, in fact, she's terrified of you, your lordship."

While she talked, Bethany began arranging the roses

in vases, pausing now and then until she had them exactly as she wanted them. "There now. Aren't they wonderful?" She turned to Kane, who hadn't spoken a word, but was staring at her with a look that might have been part amusement, part amazement. "Mistress Dove said I might use a couple of these vases. I hope you don't mind."

It occurred to him that she'd been here scant hours, and she already knew the names of his maid and gardener, and practically their entire family history.

"Where do you intend to put them, Miss Lambert?"

"This one—" she chose a tall silver vase massed with white roses "—will go nicely right here on your desk." She placed it just so, then nodded. "It won't block your view of the door, and the perfume will make your work seem so much sweeter, don't you think?"

He couldn't help breathing in the fragrance. He nearly smiled before he caught himself. "And the others?"

"I thought I'd give the pink roses to Mistress Dove, perhaps for a parlor table. And the red roses for your dining table. Do you mind?"

He shook his head. "That would be...perfectly acceptable."

"Well, then." She picked up two of the vases and flounced away. Minutes later he heard her footsteps descending the stairs, and her voice, soft and breathless, calling to his housekeeper.

He started to write in the ledger, then paused to inhale the perfume of roses. It awakened a long-buried memory of his mother, kneeling in the garden, tending her roses. She'd loved them so. And his father constantly teased her about them. But, as Bethany had said, they'd not only survived this harsh land, but thrived. Perhaps they were a symbol, he mused. His thoughts were interrupted by a knock on the door.

Huntley entered. "Mistress Dove has your midday meal ready, your lordship."

"Thank you, Huntley. Find Miss Lambert and bring her to the great hall."

"Aye, your lordship."

When his butler exited, Kane pushed away from the desk, grateful for the interruption. There was no room for such flights of fancy. Next he'd start believing in enduring love and happily-ever-after. With a frown he made his way to the dining hall, with his dog by his side.

"Here you are, Miss Lambert." Huntley stood aside while Bethany preceded him into a room that could comfortably hold two hundred people. Inside, fires blazed at either end of the room. In the center was a long table, set for two.

Kane was already seated at the head of the table. Storm lay at his feet.

Huntley held the chair beside his.

Bethany glanced around. "Are we the only two who will be eating?"

"Aye."

At the look on her face he realized how strange it must look to one not accustomed to such formality.

The butler gave a signal and a parade of servants filed in, each bearing a tray for the master's inspection. In a trembling voice the housekeeper announced each dish, and waited for Kane's approval or rejection.

"Roast goose, your lordship."

At Kane's nod, the butler placed a small portion on his plate, then on the plate of his guest.

"Salmon, your lordship. And this is mutton. Summer

vegetables, your lordship, from the gardens here at Penhollow Abbey. Fruit conserve for your biscuits, your lordship. Ale, your lordship. Tea for the lady?''

Bethany watched as the food continued to pile up on her plate as well as his.

Finally, when the housekeeper asked, ''Is there anything more you'd like, your lordship?'' Kane glanced over.

''Is there anything more you require?''

Bethany's lips twitched. ''Perhaps someone to help me eat all this.''

At that, several of the servants giggled, then coughed to hide the sound.

Kane turned to the housekeeper. ''Nothing more for now, Mistress Dove.''

''Very well, your lordship.'' With a stern look, the old woman signaled to the servants, who hurried from the room, leaving them alone with only the butler, who stood a discreet distance away.

''Tell me.'' Bethany glanced over at him, her voice a whisper. ''Do you eat like this every day?''

''Doesn't everyone?''

Was he teasing her? She couldn't be certain.

''Why are you whispering, Miss Lambert?''

''Because—'' she glanced toward Huntley, whose hands were locked behind his back, his gaze fixed on a distant wall ''—this room is so big, I'd swear I was in a cathedral. I don't feel at all comfortable speaking aloud.''

''Trust me, Miss Lambert. You may say anything you please here.'' He sipped his ale. ''What do you eat at MaryCastle, Miss Lambert?''

''Fish, mostly. Since we're all sailors. My father was captain of the *Undaunted,* until his death, along with my brother, James, two months ago.''

"So recent? I'm sorry." He could read the pain in her eyes. A pain he understood all too well. "That must have been a terrible blow."

"Aye." She uncurled her fingers which she'd balled tightly into a fist and forced herself to focus on the beautiful red roses gracing the table. "But out of even that tragedy, some good came to us. In the form of Captain Riordan Spencer. After bringing us the sad news, he stayed on to win my sister Ambrosia's heart. They were wed here in Land's End just a fortnight ago."

"Riordan Spencer is wed to your sister?"

"Aye. Do you know him?"

"I do."

"We adore him." Now her smile bloomed, and he had a chance to see the light that came into her eyes when she was happy. "Now that he's part of our family, he occasionally acts as captain of the *Undaunted.* But he also captains his own ship as well. He's named it the *Warrior,* in honor of the first ship of that name that was destroyed by pirates. Right now, he and Ambrosia are enjoying a honeymoon cruise aboard his ship. He's promised to take her to all sorts of exotic lands."

Kane waited until she paused to catch her breath. Each time she spoke it was if a dam broke and more of herself spilled out.

He loved hearing that slightly breathy voice. A voice that whispered over his senses like a cool morning breeze. "Do you sail, Miss Lambert?"

"Oh, aye. That is…occasionally." She felt the beginnings of a blush and cursed herself. Deception had never come easily to her. "Do you sail, your lordship?"

"I do. I've often thought that if I had not been required to carry on my family legacy, I would have gone to sea."

"Really?" She brightened. This was something she

could talk about without ever growing weary of the topic.
"Then you've been to sea?"

"Many times. And each time, I found it more difficult
to return to land."

She nodded. "Newt calls it the siren song of the sea.
Newt said that once a man loses his heart to the sea, he's
never truly happy unless his feet are planted on the deck
of a ship, the taste of salt on his lips and the tang of sea
air in his lungs."

He sipped his ale. "Though you're not a man, Miss
Lambert, I get the feeling that you know exactly what he
means."

"I...do indeed."

Seeing the flush of color on her cheeks, he sat back.
"You're not eating your meal. You wouldn't want to hurt
Mistress Dove's feelings, would you?"

"N-nay." Though her heart was beating overtime, she
managed to take several bites of food. She looked up in
surprise. "This is quite wonderful."

"I'll convey your compliments to my housekeeper."
He ate a little, and watched with approval as Bethany
managed quite a bit before giving up.

As soon as they were finished, the butler went to the
door to summon the housekeeper.

She returned, followed by a line of servants. "Will
there be anything else, your lordship?"

He glanced at Bethany, then shook his head. "I believe
we've had sufficient, Mistress Dove. But our guest
wishes to convey her compliments to you and the staff."

The old woman beamed with pleasure at the unexpected compliment. "Thank you, miss."

Kane turned to Bethany. "I must return to my ledgers
now, Miss Lambert."

"So soon?"

He caught her look of dismay. "If you wish, you may wander the halls and have a look around. There's a great deal to see here at Penhollow Abbey."

"Thank you, your lordship." Her smile returned.

As he watched her walk away, he wondered at the fact that, because of that singular smile, his heart felt so much lighter.

"Huntley." It was late afternoon when Kane summoned his butler to the library. "Where is Miss Lambert now?"

"The last I'd heard, she was out in the stable, your lordship."

"Doing what?"

"Chatting up the stable master while she looked over the horses."

Kane turned from the window. "Summon her here. I can see the wagons moving out of the forest. One of them should be here shortly to fetch her home."

"Aye, your lordship." The butler hurried away.

When Bethany returned to the library, Kane was seated at his desk, the ledger open in front of him, his dog beside him. He looked up. "Huntley tells me you visited the stables."

"Aye. Your stable master, Richmond, was most kind."

"Richmond?" He waited, wondering if she'd learned his family history as well.

"He told me that all four of his little daughters have red hair, though not as red as mine."

He need not have wondered, he realized. This young woman just had a way about her that made people open up to her at first meeting.

"And his wife, Cara, is expecting another wee one. He

said most of the servants here at Penhollow Abbey assume he's hoping for a son. But in truth, he wouldn't mind another daughter. He thinks having a house filled with females is a most pleasant thing. That's what my own father used to say. Isn't that lovely?''

''Aye. Lovely.'' He wondered why the sound of that voice always made him want to smile. ''What did you think of the horses?''

''They're magnificent, your lordship.''

''Do you like to ride?''

''Aye. On land it's one of my greatest pleasures.''

He smiled. ''I thought as much. You look like a woman who can do many things well. Ride. Sail.''

''I like nothing better than to ride wild and free along the beach, just beyond MaryCastle, when the rest of the family has settled in for the night.'' Her voice lowered with feeling. ''Then I pretend I'm the only one left in the world. It's a feeling like no other.''

''Shouldn't you be worried about being accosted at that time of night?''

''Since our home is far from the village of Land's End, I never encounter other riders at that time of evening.''

''What about the highwayman, the Lord of the Night?''

She shook her head. ''I have nothing he would want. It's said he steals only from the wealthy.''

''There are things of value beyond gold and jewels, Miss Lambert.'' He saw her blush before she looked down. ''There is a rumor that he stole a kiss from you.''

Did the whole world know of her humiliation? She forced herself to meet his look. ''It meant no more to him than it did to me. No more than the rustle of the wind through the leaves.''

''Are you certain of that, Miss Lambert?''

Her eyes flashed fire. "Aye."

For a moment he merely stared at her in a way that caused her heart to beat overloud. Then the sound of a horse and wagon filtered up from the courtyard.

She felt a wave of relief. "It seems that Newt is here for me."

"Aye, Miss Lambert. I look forward to seeing you on the morrow."

"Good day, your lordship." She danced out of the room and down the stairs, where Newton was waiting.

As she climbed up to the wagon seat beside him, she glanced up and saw the shadow of a man behind the billowing curtains. Once again she had the strange feeling that the earl of Alsmeeth was watching her departure.

She lifted her chin and stared straight ahead until they had left the estate far behind.

Chapter Five

"Tell us everything," Darcy urged as the family took their evening meal together. "What did you do?"

"I toured the earl's gardens with his gardener Quinlan. And looked over his stable of horses with his stable master Richmond. The estate is so vast, it would probably take an entire summer to see it all."

"You jest," Miss Mellon said sternly.

"Nay, Winnie. I caught just a glimpse of the land when we arrived. But it seems to go on forever."

"I want to hear more about the earl." Darcy lifted her cup to her lips, regarding her sister over the rim.

Bethany frowned. "He seems to do nothing but tally numbers in his ledgers. He spent the entire day in his library."

"I care not how he spends his time. I want to know about the man himself." Darcy glanced at the others. "Is he tall or short? Fat or slim? Old or young?"

"It's difficult to know. He never stands in my presence. He remains behind his desk. He wears a dark waistcoat. His hair is dark. His eyes appear dark. And he seems to prefer the dark. The room where he sits has heavy draperies, always drawn against the sunlight."

"Perhaps he is deformed," Miss Mellon said gently. "Or scarred in some manner."

"I hadn't thought of that." Bethany nodded. "You may be right, Winnie. I asked his butler if the earl was infirm and he told me he is, in fact, quite robust. But if he is scarred or maimed in some way, that would explain why he seems to hide away."

Their housekeeper, who had held her silence until now, said, "It would explain, also, why his bride may have killed herself on their wedding night."

"Mistress Coffey." Bethany looked up in alarm. "We agreed not to repeat Edwina's hateful gossip."

"Aye. That we did. But I find it hard to forget. Especially now that you're being forced to spend time with a man who could be a...monster, for all we know."

Bethany ducked her head to sip her tea. In truth, she was finding it difficult to forget as well. Each time she saw him in his room, she wondered if he was hiding away. But if it was true that he was scarred, not just in body, but in soul as well, it would explain why none of the servants seemed willing to talk about him. And why his housekeeper was decidedly unnerved in his presence. Still, he didn't strike her as cruel. He seemed merely... distracted. Or perhaps wounded.

"You can thank the earl of Alsmeeth for one thing." Darcy's voice broke through her reverie.

"And what is that?" Bethany asked.

"Because you must leave early on the morrow, Mistress Coffey has decided to excuse you from the Psalm readings tonight. I must go to the vicarage in your stead."

Darcy's little frown had Bethany grinning. "I must remember to thank his lordship on the morrow."

As he had on the previous day, Huntley greeted the villagers and Bethany upon their arrival at the forest. But when he started to help Bethany into the sumptuous carriage, she resisted.

"Would you mind if I drove the team, Huntley?"

The poor man was so taken aback, he could do nothing more than stare in surprise. "Drive the team, miss?"

"Aye." She pulled herself up to the driver's seat and took the reins. "I've never handled a team of such lovely horses before. Do you know, they even prance in unison?"

"Indeed they do, Miss Lambert." He had all he could do to pull himself up beside her before she flicked the reins and the horses took off smartly.

"Ah." She glanced over at the stiff-backed servant. "Just as I'd thought. They move as one. Aren't they marvelous?"

"Aye, Miss. They are." He prayed the earl was too busy to note their arrival. Otherwise, he'd have hell to pay for this.

As they moved along the grand drive leading to the earl's estate, Bethany turned to the butler. "How is his lordship feeling this morrow?"

"Fine, Miss. Why do you ask?"

"I was hoping he might want to do something today. Ride or walk or perhaps take a drive over the land."

"I doubt he'd even consider such a thing, miss. He almost never leaves his library except to eat."

She sighed as the team came to a halt in the courtyard. "What a shame."

As before, the housekeeper was awaiting their arrival. This day, her nerves had her twitching like a puppet on a string. "I'm afraid you won't be able to see his lordship right away, Miss Lambert. He's with his cousin, Oswald Preston, just now."

Bethany saw the housekeeper and butler exchange knowing looks. And though not a word was exchanged, she had the distinct impression that neither of them was pleased by this early-morning visit.

"Perhaps you'll have some tea while you wait, Miss Lambert."

She nodded. "Thank you, Mistress Dove. That would be lovely."

"What do you mean, you need money?" Kane regarded his cousin, who settled himself in the chair across from his desk and stretched out his legs in a lazy pose. "What about the money I gave you before leaving London?"

"I'm far from London now, and in need of an quick infusion of gold."

"If you knew you were coming here, why didn't you bring enough with you to sustain your visit?"

Oswald merely smiled. "I'd intended only a quick visit. I hadn't realized I'd find Land's End so…attractive. These country wenches are most…accommodating. I simply can't tear myself away."

Kane's eyes narrowed. "It's not my place to remind you that you have an obligation as a gentleman to leave these maidens as you find them."

His cousin's smile remained. But his eyes blazed. "As you said, it's not your place to offer advice. As for the maidens…" He shrugged. "I can't help it if they throw themselves at me. They have so little opportunity to meet men of wealth and refinement in this wasteland."

"They're simple people. With simple tastes." Kane had had plenty of opportunities to watch his cousin dazzle the women. What always amazed him was the fact that so many were willing to be fooled by a charming smile and a shallow mind, wrapped up in the latest fashions.

"I have no interest in your lectures." Oswald sat up straighter. "Put yourself in my place. If my father had been born before yours, I would be the one sitting behind that desk, collecting all that gold, and you'd be sitting here, begging for a few shillings."

Kane shot him a chilling look. "Your father was given several of the finest estates in England, and the means to maintain them. Since his death you've managed to squander a king's ransom in gold on every vice known to man. And you dare to suggest you ought to be given more?"

"A loan, then. You can put it against my estate in London. When I return I'll pay a call to your solicitor to return the loan."

"You haven't even paid back the last one. Nor the time before that."

"What do I have to do? Beg? Will that satisfy your need to humiliate me?"

"I have no desire to cause you pain, Oswald. What I do desire is that you take responsibility for your life." He sat back, studying the dour young man. "Your problem is not a lack of money, but a lack of character."

"You see? Another lecture. I came here for gold, and I'm offered empty words."

"Hardly empty, except to the one who refuses to heed them." Kane opened a ledger and began to write, while his cousin watched with naked hunger. As he blotted the document, and handed it over, he added, "Take this to the banker in Land's End. He'll see that you're given a thousand pounds."

Oswald snatched the document from his hand. Before releasing it, Kane added, "If you were earl of Alsmeeth, Oswald, you can be certain of one thing. I wouldn't be accepting this from you. Nor would I be in need of your help to survive. I would be back in London, working diligently at making my estates as profitable as possible.''

''And you'd still be the most miserable man in England. And the loneliest.''

With that parting shot, his cousin strolled across the room. At the door he turned. ''I'll wager that all your gold doesn't keep you as warm as the lovely maidens in Land's End are keeping me.''

Mistress Dove bustled into the parlor, her fingers worrying the folds of her apron. ''His lordship will see you now, Miss Lambert.''

''Aye, Mistress Dove.'' Bethany sighed as she got to her feet. ''In the library.''

In the hallway she found Huntley, who led her up the stairs and cautioned her to wait while she was announced. ''Miss Lambert is here, your lordship.''

Kane, seated behind his desk, was still fuming from his visit with his cousin. He glowered at his butler. ''Did I see her driving the team?''

''You did, your lordship.'' The older man felt heat rising to his normally pale cheeks. ''I couldn't stop her, your lordship. She simply…took the reins and I was forced to go along.''

Kane's frown eased a bit. ''I should have known it wasn't something you'd approve. She does seem a bit headstrong. Show her in, Huntley.''

''Aye, your lordship.'' With a sigh of relief the butler stepped aside and Bethany came bounding in.

His dog watched with avid interest, but made no warning sound.

''Good morrow, Miss Lambert. Would you care for some tea?''

"Good morrow, your lordship. I had some in the parlor while I waited. Perhaps I'll have more in a little while. Have you taken a look outside?"

"For what reason?"

"Simply to admire the day. The sun is shining. The weather is so gentle, Newt would call it a day heaven made for sailing."

"Would he?" He set down the quill he'd been holding in his hand, while he studied her. He'd thought of nothing else the entire night. Thoughts of her, dashing into his room, her cheeks pink, her arms laden with roses, had played havoc with his system. And now she was here, her cheeks the color of ripe apples, her hair wind-tossed. She looked so fresh and clean. And sweet.

It occurred to Kane that she was the first woman he'd ever met who hadn't dressed to impress him. And by doing so, she had impressed him even more. That mass of red hair, all tied up so neatly, and that prim little shirtwaist buttoned clear to her throat, delighted and intrigued him. Not even such a simple frock could hide the lush body underneath.

It would be so pleasant to simply spend an entire day looking at her. And listening to that soft, easy voice soothing his temper. But there were the books and ledgers. The accounts of the tenant farmers. The reports on his far-flung properties. Still, he could take one minute.

Before he could stop himself he said, "Then I must see this day that makes you so happy. Come, Miss Lambert. We can glimpse it together from the balcony."

Lifting aside the heavy draperies she stepped out onto the balcony and glanced around admiringly. "Oh, this is simply stunning."

She studied the green rolling hills in the distance, and the forest that ringed the estate, then peered down at the lovely gardens below. "I don't believe I've ever seen anything so beautiful."

"I quite agree."

At the tone of his voice she turned. He'd followed her to the balcony. But she realized that it wasn't the countryside he was looking at. He was staring at her in a way that had the heat rising to her cheeks.

This was the first time that he hadn't taken refuge behind a desk or table. In the dazzling sunlight, he wasn't at all what she'd expected. He was tall and lean, and as Huntley had said, appeared to be quite robust. There was nothing of the invalid she'd suspected. He wore lean black breeches tucked into expensive kid boots. His white shirt, of finest lawn, looked slightly rumpled, the sleeves rolled above his elbows. His hair, jet-black, tumbled over his forehead, as though he'd run his hand through it in frustration. His eyes weren't brown, but gray. In the sunlight, they gleamed like silver. He revealed no deformity. He was, she realized, devastatingly handsome.

She felt the heat rise to her cheeks and realized she was staring. At once she turned away, pretending to be interested in the view. "What must it feel like to know that everything, for as far as you can see, is yours?"

He stepped closer. His tone lowered. "Not everything I see is mine. At least not yet. But perhaps, if I should be so fortunate…"

She caught her breath at his boldness and recalled Miss Mellon's fear for her. "I…believe I'd like that tea now."

He smiled easily, enjoying the fact that she was flustered. It was a most endearing trait. "Of course."

He led the way inside and poured, then handed her a cup. When their fingers brushed she felt a wave of heat and blamed it on the weather.

"I would be hard-pressed to stay indoors with such a

lovely view as this, your lordship. How do you stay at your desk and deal with your paperwork with such a temptation just beyond your door?''

''There's been little in my life to tempt me to forget my obligations, Miss Lambert. Until now.''

Again that arched brow. But it was softened by the hint of a smile on his lips. She ducked her head and sipped her tea, struggling to ignore the most amazing flutter in the pit of her stomach. Without thinking she reached down and began to rub the head of the big dog. At once he gave a warning growl. Alarmed, she lifted her hand.

''Storm never allows anyone to touch him except me, Miss Lambert.''

''Why is that?''

''I seem to be the only one he trusts. I suspect he was abused as a pup. He has no use for mankind.''

''Then why does he trust you?''

''Perhaps it isn't so much trust as need. He needs me.''

''How did you come by him?''

''I found him in a storm. I heard a whimpering sound, and discovered that he was buried beneath a heavy tree limb. So I removed it and freed him.''

''And he thanked you by staying with you?''

''He thanked me by biting my hand.''

''He bit you?''

''That's what animals do when they're afraid, Miss Lambert. They bite. But I carried him home and bound his wounds. When I later tried to free him, he refused to leave.''

''And so he became your pet.''

Kane shook his head. ''Storm is no pet, Miss Lambert. He is my companion and my fierce protector. But not my pet.''

''I see.'' She set aside her tea. ''I thought, while you work on your ledgers today, I might explore the ruins I spotted in the distance. That is, if you don't object.''

''Nay. I have no objection, Miss Lambert.'' His gaze returned to his ledgers. He walked to his desk. ''If you need anything, ask Huntley or Mistress Dove.''

She realized she'd just been dismissed. With a sigh she crossed the room and let herself out. As she did, she glanced back and saw that he was already immersed in his work. Storm had settled down at his feet.

Kane looked up as his butler knocked and entered with an air of distraction. ''Mistress Dove seems to have lost her senses. She informed me that Miss Lambert wishes to have a table set in the gardens for the midday meal, your lordship. I told her it would not meet with your approval.''

''A meal in the garden?'' He considered for a full minute, a frown darkening his features. Then he suddenly nodded. ''I suppose I could tolerate it.'' If Kane noticed his butler's look of surprise, he paid no heed.

''Very well, your lordship. I'll tell Mistress Dove at once.''

When Huntley was gone, Kane sat back, steepling his fingers, deep in thought. Then he pushed away from the desk and made his way below stairs, with the dog moving like a shadow beside him.

Bethany met him at the door. ''I'm so relieved that you agreed to dine in the garden. I couldn't bear the thought of that long table, in that dark, cavernous room, on such a day.''

''I understand. I asked Mistress Dove to prepare something impressive for you today.''

She was surprised and pleased. "Will I be impressed?"

"You will, indeed. We've had no guests here at Penhollow Abbey since I arrived. You're the first. So I'm afraid that dear old lady intends to overwhelm you with the bounty of our larder."

Bethany shook her head, remembering yesterday's feast. "Then I hope you intend to invite the villagers who are working in your forest to help me eat it."

He chuckled. A deep, rich sound so unexpected, it had Bethany turning to stare at him. "It occurs to me, Miss Lambert, that you are exactly what has been missing for too long in this place."

"Is that why I'm here?"

His smile faded. "You're here because I desire it."

"And do you get everything you desire, your lordship?"

"Haven't you heard?" His tone rang with sarcasm. "I'm a pampered rich man. I need only ask and it's mine."

"Why have there been no guests?" She followed along the grassy path, taking care to give the dog a wide berth.

He merely smiled. "Because the master of Penhollow Abbey knew of no one he wished to entertain. Until now."

"But ours is simply a business arrangement, is it not?"

His face settled into a closed, shuttered look. "Aye. Of course."

In silence she removed her shawl and folded it over her arm as they walked toward the rose garden. Her tone grew pensive. "There are so few days as perfect as this. Perhaps that's why each one seems so special. Because they're so rare."

His footsteps faltered. He turned, a trace of excitement in his eyes. "Exactly. Have you ever wondered about people who live in lands where the sun always shines? Do they realize they're living in paradise? Or do they simply accept it as their due, believing that everyone lives as they do?"

She shrugged, puzzled by the question. "If they've never had the opportunity to see other lands, and to see how others live, how can they question?"

"Aye. You're right, of course." His voice lowered, as though thinking aloud. "They must first see how others live. Then, and only then, will they realize whether their own life is blessed or cursed."

He seemed deep in thought as they made their way along the curving ribbon of grass.

Bethany left him to his thoughts until they came upon a scene so beautiful, she couldn't help exclaiming. "Oh. How perfectly lovely."

In the shade of a gnarled tree a table had been set with fine linen. A stone bench had been drawn up for seating. Sunlight filtered through the leaves, glinting off china, crystal and silver.

As they were seated side by side on the bench, a serving wench came toward them bearing a silver tea tray. Behind her came a staff of servants, each carrying a tray of meat, fish, breads and assorted pastries. As before, each dish was presented to the master for his approval, then Huntley served their plates.

When she took the first bite Bethany looked up. "Oh, Mistress Dove, this is excellent."

"Thank you, Miss Lambert." The housekeeper's smile was dazzling. "Would you care for tea?"

"Aye. Please."

Huntley took the teapot from a tray and poured, then

returned it to a servant. Afterward, the entire staff departed, leaving them alone in the garden, with only the butler, who stood a discreet distance away.

Bethany lowered her voice. "Do you ever grow weary of having so many people around you?"

"I do indeed." Kane leaned toward her. "All my life I've been surrounded by people. Nursemaids when I was very young. Tutors. Servants. And, of course, Huntley. He's been with me since I was a lad. And all of them calling me your lordship."

"That's what you are."

"Nay. That's what my father was. I am Kane Preston."

She heard the trace of anger in his tone and turned away, catching a glimpse of Huntley, standing at attention in the sunlight. "Do you ever have a desire to be alone? Completely alone?"

Kane nodded. "I do. And there are ways, if one is clever."

"Ways?"

She saw the hint of a smile on his lips as he placed a hand over hers. At once she felt the jolt and then the slow, simmer of heat. She looked up, wondering if he felt it, too. But all she could see in his strange silver eyes was a glint of humor.

He nodded toward her plate. "If we don't soon eat some of this food, poor Mistress Dove will think we don't appreciate all the work she's gone to."

It was no effort for Bethany to do as he urged. Now that the moment had passed, her heartbeat gradually returned to normal.

The food was heavenly. Thin slivers of roast beef. Salmon fresh from the ocean. Biscuits still warm from the oven. The morning's walk to the ruins had sharpened her appetite and she found herself enjoying their meal.

She sipped her tea. "Was your life in London very different from your life here in Cornwall?"

"Completely different. There are…certain expectations in a city the size of London. Protocol to be observed. Business to be conducted. Social obligations to be met."

"Do you miss it?"

"Not at all."

"But I suppose you shall return there?"

She saw a faraway look come into his eyes, along with a sadness, and realized that he had once again gone somewhere in his mind. Where did he go? What burden did he carry? Was he remembering his time spent in prison? Mourning the loss of a father and a bride? She thought about all the dreadful things Edwina Cannon had told her. She hated the fact that a seed of doubt had been planted. A seed that she couldn't seem to dispel. Still, despite the fact that he was a man who displayed arrogance, willfulness and a definite temper, she found it impossible to believe that he could behave like a brute or a bully toward his bride. There had to be another reason for what happened. If indeed, it did happen. Knowing Edwina's love for gossip, the entire tale could have been completely fabricated. Aye. She would put it out of her mind as much as possible and get through these next few days. Once the timber was harvested, she would have no occasion to see the earl of Alsmeeth ever again. She ignored the little twinge around her heart. Disappointment? Not likely. Especially since they were from two very different worlds. Hadn't he admitted that she was simply here for his entertainment?

She breathed in the fragrance of roses. "When Quinlan

told me about your mother's roses, it reminded me of my mother. She loved roses, but despaired of ever growing them at MaryCastle. The brutal winds and salty air conspired to kill all but the hardiest of her flowers. She often said that little could survive the rocky coast and the bitter Atlantic.''

He touched a hand to a wisp of hair that had pulled free of the knot at her nape, loving the softness of it. ''Your mother had no need of roses, Miss Lambert. She left something far more precious.''

Bethany wondered if he had any idea what his touch was doing to her. She felt the jolt all the way to her toes.

''You haven't tried the pastries.'' He placed a small tea cake on her plate. ''You'd better eat at least one, or Mistress Dove will be sad.''

''We wouldn't want that.'' She tasted and gave a sigh of pleasure. When she reached for a second, she saw his smile. ''I must make the sacrifice for the sake of your poor housekeeper.''

''I do admire a woman with a noble heart.''

They shared an easy smile.

As she finished her tea she nodded toward the ruins in the distance. ''I found them fascinating. Can you tell me about them?''

His smile faded. His tone was suddenly gruff. ''Perhaps another time. I fear I must return to my work.''

''His lordship summons you, Miss Lambert.''

Bethany left the upper rooms, where she'd been studying the land far below, and hurried to the library.

Kane turned from the balcony. ''Your wagon and driver are approaching, Miss Lambert.''

''Then I'll bid you good day, your lordship.'' She started toward the door.

"Good day, Miss Lambert. Will you ride tonight?" he called.

She paused. "I suppose."

"Along the beach near MaryCastle?"

She nodded, wondering at the intensity of his tone. "Aye. Along the beach."

When he said nothing more, she turned away. "Good day, your lordship."

She hurried out and down the stairs. In the courtyard, she climbed up to the wagon and sat staring straight ahead as Newton urged the team into a trot. And though she never looked back, she had the strangest feeling that he was standing where she'd left him. Watching her. Always watching her.

Chapter Six

The night had grown cool. The sea was calm. Overhead, clouds scudded across a full moon. Bethany had changed from her shirtwaist into an old gown that had long ago outlived its usefulness. If the bodice was a little tight, and the sleeves a bit frayed, all the better. For she intended to ride along the beach, without benefit of saddle. If Lacey should splash through the surf, or kick up dirt in the sand, it wouldn't matter in this old thing. She slipped out the back door and made her way to the stable.

"Hello, old girl," she murmured as she fed her horse a carrot before leading it from its stall. "We're going to ride. Just the two of us."

The mare picked up her ears, eager for what was to come. This had been their ritual for years, ever since Papa had given the animal to his middle daughter for her tenth birthday.

"Why can't I sail like James?" she demanded, holding back tears on her birthday.

"Because it's too dangerous for my daughter."

"But not for your son?"

"Aye. It's dangerous for anyone who chooses the sea,

*Bethany. But James is...James. He's bound and deter-
mined to follow in my footsteps.''*

"And you're proud of his decision.''

"Aye.''

"Then why can't I?''

*"I know it's what you crave, Bethany. But I'll not have
my daughter living and working among hardened sailors.
And so, to soften the blow to your heart, I've brought
you this.'' He'd led her outside, where old Newton stood,
holding the reins to a beautiful roan filly. "Her name is
Lacey. I bought her from a farmer in Bretton, because
she reminded me of you. That proud bearing. And all
that lovely red hair,'' he added with a smile. "There was
nothing to do but bring her across the sea aboard the*
Undaunted. *So she's had a taste of the life at sea which
you so desperately crave. When you have a need to be
free of us, ride her to the sea, Bethany. And whenever
you do, think of me.''*

"Oh, Papa.''

She'd fallen into his arms and wept for joy. And then
she'd pulled herself bareback onto the mare and the two
had spent a glorious afternoon playing in the surf.

Now, as she pulled herself onto Lacey's back, she
looked up at the darkened sky and thought about the father she'd lost at the hands of vicious pirates. That loss
had forever changed the lives of her and her sisters. With
the blessing of King Charles, they continued to sail the
Undaunted, as both cargo ship and privateer in the service of their king. They were earning enough to live quite
comfortably, as long as the *Undaunted* remained seaworthy. Their larder was full. Their servants well-paid.
And Grandpapa, Winnie and Mistress Coffey need not
fear for their old age.

You're still looking out for us, aren't you, Papa?

Lacey picked up speed as they left MaryCastle behind and followed the line of the beach. Bethany dug her hands into the mare's mane and laughed aloud at the sheer joy of riding hard and fast. It was, in her mind, the next best thing to skimming the waves of the Atlantic aboard ship.

She leaned down low over the mare's neck and crooned words of encouragement as they left the beach behind. Minutes later they crested a hill, and horse and rider paused for a moment, gathering their energy for the next thrill.

"Look, Lacey." Bethany stared at the *Undaunted,* lying at anchor in the harbor, its white sails like beacons of light against the darkness. "It's Papa's ship. The one that brought you to me."

The horse stood perfectly still, as though understanding every word being spoken.

"And it will be Papa's ship that will take me to foreign shores and home again." She leaned down and ran her hand along the horse's neck. "You miss the water, don't you, girl? As do I. Let's go to it, girl. Let's feel the water beneath our feet."

The mare started forward, down the hill, across the beach, and into the surf, sending up a glorious spray as horse and rider raced through the shallows.

It was, in Bethany's mind, the perfect way to empty the mind of all its problems, and to free the heart of all its troubles. She could go on like this for hours.

They flew along the sandy beach, the horse's hooves leaving deep prints that were instantly erased by the waves rolling in.

Suddenly, Lacey pulled up so abruptly, it took all of Bethany's skill to keep from toppling headlong into the water. With her knees gripping tightly, and her hands fisted in Lacey's mane, she managed to stay upright, but barely.

A horseman, clad all in black was mere inches away. Bethany's breath caught in her throat. There was no mistaking the Lord of the Night.

"Forgive me." His voice was that strange whisper, that caused a prickling at the nape of her neck. "There was no time to warn you of my presence."

"You could have tried shouting."

"I could have. But you'd have never heard me over the sound of your horse's hooves."

She regarded horse and rider carefully. The stallion was blowing and snorting, as though it had been ridden hard and fast. Despite the hat pulled low on the rider's head, and the scarf that hid the lower part of his face, she could see that he was breathless as well. His chest rose and fell with each measured breath. It was obvious that they'd come from a great distance.

Now that she'd caught her breath, she found her fear fading, and her anger rising. "You're a long way from the rich and titled who are usually accosted by you."

"They hold no appeal for me this night. It's you I came to see, Bethany."

His words caused a different sort of fear. "How long have you been here, watching me?"

"Long enough to see you silhouetted on the hill in the moonlight." The sight of her had robbed him of breath. "And long enough to watch you racing through the surf." It had brought a smile to his lips. She was, quite simply, the most fearless, the most magnificent creature he'd ever seen. "I envy you your freedom, Bethany."

She felt her throat go dry at the way he was watching her, as though devouring her with those dark, mysterious eyes. To cover her nerves she asked, "Aren't you equally free? You're here, after all."

He inclined his head. "So I am." If she only knew what he'd gone through to be here. But that only made the goal all the sweeter. He'd always loved the challenge of slipping away by himself under cover of darkness.

"If you're here, it must mean you've come to ride, since I have nothing of value to steal." She gave the slightest nudge of her knee to Lacey's side and the mare started forward, eager to run. "Just so you understand, I'll not be caught. By you or by anyone," she called, giving him no time to argue.

Her horse danced through the water and along the shore, gathering speed as she ran. He watched them for the space of a minute, then, feeling his stallion's quivering response to the mare's challenge, he gave him his head. They were off like a shot, horse and rider speeding across the sand, gaining momentum with every step. In no time, his mount had eaten up the distance between them. When they were racing side by side, he turned his head to glance at the woman beside him. Her gown was damp, and plastered against her like a second skin. Her skirts were hiked up to her thighs, revealing a daring amount of flesh. Her hair streamed out behind her like a fiery cloud. Her eyes danced with unconcealed joy. Her laughter rippled in the night air, as clear as a bell. Then she leaned low over the mare and shouted something unintelligible, and horse and rider streaked ahead. By the time the highwayman and his horse reached the harbor, Bethany sat astride her mount, laughing.

"I told you I'd not be caught."

"Aye. You've a horse that matches your spirit, Bethany. What do you call her?"

"Lacey. She was a gift from my father."

"She suits you. There's a wild streak in her."

"Aye." Bethany laughed with delight. "And like me, she hates to lose."

"I surmised as much. I've never before met a woman so competitive." He drew closer. "Do you know, you quite simply take my breath away?"

"Don't—" Before she could respond he cupped her head and dragged her close, in one instant removing his scarf and covering her mouth with his.

This kiss was unlike the others. Before, he had been testing. Tasting. Keeping his feelings on a short tether. This kiss was rough, almost savage in its intensity. It spoke of need, long suppressed. It was a kiss that drained her, then filled her. And demanded more.

"Stop." She drew back, sucking in great gulps of air.

He slid from his horse and reached up, dragging her into his arms. They found themselves standing in water nearly to their hips.

"Nay. What are you—?"

His mouth covered hers, cutting off her protest.

The two horses danced nervously around them in the surf. The waves rolled in on the tide, nearly swamping her. But his big hands held her firmly, stronger even than the pull of the Atlantic. It was a kiss that was all heat and flash and passion. A kiss so hot, so hungry, all she could do was cling to him.

"You are the most magnificent woman I've ever known." He spoke the words against her mouth, then inside her mouth as he dragged her closer and kissed her again and again. "You touch a chord deep inside me, Bethany. You awaken things I'd thought forever buried. God in heaven, I want you. As I've never wanted anyone, anything in my life."

Dazed, she knew she ought to resist. But each kiss,

each touch of his hands, seemed to unlock some hidden feeling inside her. Feelings she'd never even known she possessed were taking hold of her senses. And robbing her of the strength to think clearly.

He saw the way her lashes fluttered. Heard the little sigh. Felt the way her pulse throbbed. Then, before she had time to catch her breath, his mouth was moving over hers with a hunger that left her dazed and breathless. He feasted on her lips like a starving man, feeding, filling himself with the sweet, clean taste of her. He ran nibbling kisses over her eyelids, her cheeks, her jaw. He traced the outline of her mouth with his tongue until she thought she would go mad with the need to feel his lips on hers. When at last his mouth closed over hers, she clutched him with a fervor that matched his, and returned each kiss with one of her own.

She couldn't seem to stop herself. She had a need to take the dark, mysterious taste of him deep inside herself. To drink her fill of him. And though she kept her hands firmly at his chest, she itched to touch him the way he was touching her.

His hands moved down her back, along her sides. When his thumbs encountered the fullness of her breasts, she gasped and pushed away. At once his touch gentled, his hands soothing, even while his kisses continued to arouse.

He loved watching her. The way her lashes fluttered, then closed, casting spikey shadows on her cheeks. The flush of desire that colored her skin. And the quick shudder when his thumbs brushed the tips of her breasts.

She pushed back, knowing she had to end this. And yet, the hypnotic pull of those lips, the need for one more drugging kiss, had her sighing with regret for her weakness. Suddenly she wrapped her arms around his neck and clung to him, offering her lips for more.

The softness of her body pressed to his was the sweetest torture of his life. Through the dampness of his clothes he could feel her breasts, crushed against his chest. Could feel the hard, taut nipples, erect in the cold night air. Could feel her thighs pressed to his, as he moved his hands to her hips, to drag her firmly against him.

The thought of lying with her in the cool sand, and ending this terrible tension, was overpowering. He wanted her. Desperately. And the need was like a demon, clawing to be free.

It would be so simple. He knew, from the way she clung to him, and offered her lips, that he had taken her over the line. Like him, she was beyond reason. As he drank her in, filling himself with the sweet, clean taste of her, he heard her little whimper and felt a wave of sudden guilt. She was a maiden. An innocent. And he had taken advantage of that innocence for his own pleasure.

"Bethany." Her name was torn from his lips as he lifted his head and held her a little away.

"It isn't fair. You know my name, yet I know not yours." The words came out on a sigh of pleasure.

"You know my name."

"Aye. The Lord of the Night." Never in her life had she felt like this. Dizzy and light-headed, and almost mad with need. The whole world seemed to be spinning. And the water that rolled over her couldn't cool the heat that simmered in her veins. "But I wish to know more. I want to know you. Everything about you."

"I must…apologize, my lady." He kept his hands firmly on her shoulders, so that the waves wouldn't swamp her. Then, taking a deep breath, he pressed his forehead to hers. "I fear I've…overstepped my bounds."

She stood very still, taking in deep breaths to calm her ragged breathing. Her heart was pounding so hard, she feared he could hear it over the sound of the surf.

He reached out and caught her horse's reins. "I'll see you back to your home."

"That isn't necessary." Suddenly stung with embarrassment at his abrupt change of heart, she pulled herself onto the back of her mare and snatched the reins from his hands.

"I said I'll see you back." He climbed into the saddle of his stallion, but she had already nudged Lacey into a run and was racing across the beach toward the house in the distance.

He watched with a sense of frustration as she and the horse were swallowed up in the darkness. Minutes later he saw their silhouettes as Bethany led her horse into a stall, then turned and ran to the darkened house.

He stayed where he was, willing his heart to return to its normal rhythm. His hands, holding the reins, were trembling.

At long last he nudged his stallion into a trot. And as he headed into the darkness, he cursed and called himself every name he could think of.

Bethany Lambert was too fine to be used in such a fashion. She deserved better than the likes of him. He had an obligation to leave her as he'd found her. She was sweet and good and innocent. All the things he could never be.

And yet, knowing all that, he wanted her. Wanted her with a desperation that had begun to border on madness.

He wasn't certain how much longer he could go on playing this dangerous game, before the madness would take him over the edge.

Chapter Seven

Bethany awoke to the morning sounds of MaryCastle. Grandpapa's door opening and closing with a slam, and his voice overloud in the hallway, asking their little maid, Libby, where his clean shirt was. Libby telling him, as she did each morning, that it was neatly laid out on his dressing table. Mistress Coffey, calling from below stairs that their morning meal was ready. Newton returning from the stables, whistling a little seafaring tune. Darcy climbing to the widow's walk to watch for a glimpse of the ship that would bring Gray, her childhood sweetheart, home to her.

Bethany's fingers fumbled as she dressed for another day at Penhollow Abbey. How could she bear to spend an entire day in the company of the earl, when her heart was still with the Lord of the Night?

Her hands stilled as she thought about what they had shared. It was much more than a few stolen kisses. There had been heat and passion and the sort of wild desire she'd never even known existed. And if it hadn't been for his strength of will, they might have crossed a very dangerous line.

She dressed quickly in a simple shirtwaist and dark

skirt, and twisted her hair into a knot. Then she stood for long minutes, staring at her reflection in the looking glass, and wondering if she looked somehow different after last night. Would the others know, just by looking at her, that she had met with the Lord of the Night? Did a few stolen kisses, a passionate embrace, make a woman look older? More sophisticated? Oh, she wished with all her might that she could look fashionable and beautiful and...seductive.

Annoyed at the direction of her thoughts, she snatched up her shawl and slammed out of her room. As she started down the stairs she was startled to hear the sound of Edwina's voice coming from the parlor.

Before she could slip past, Edwina spotted her and rushed out into the hallway, attaching herself like an eel. "Bethany. You simply won't believe this. I was just telling the others...." She dragged the young woman into the parlor, where the rest of the household had gathered at her insistence to hear the news.

"We've just received a missive from a Miss Jenna Pike, of the Mead Foundling Home, in the village of Mead. Do you know of it?"

While the others shook their heads, Geoffrey Lambert nodded. "Mead's a small fishing village, a good distance from here. But I've never heard of this foundling home."

Edwina lowered her voice conspiratorially. "Nor has anyone else. This Miss Jenna Pike has invited Mama and me to come and claim our valuables."

There was a gasp from the others.

Edwina smiled, loving the fact that she had their undivided attention. "It seems there was a parcel left on the doorstep of the foundling home last night. And inside were a score of jewels and other precious items, along with the names of those from whom they'd been stolen. And it was signed by the Lord of the Night.''

''Could this mean that the highwayman has had a change of heart?'' Geoffrey mused aloud.

''I hardly think that.'' Edwina started toward the door. ''Oswald said that more than likely it means that the king's soldiers are close to catching him, and he fears being caught with the evidence on his person as he flees Cornwall.''

''Oswald?'' Bethany had been hearing rumors about Edwina and the earl's cousin.

''Aye. Haven't I told you?'' Edwina lowered her voice. ''Oswald Preston has been spending a great deal of time in my company. He claims I'm the reason he hasn't already returned to London. Mama and I both think he might soon ask for my hand.'' She gave them a look of triumph.

''Well.'' Bethany couldn't think of anything else to say. The attraction of any woman to such a shallow man mystified her. But then, she thought, it was so typical of Edwina.

''As to this strange turn of events,'' Edwina said importantly, ''whatever the reason, Mama and I will have our jewelry back. Oswald said we will leave this very morning for the village of Mead, and the Mead Foundling Home.'' With a rustle of petticoats, and a cloud of French perfume, she was gone.

As they speculated about this latest twist in the mystery, the others followed Mistress Coffey to the dining room, where their morning meal was ready. Bethany found her mind wandering to her strange nighttime encounter with the Lord of the Night. Both he and his mount had displayed signs of a long, hard ride. It made perfect sense if they were coming all the way from the village of Mead. But he hadn't seemed like a man running from danger. In fact, he'd acted like a man at peace with himself. A man who had all the time in the world.

Her sister's words brought her out of her musings.

"Do you think Edwina is correct?" Darcy nibbled a biscuit. "Do you really believe the Lord of the Night has left Cornwall, Grandpapa?"

Bethany turned to her grandfather, who sat sipping his tea.

"I should hope so. It will give some people around here a great deal of peace of mind."

"Were you ever worried, Grandpapa?" Bethany asked.

He shook his head. "Only the nobles need worry. I have little of value to a highwayman."

"Well." She circled the table to kiss his cheek. "You have a great deal of value to us."

Surprised and touched, he patted her hand. "Now what brought that on, lass?"

"It's just that I love you, Grandpapa. And I've been thinking that I don't tell you that nearly often enough." She brightened at a sudden thought. "Why don't you and Winnie come with me to Penhollow Abbey today?"

"Oh, how I wish we could." The old nursemaid exchanged a smile with the man across the table. It was, Bethany thought, the smile of a woman who was smitten. It seemed to confirm her opinion that their grandfather and their old nurse had grown closer of late. Considerably closer. "But I'm afraid today is impossible. Geoffrey and I promised young Deacon Welland that we'd go to the vicarage. He's planning a special blessing of the ships in the harbor on Sunday. He asked to confer with a real ship's captain before giving his sermon."

The housekeeper gave a huff of disapproval as she

circled the table pouring tea. "The one who ought to be accompanying you to the vicarage is Bethany."

"Whatever for, Mistress Coffey?" Darcy asked in all innocence.

"What the young deacon needs, as everyone in Land's End knows, is a wife. And what our Bethany needs is the calming influence of a fine, sensible young man like Deacon Welland."

Bethany rolled her eyes and started toward the door. "Excuse me. I believe I hear the rumble of wagon wheels."

"Don't try to evade the issue, young lady," the housekeeper called. "You could do a lot worse than a man of the cloth. He'd be steady and dependable, and sober," she added as an afterthought.

Bethany heard the sound of Newton's voice and nearly ran in her haste to escape. "Here's Newt now, looking for me. I'm holding up the others. I should be home by dark."

"See that you are," her grandfather called. "And tell the earl I'll accompany you tomorrow, if there's still timber to be harvested."

"Aye, Grandpapa. Thank you." She ran out the door and pulled herself up to the seat of the wagon.

"Looks like ye're in a hurry, lass," the old sailor flicked the reins.

"Aye. You came along just in time to save me. Mistress Coffey is matchmaking again."

"Who's the lucky one this time?"

"Deacon Welland. She thinks he'd make the perfect husband for me."

"Now there's a pair." He shook his head and chuckled. "It'd probably take him the first five years of marriage just to find the courage to hold yer hand, lass."

She joined in his laughter. ''Aye. And the first time he saw me strapping on a sword and tucking a pistol in my pocket, he'd probably have to trade his collar and robes for sackcloth and ashes to do penance.''

The old man nodded. ''Don't let that old hen choose yer mate for ye, lass. Ye'll do a fine job of that all by yerself.''

She shook her head. ''I'm not so sure, Newt.'' She turned to him. ''How does a person know if it's really love, or if it's just...'' Her words trailed off in embarrassment.

Though she'd spoken the words lightly enough, the old man heard the underlying note of concern. He'd noticed the telltale signs of growing nervousness lately. And he'd seen the high color in her cheeks.

He grew silent a moment, before saying, ''Love, real love, means caring about the other more than yerself. Wanting what's best for the other, even though it might cause you pain. I watched Riordan Spencer fight a terrible battle with himself because he wanted yer sister, Ambrosia. But what he wanted even more was to do the right thing by her.''

''How did they resolve it, Newt?''

He grinned. ''I think Ambrosia simply wore him down. The poor lad never had a chance after she set her cap for him.''

Seeing the look on her face he closed a gnarled old hand over hers, held tightly together in her lap. ''Don't worry about Mistress Coffey's matchmaking. It's of no consequence. Those who go looking for love rarely find it, lass. Love, real love, has a way of sneaking up on ye when ye least expect it.''

''Has it ever sneaked up on you, Newt?''

"Aye. And caught me purely by surprise." He winked, then turned his attention to the team.

Bethany found herself wondering why the closer they got to the forest the more restless she became. She was actually looking forward to spending another day in the company of the earl. But how could this be? At night she gave her kisses to a highwayman. By day she talked and laughed, and if truth be told, nearly flirted, with the earl of Alsmeeth. Did that make her as silly as Edwina Cannon?

Her nerves increased when they reached the forest and found Huntley standing beside the earl's fancy carriage. As before he greeted Newton and the men, and then assisted her into the carriage for the ride to the estate. And, as she had the previous day, she took the reins and handled the team, grateful for the release that task offered.

"You shouldn't be doing this, Miss Lambert," Huntley warned sternly. "And if I had any sense at all, I'd not permit it."

"I won't tell a soul, Huntley. It'll be our little secret."

He clamped his jaw, knowing full well the earl would be watching their approach.

"Welcome, Miss Lambert." As before, the housekeeper greeted her in the courtyard, then hurried off to attend to her duties while Huntley led Bethany up the stairs to the library, where he announced her.

"Miss Lambert is here, your lordship."

"Thank you, Huntley."

The butler stepped aside and Bethany walked into the room. She came to a sudden halt when she realized that they weren't alone. Four men, all in dark waistcoats, were seated around the earl's desk.

Kane pushed back his chair and came around the desk. Seeing the flush on her cheeks, and the tendrils of fiery hair that had pulled loose from her nape, he had to bite back a smile. "It appears the wind has picked up a bit."

"Aye." She heard the butler's discreet cough and stared at a spot on the floor.

Kane glanced toward the others, then back to her. "Forgive me, but I find that I must deal with my solicitors, who have just arrived from London."

"I see."

He could read the disappointment in her eyes. It matched his own. But it was just as well, since looking at her made him ache to touch her. And touching her might lead to all sorts of other...complications. "Feel free to explore whatever captures your interest here at Penhollow Abbey. And if we've finished our business in time, perhaps I can join you for a midday meal."

"Of course." Swallowing back her disappointment, she turned away and let herself out of the library. As she was closing the door, she caught sight of Kane already seated behind his desk, opening the first of many ledgers that were piled to one side. It appeared that he had already forgotten about her.

With a sigh she made her way below stairs. Then on a whim, she followed the sound of voices coming from the kitchens.

Kane pushed away from his desk and offered a handshake to each of the solicitors. "I'm grateful for your prompt attention to this matter. I hope your journey back to London is uneventful."

When they were gone, he pressed a hand to the tension at the back of his neck. He hadn't expected to spend so many hours in their company. But it couldn't be helped.

Perhaps, he thought, it was just as well. Bethany had looked so tempting when she'd arrived, all pink-cheeked and windblown, that he might not have been able to resist the desire to kiss her. The hours spent going over the ledgers, no matter how tedious, had given him time to cool his ardor. If he made the effort, he ought to be able to keep his hands off her for what was left of this day.

With Storm by his side he wandered down the stairs and heard the sound of raucous laughter coming from the direction of the kitchens. Though he'd never had occasion to go to this section of the house, he decided to investigate. He peered into several rooms and found them empty. But up ahead, he could still hear the voices raised in laughter. He paused in the doorway and found himself staring in surprise.

Bethany was standing with her back to him, surrounded by the servants, including Mistress Dove and Huntley. All were listening with rapt attention as she relayed a funny incident from her childhood.

"...and there we all were, Ambrosia, Darcy and I, soaked to the skin after our spill in the sea, forced to wear castoffs from Papa and James. Ambrosia, as I recall, was wearing Papa's shirt and a pair of our brother's breeches. I thought she looked rather good in them. I, on the other hand, had on a pair of Papa's breeches which were big enough for two of me. And poor Darcy was so small, she was swimming in one of James's shirts. And as we stepped off the ship onto the beach, who should be waiting to greet us but the lord mayor of Land's End. Poor Papa. Left to explain why his daughters looked like ragamuffins."

The servants were shaking with laughter.

"But the worst of it was the fact that the mayor had brought along his spinster sister, who'd set her cap for Papa. You can imagine how quickly she changed her mind when she realized just what sort of baggage she'd be taking on. Not only would she have to deal with our home, which everyone in the village referred to as Lambert's Folly, but the entire Lambert clan as well. And she'd pretty much decided after one look at us that we were all quite mad.''

Even Kane couldn't help laughing at the image she'd painted.

Bethany saw the others glance beyond her and fall silent. She turned to see Kane standing in the doorway.

"Forgive me, your lordship." Mistress Dove began backing from the room.

The servants scattered. Even Huntley cleared his throat, then took himself off to find some chores.

When they were alone, Kane leaned against the doorway and crossed his arms over his chest. "That was quite a tale. Was it true?"

"Aye. Things like that always seemed to happen to our family."

He was beginning to understand why she was so unique. "I'm sorry I didn't know you then. Do you have many of those mishaps now?"

"Constantly," she said with a sigh.

He smiled and stepped closer. "I'm sorry I missed our midday meal."

"I don't mind. I took my meal in here with your staff."

"So I see. Now I'm doubly sorry I missed it."

"Have you ever eaten here with your servants?"

"Nay. But I can see that I've been missing some…interesting moments."

She looked down, running a finger around the flour that dusted the tabletop. "They're delightful."

Without thinking he touched a hand to her cheek. "I believe they would say the same of you."

She tried steeling herself against his touch, but it was no use. The mere press of his hand had her skin burning.

"Did you..." She took a step away and continued staring at the tabletop. It was easier than looking at him, knowing he would see the betraying flush on her cheeks. "Did you hear the news?"

"What news?"

His voice was nearer, and she realized he was standing directly beside her. Though she didn't turn, she could feel his gaze boring into her. She swallowed, and the sound was overloud in her own ears. "Edwina Cannon and her mother received a missive this morrow from a Miss Jenna Pike at the Mead Foundling Home, stating that they could claim their treasures which had been stolen by the Lord of the Night."

"Interesting." Even more interesting was the tendril of hair that had pulled loose from the knot at her nape. He couldn't resist touching a finger to it, and rubbing it between his thumb and finger. It was softer than down.

Heat spiraled from Bethany's head, all the way to her toes. She drew her arms about herself to keep from shivering. "Edwina says your cousin Oswald suspects that the Lord of the Night is about to be captured by the king's own soldiers, and fears being caught with the evidence of his crimes on his person." Very slowly she turned. The look she saw in his eyes caused a jolt to her heart. "What say you?"

For the space of a heartbeat his mind was wiped clear of all thought. All he could see were those green eyes staring into his. He had thought he could carry this off. He would simply keep his distance. But right now, this moment, all he wanted was to crush her in his arms and kiss her until they were both breathless. And to take the kiss to its inevitable conclusion.

With great effort he pulled himself together. "I know of the Mead Foundling Home."

Her eyes widened. "You know of it?"

"Aye." He paused for a moment, then came to a sudden decision. "Would you care to see it?"

"Could we? You wouldn't mind?"

"It might be an enjoyable experience. For both of us." And it would give him something to do besides stare at her like a lovesick fool. He turned away almost gratefully. "I'll have Huntley arrange for my carriage."

It was a beautiful day for a ride. A gentle breeze ruffled the leaves of the trees as they sped along a sun-dappled trail. Storm had leapt up on the seat of the rig, positioning himself between Kane and Bethany. And much to Kane's amazement, after a few minutes the dog had even allowed her to pet him. Not just touch his head, but to rub his fur until he was practically purring.

"What do you know of Mead, your lordship?"

"It's a small village. And quite poor. I send Huntley there several times a week with Mistress Dove, to buy fresh fish."

"Grandpapa said it's a fishing village. No wonder we've never been there. We catch our own fish for supper. We've never had to buy from others."

He flicked the reins, and the horse broke into a trot. "That's true of most of Cornwall. Which is one reason why Mead is so poor. They have few coming to their docks to buy their wares."

She turned to look at him. "How did you know of it?"

"My father went there often." They crested a hill and looked down on a tiny harbor, where a few fishing boats bobbed near shore. "For the longest time I wasn't permitted to accompany him."

"Why?"

"I suppose the contrast between our wealth and the little village was too great. But as I grew older I found my way here."

As they drew close, she could see that the houses were tidy, but not nearly as prosperous as those of Penhollow Abbey. Their cart rolled along the wharf, where men sat in the sun, mending their nets, and women picked among the buckets of fish, shopping for their supper.

Kane brought the cart to a halt and stepped down, to be warmly greeted by a weathered old man who accepted his gold and carried a bucket of wriggling fish to the back of the cart.

"Reide," Kane said, "this is Miss Bethany Lambert."

"Miss Lambert." The old man doffed his hat and gave a toothless smile, then turned to Kane. "Miss Pike will be disappointed if you don't stop by for a visit. Not to mention the children."

"Aye. I'll see them now." Kane clasped the old man's hand before climbing up beside Bethany.

As they started up the lane she turned to him. "You know Miss Jenna Pike?"

"Aye. A good woman," he said simply. "Maybe the best woman I've ever known. Like her mother, she's beautiful and kind and generous."

Bethany felt a quick stab of something that startled her. Jealousy? Impossible. She'd never known such an emotion in her life. Besides, she certainly didn't care who the earl of Alsmeeth spent his time with. But as they rolled through the sleepy little village, she was prepared to dislike this woman whom he held in such high esteem.

The horse and cart meandered up a hill, past an ancient church with crumbling stones and ivy that had grown wild and covered half the foundation. Just beyond was a sprawling old house that looked to be the vicarage. Despite the fact that it, too, was crumbling, the gardens had been carefully tended, and the fragrance of bread seeped from the open windows, perfuming the air.

Before Kane could bring the horse and cart to a halt, voices were heard raised in excitement, and the door was thrown open. A beautiful young woman stood on the threshold and opened her arms wide. To Bethany's amazement, Kane stepped down and clasped the woman's hands in both of his, while a score of little children tumbled out the door and circled around them, shouting, squealing, shrieking. When Kane and the woman stepped apart, she said something in a soft tone and the children fell into a respectful silence.

"Who is this?" The woman smiled as she studied Bethany.

"Come, Miss Pike." Kane caught her hand and led her to the cart. "This is Miss Bethany Lambert. Miss Lambert, this is Miss Jenna Pike."

"Miss Pike." Bethany offered her hand and it was caught in a firm grasp as the woman stared up into her eyes.

"Miss Lambert. We're honored by your presence." She turned. "Children, can you give a proper greeting to our guest, Miss Lambert?"

In singsong voices the children greeted her with, "Welcome, Miss Lambert."

Bethany couldn't help but be charmed. Not only by the children, but by the warmth she could read in this young woman's eyes. "Thank you. I'm most happy to be here."

"Your lordship, why don't you bring Miss Lambert inside? I've baked bread. We'll have tea."

"Thank you." He offered his hand and helped Bethany from the cart.

She turned. "What about Storm?"

Kane shook his head. "I'm not sure he knows how to behave around children."

"There's one way to find out." She clapped her hands and the dog leapt down and trailed behind them.

They walked through a house that was as tidy inside as the gardens outside. At a long wooden table they sat, with the children crowded around them, while Jenna fixed tea and sliced freshly baked bread still warm from the oven.

Bethany found herself counting the children. There were ten, ranging in age from a curly-headed toddler to a boy of perhaps ten and two. She couldn't resist picking up the little toddler and cuddling her on her knee, feeding her bits of bread and fruit conserve, and giving her sips of tea.

"I hope you don't mind," she asked softly.

Jenna smiled. "Mind? Miss Lambert, the children take great delight in being treated to company. Especially if it's someone who doesn't mind so many wriggling little bodies."

"I'm enjoying myself thoroughly. How could I not enjoy this?" Bethany found herself smiling at a shy little boy, and kissing the cheek of a girl who reached up to touch her hair.

She noted that the children were busy feeding bits of bread to Storm, who was lying under the table, his tail wagging like a pendulum.

Jenna took a seat at the table and said, "I must tell you our news." Her eyes were bright with excitement. "This morning young Noah found a parcel on our front step. Inside was a sack of gold and some lovely jewels.

There was also a missive listing the names of people in nearby towns and villages who had once owned these treasures. It instructed me to notify these people that they could claim their possessions any time they chose to visit. And it was signed by the notorious highwayman, the Lord of the Night.''

''Fascinating.'' Kane smiled. ''Do you know this outlaw personally?''

That brought a chorus of laughter from the children.

Laughing with them, Jenna shook her head. ''I'm sure I'd remember if I'd ever met such a man.''

''Have any of the people come to claim their possessions?''

''So far, only two have come. A Miss and Mistress Cannon, from Land's End. Accompanied by a young man claiming to be your cousin.''

Kane winked at the oldest lad and handed him half a biscuit. ''What was their demeanor?''

Jenna smiled at the sight of the man and boy sharing bites of biscuit. ''They seemed quite taken aback by the fact that there were so many of us living here. But they were so grateful to have their jewelry back that they bought several loaves of our bread. And the young gentleman gave us a gold piece for our trouble. ''

''A single gold piece?'' Kane kept his smile in place, for the sake of the children. But it was an effort.

''Don't scold, your lordship. It's more than we had before they came here.'' Jenna dropped an arm around a little girl and drew her close. ''The ladies told us the gold and jewels had been stolen at the point of a pistol. And that the highwayman had been a cruel monster. Why do you suppose such a brute would leave his bounty on our doorstep?''

Kane shrugged. "Perhaps he thought you might put it to some good use."

"You jest. He knew we wouldn't keep it. He even went to the trouble of giving us the names of his victims, so they could claim their valuables." She shook her head. "I wish I understood what it all meant."

Kane drained his cup and got to his feet. "Perhaps in time you'll figure it out, Miss Pike. Now I'm afraid Miss Lambert and I must leave." He reached into his pocket and withdrew a handful of coins, which he began to pass around to each of the children. Then he pressed a small pouch into Jenna's hand.

"You're far too generous, your lordship."

"Nay. Not nearly as generous as you." He turned to the older boy. "Noah, are you keeping the bargain we struck?"

The boy flushed. "Aye, your lordship."

"I'm proud of you." He motioned. "There's a bucket of fish in the back of the cart. It ought to make a fine supper with this bread."

The boy hurried out and returned with the bucket of wriggling fish.

At the door Kane paused to lift Jenna's hand to his lips.

She seemed touched by his gesture. "Now what was that for?"

"For being yourself." He helped Bethany up to the cart, then climbed up beside her and picked up the reins.

After enduring hugs from all the children, Storm leapt up beside them.

"Hurry back, your lordship," Jenna called. "And you too, Miss Lambert."

"Thank you. I'd love to come back."

Bethany turned and waved to the children as the horse

started forward. The oldest boy ran alongside them until they reached the end of the lane. Even then he looked as though he'd run for miles just to keep them in sight.

When they passed the crumbling old church she said, "Who is Jenna Pike? And why does she take in so many children? Surely it can't be easy for her."

Kane shook his head. "Nay. It's a daunting task for one woman. But she simply can't refuse a child in need. She's just a kindhearted teacher who, like her mother before her, wanted to make a home for some of Cornwall's poorest of the poor."

"Are they all orphans?"

He shrugged. "Most are. She told me that one of them had been abandoned by her mother, because she could no longer provide food or shelter."

Bethany shook her head. "That's just heartbreaking. But they seemed so happy." She flushed. "I suppose I'd always thought that foundlings would be sad and lonely and treated to a miserable existence."

"They would be. Without Jenna Pike. She never counts the cost, both in gold, and in her personal life." He slowed the team to a walk. "How many men would be willing to offer marriage to a beautiful young woman who was responsible for a score of children?"

"I hadn't thought of that."

"Nor does she. That's what makes her so remarkable. She sees a need and answers it, without regard to the consequences. But she pays dearly for that kind heart. I suspect she often goes without, so that the children will have a little more."

"And so you help her with food and gold."

"It's little enough, when you consider all that she does. She bakes bread and she and the children carry it to the village in a little cart, where they sell what they can. But it's a poor village.''

''Aye. Even their church appears to be crumbling.''

''That's because their last vicar died more than five years ago, and there's been no one to replace him.''

''What a sad little village.''

''Not so sad. Just poor. But if enough people came to know Mead, and its people, they might make a difference.'' He flicked the reins. ''Now we'd better hurry back to Penhollow Abbey. I've a feeling old Newt will be waiting to take you home.''

As they rolled along the country lane in the late-afternoon sunshine, it occurred to Bethany that the earl of Alsmeeth actually seemed to care deeply about this young woman and her foundlings, as well as the village where they lived. It was a completely different side to him than he allowed the rest of the world to see. A side of him that touched her heart.

When they arrived at Penhollow Abbey, the wagon loaded with timber was already standing in the courtyard. Kane handed the reins of the carriage over to a stable lad, and he and Bethany went inside in search of old Newton.

They found him in the kitchen, seated at the wooden table beside Mistress Dove. The two were laughing together, drinking tea and nibbling freshly baked biscuits slathered with honey.

''Oh. Your lordship.'' The housekeeper got to her feet so quickly, she nearly knocked over her chair. Her cheeks, Bethany noted, were flushed.

''We were just enjoying a bit of tea while we waited for you.''

''So I see.'' He turned to the old sailor. ''You'd be Newton.''

"Aye, yer lordship." Newt got to his feet and offered his hand. "Newton Findlay."

"Miss Lambert speaks of you often."

"She and her sisters are like my own." The old man turned to Bethany. "Good news, lass. We've cut the last of the timber. We can start work on the *Undaunted* on the morrow."

"That's good news indeed." She turned to the housekeeper. "Well, you'll not have me underfoot anymore, Mistress Dove."

"Nonsense, miss. You were never underfoot."

"I do thank you for all your kindness."

"You're welcome, Miss Lambert. It's been a pleasure to have you here at Penhollow Abbey." The old woman glanced at Kane, who hadn't spoken a word. "If you wouldn't mind, your lordship, I'm certain the servants would like to bid goodbye to our guest."

He gave a curt nod of his head. "Why don't you have them assemble in the courtyard?"

"Aye, your lordship." Pleased, the housekeeper hurried away.

Minutes later Bethany and Newton followed the earl outside, to find the others hastily gathered. Bethany bid goodbye to the servants, and then turned to Huntley, who stood at rigid attention beside the earl. "Goodbye, Huntley. Thank you for everything. Especially for allowing me to drive the team, even though it was against your better judgment."

The man flushed, a sure sign that he was losing his composure. "It was my pleasure, Miss Lambert."

She turned to Kane, who was staring at her with such intensity, it made her cheeks burn. "I thank you, as well, your lordship. For the lovely tour of your gardens and your estate. And for taking me to Mead today."

"You are most welcome, Miss Lambert."

She knelt down and petted Storm, and the dog surprised her by licking her hand. She turned away and Newton handed her up to the driver's seat, then climbed in beside her and took the reins. The team strained against the harness and started off at a slow, plodding pace.

Bethany turned to give a last wave of her hand. And then the horse and wagon dipped below a hill, and the servants, murmuring among themselves, returned to their chores.

Only Kane remained alone in the courtyard, with the dog at his heel, watching the dust begin to settle. Finally he turned away and climbed the stairs to his library. On his face was a thoughtful, pensive look.

Chapter Eight

"I do so enjoy hearing Deacon Welland reading from the Book of Psalms." Mistress Coffey studied Bethany, seated across from her in the carriage. "Don't you just love his deep, rich voice?"

Bethany was more interested in the clouds, moving lazily across the moon in the darkened sky. It would have been such a fine night for riding Lacey along the beach. But her plans had been changed abruptly when the housekeeper had caught her and insisted that she fulfill her duty at the vicarage. "I think Deacon Welland's talents are being wasted here in Land's End."

Mistress Coffey was scandalized. "Bethany. How can you say such a thing?"

"Well, think of it. Vicar Goodwin conducts almost all of the Sunday services. He performs all of the marriages. Christens all the newborns. And he occasionally permits the young deacon to preach or bless a ship. Did you know, Mistress Coffey, that there are poor villages whose churches are crumbling, and whose flock are going unattended, because they have no vicar?"

"I find that hard to believe." The older woman pursed her lips with distaste. "If there were such a place here in Cornwall, I'm quite certain Vicar Thatcher Goodwin would be willing to share the talents of his fine young deacon. As he often says, we're all part of God's family.''

"He does say that, doesn't he?" Bethany smiled as a thought began to take shape in her mind. Of course. It was all so simple. She leaned across the seat to squeeze her housekeeper's hand. "Oh, Mistress Coffey. You've just given me a wonderful idea."

"I have?" The old woman arched a brow in puzzlement.

"Aye. Thank you."

"You're welcome." Mistress Coffey sat back, wondering what she'd said to make Bethany so happy.

When they arrived at MaryCastle, Bethany climbed the steps behind the housekeeper, and gave a last, lingering look at the night sky. She wanted, more than anything, to ride Lacey before going off to her bed. But the sky had gone dark. Storm clouds threatened. Instead, she made her way to her room and slipped into a nightshift. As she brushed her hair long and loose, she walked to the window and stared out at the beach.

Her heart nearly stopped. She'd thought, just for a moment, that she'd spotted a horseman. Then a bank of dark clouds scudded past the moon, casting the land in darkness. She knelt beside the window and strained to see. Finally, as the clouds parted, she saw him. A figure all in black, astride a black stallion. Without giving a thought to what she was doing, she dropped the hairbrush and began to run. She raced out of her room and down the stairs. Once outside she raced barefoot across the sand.

He sat perfectly still, watching as she drew near. She might have been an angel, with her white shift fluttering around her ankles, her hair dancing around her face and shoulders like a halo.

"How long have you been here?" Her voice was low, breathless.

"For hours. I'd hoped we could ride together one last time, Bethany."

"Last—?" She drew up short and stared at him.

He nodded. "I came to tell you that I must leave Cornwall."

She walked closer. "Because the authorities are closing in?"

He smiled. "Aye. That's reason enough."

"There are other reasons?"

"Perhaps I find myself caring too much for you."

"Is that a reason to leave?"

"Aye. The most important one of all. For we can have no future."

"You could mend your ways. You could…"

He held up a hand. "It can never be. You're too fine to be tied to an outlaw. I came to say goodbye, Bethany. And to tell you that you'll never see me again."

"Never?"

He shook his head and stared at her as though memorizing every line and curve of her lovely face.

"This isn't fair. I don't even know your name."

"Nor will you ever."

She sighed at the fierceness of his whisper. "I'll not forget you."

"Nor I you." He started to turn his horse.

"Wait." She stepped closer, clutching the reins. "Why did you return all the jewels and gold you'd stolen?"

"I had no use for them."

"No use? But then…" She pondered this a moment.

''If you don't need them, why did you go to the trouble of stealing them?''

''Perhaps for the sheer pleasure of making their owners uncomfortable. Or because I wanted to shake up their placid lives.''

''I don't understand.''

''I'm not sure I do, either.''

She continued holding the reins. ''Will you at least kiss me one last time before you go?''

She could see a smoldering look come into his eyes. ''After our last…encounter, that wouldn't be wise.''

''Why?''

''You have a powerful effect on me, Bethany.''

She knew she was close to tears, but she didn't care. She closed a hand over his. ''If I can never see you again, then at least give me one kiss to carry with me for a lifetime.''

She felt his hand tighten. Then, before she could blink, he lifted her in his strong arms and tugged aside his scarf. His mouth covered hers in a savage kiss. It spoke of hunger. Of need. Of a desperate, driving desire to take and take until they were both sated.

It was the most amazing feeling to be held like this. As though she weighed nothing at all. There was such strength in him. And such control. She could feel it, as he held back, struggling not to give in to the feelings that he'd revealed the last time they'd been together like this.

With a sigh she brought her arms around his neck and kissed him back, pouring all her heart and soul into it. Her mouth moved over his, her lips warming and softening, before opening to his probing tongue.

For the space of several minutes he gave in to the pleasure, filling himself with her. Thrilling to the easy way she offered herself to him. But as the kiss deepened, and the passion rose, leaving them both trembling, he pulled back. Their breathing was already labored. Their chests heaved with churning emotions. Emotions that were far too close to the edge.

Abruptly he lowered her to the ground and stared at her for the space of a full minute, before urging his mount into a run. With sand churning, horse and rider raced along the beach. Bethany remained where she was, until darkness swallowed them up. Then, with tears rolling down her cheeks, she made her way back to the house. But even after she'd slipped between the covers, sleep wouldn't come. Instead, she tossed and turned and cursed herself for losing her heart to a highwayman. Hadn't she known there could be no future in such foolishness? But it was out of her control. As old Newt had warned her, love had come sneaking up on her. And now she would have to live with the knowledge that such a thing might never come her way again.

"Well." Mistress Coffey stood with her hands on her hips as Bethany stepped into the dining room. "Did you think, now that the timber was cut and your task with the earl completed, that you could sleep the day away?"

"I'm truly sorry." Bethany took her place at the table and glanced around at the others. "I didn't mean to keep you waiting. I...slept badly."

"Did I hear you go outside after you returned from the vicarage?" Darcy broke open a biscuit and glanced at her sister across the table.

"I—" Bethany was relieved to hear a knock on the door. At the moment she would welcome any sort of interruption.

"Now who could that be?" The housekeeper waved a

hand at their little maid. "Libby, see to the door while I pour the tea."

A moment later the maid returned, looking ashen. "You have a visitor."

Geoffrey cupped an ear. "Eh? A visitor, you say? Well, don't just stand there. Show him in, Libby."

"But it's—"

"Show him in, girl," the old man said with a trace of impatience.

A moment later the maid returned, trailed by a tall, well-dressed man who had the others staring in stunned surprise.

"Captain Lambert." Libby's voice was trembling. "Your guest is the earl of Alsmeeth."

For the space of several moments there was complete silence, except for the scraping back of Geoffrey's chair.

"Your lordship." Bethany couldn't hide her surprise as she got to her feet. "May I present my grandfather, Captain Geoffrey Lambert."

"Your lordship." The old man extended his hand.

"Captain Lambert." Kane accepted the handshake.

"And this is my sister, Darcy."

He nodded graciously. "Miss Lambert."

Darcy nearly swooned at the sight of him.

"You've met Newton Findlay. And this is our nurse-maid, Miss Winifred Mellon."

He bowed slightly. "Miss Mellon."

The old woman blushed clear to her toes.

"And our housekeeper, Mistress Coffey."

The housekeeper nearly dropped her teapot. When she finally managed to set it down, tea sloshed over the snowy linen cloth and she was forced to grip the edge of the table to keep from sinking to her knees as she attempted a curtsy.

Geoffrey Lambert indicated the empty chair beside Bethany. "We were just breaking our fast. Will you join us at table, your lordship?"

Their housekeeper nearly fainted. The earl at their table? It was unthinkable. She was stunned when he accepted the invitation.

"Thank you. That's most kind." Kane held Bethany's chair, then took the seat beside her.

Mistress Coffey nearly ran to the kitchen, where she began shouting orders to the cook to slice more beef, cook more eggs, heat more biscuits. When she returned to the dining room, she was out of breath as she began to circle the table with a fresh platter of food.

Kane helped himself to beef and eggs, and broke open a steaming biscuit. After one taste he looked up. "My compliments to your cook, Mistress Coffey. These biscuits are the finest I've ever tasted."

"Oh, your lordship." Her face was bright with color, and she looked as though she might weep with relief. "If I'd known you were coming, I'd have had our cook make her bread pudding. No one in Cornwall makes better."

"Then you're most fortunate to have her. Just as I'm sure the Lambert family is fortunate to have you."

"You're much too kind, your lordship." The old woman bobbed her way out of the room, much to the delight of Darcy and Bethany, who glanced at each other and had to cover their mouths with their napkins to keep from giggling.

"You're up and about early, your lordship." Geoffrey Lambert studied the man who had elicited so many rumors and whispers since his return to Cornwall.

"Aye. I'm pleased to see that your family is also up and about early."

"We're a seafaring family, your lordship. We're guided by the moon, the stars and the tide."

Kane nodded. "I like the sound of that, Captain Lambert. I think it would be a comfort to know one had such competent guides through life."

"They're there for anyone who wants them, your lordship." The old man sipped his tea and glanced from the earl to his granddaughter. "Have you come here for a reason, your lordship?"

"I have." Kane set down his cup. "But I'd prefer to speak with you about it in private. I wonder if I might meet with you in the parlor after we've eaten?"

"By all means, your lordship."

Bethany found that her appetite had fled. Was he here to complain because she had brazenly driven his team? Or was he angry because she'd taken her meal with his servants? Whatever her offense, he was here to announce that she had overstepped her bounds. Would he demand the return of his timber?

Nonsense. She had lived up to the terms of their agreement. At least the first half. And when the *Undaunted* was repaired, she fully intended to take the earl on the cruise he'd insisted upon. Perhaps it wouldn't be as long or as difficult as he hoped, but he would get his journey aboard ship. And she would fulfill the terms of their agreement.

Though her nerves were jumping, her grandfather seemed not the least concerned about what the earl was doing here. With maddening thoroughness, he continued enjoying his beef, his biscuits, his tea, as though he hadn't a care in the world. When at last the interminable meal ended, Geoffrey set down his napkin and said to their housekeeper, "A fine meal as always, Mistress Coffey."

He turned to Miss Mellon. ''I'll meet you in the garden in a little while, Winnie.''

''Aye, Geoffrey.'' The old woman smiled and pushed away from the table. ''Bethany and Darcy, perhaps you'll join me for a stroll in the garden?''

''I thought I'd stay with Grandpapa,'' Bethany said.

The old man patted her hand. ''Go with Winnie, my dear. The earl and I have matters to discuss.''

''But—''

He shook his head. ''Go along now.'' He glanced at their guest. ''If you'll follow me, your lordship.''

The two men made their way to the parlor, and closed the door. With a sigh of disgust, Bethany followed her sister and old nurse to the garden, where she was forced to endure a long-winded lecture on Winnie's latest theory of cross-pollination.

Bethany was seated on a stone bench in the garden when she looked up to see her grandfather and the earl walking toward her. Judging by the stunned look on Geoffrey's face, the business they had discussed had caught him by surprise.

Concerned, Bethany hurried forward to grasp his hands. ''What is it, Grandpapa? What's wrong?''

''Lass—'' He studied her a moment, then cleared his throat. ''The earl has come here to ask if he might court you.''

''Court—'' She knew her jaw had dropped. Knew the others were staring at her. But she couldn't seem to find her voice. Of all the things she'd imagined, this hadn't been one of them.

The old man lay a hand on her shoulder. ''I told our young gentleman that I have no objections. But if you should object...'' He studied her closely, looking deeply into her eyes. "I'll not give my approval until I know your feelings, Bethany."

Feelings? She had to struggle with so many confusing, conflicting emotions. She'd expected to be reprimanded. Instead, she was to be courted. By the wealthiest man in Cornwall. She could see the housekeeper clasping her hands together and looking overwhelmed at the implications. Winnie was beaming with happiness. This would appeal to her romantic old heart. As for Darcy, she was grinning from ear to ear. But what did she herself think of such a thing? What did she feel?

At last she found her voice. "Why would you wish to court me, your lordship? I'm not a highborn woman. Nor do I have a dowry."

"Such things are of no concern to me, Miss Lambert."

"But they ought to be. There will be those who will say you keep company with a woman beneath your station."

"Let them say whatever they please. I have never chosen to live my life according to what others may say. I prefer to keep my own counsel." He paused. "Do the words of others matter to you, Miss Lambert?"

She thought about the rumors and whispers. "Nay."

"I thought as much." He waited for the space of a heartbeat before asking, "May I pay you court, Miss Lambert?"

"I—" She thought of those rare times when he smiled. And what it did to her insides. And of the few times when he'd touched a hand to her. The warmth that spread through her at his simple touch was unbelievable. She'd had to fight a strange yearning to touch him back. But that was a long way from love.

And what about her feelings for the Lord of the Night? Wouldn't it be dishonest to allow one man to court her when her heart already belonged to another? *An outlaw,* she reminded herself. A man who could never declare his love for her in return. A man who, except for a few stolen kisses, could never offer her a future. Hadn't he said as much, when he'd left her last night? Left, as he'd told her, forever.

Forever. The finality of his words had left no room for a second chance.

She took a deep painful breath and realized that her feelings for the outlaw must be buried. Deeply and completely. Forever. With no hope of ever being resurrected. As for her feelings for this man, she had no idea what they were. Oh, she felt so confused. She wished Ambrosia were here. Or Mama. They would know what to do.

She lifted her chin a fraction. "I...can think of no reason to object, your lordship. But I can think of many reasons why you shouldn't consider such a thing. First of all..."

"Not now, Miss Lambert." He shook his head and gave the merest hint of a smile. "I'll see that you have plenty of time to tell me all your faults. And I'll list all of mine, as well. As for the present, if you have no further objections, I'll send Huntley with the carriage tonight, to fetch you and your family to Penhollow Abbey for a celebratory dinner."

He turned to Geoffrey Lambert. "Thank you, sir, for your approval."

"You have it. So long as you give your word, as a gentleman, that you will honor and protect my granddaughter's virtue," the old man said firmly.

It occurred to Bethany that her grandfather had not missed a single word that had been spoken.

The earl nodded and offered his handshake. "I give you my word, Captain Lambert. As a gentleman."

Bethany stood as still as a statue as the two men formally shook hands. Despite the sunshine, she felt a sudden chill. What had she just done? Oh, sweet heaven. What had she done? While grieving the loss of one love, she'd just agreed to encourage another. She wondered if her poor heart would ever be the same.

"Who would have believed we'd be spending an entire evening at Penhollow Abbey?" Mistress Coffey was wringing her hands and studying her reflection in the hall mirror. Her hair slicked back in a tight little knot. Not a single strand allowed to slip free. Her perfectly starched gown of black satin was adorned by her only piece of jewelry, the brooch from her beloved Ned.

Miss Mellon was seated on a hall bench nearby. She had chosen a gown of pale peach, with a matching shawl. Her white hair was like a wispy cloud around her pale face. "Wasn't it sweet of our Bethany to insist that we be included in the invitation?"

"Aye. But that's her charm. Bethany's always been so generous. It's only natural the earl of Alsmeeth would have taken notice. After all, he's had several days to observe her." The housekeeper suddenly turned away from the looking glass. "Do you think he's been watching our Bethany with an eye toward courtship?"

"I wouldn't be at all surprised." Winnie gathered her shawl around her. "Bethany would be difficult to ignore."

"Aye." Mistress Coffey sighed. "I'd as soon try to ignore a storm off the Atlantic as ignore our Bethany."

The two women were still smiling when Bethany and Darcy descended the stairs.

"You're not wearing that gown?" The housekeeper gave her a horrified look.

Bethany was dressed in a simple gown of pale-green silk, with high neck and long, fitted sleeves. The waist was nipped with a darker green sash.

"And why not?" She looked down at herself. "What's wrong with this?"

"It isn't your best gown. Or even your second-best."

"It'll do, Mistress Coffey." Bethany glanced around. "Where are Grandpapa and Newt?"

"Waiting outside. They wanted a breath of air."

"As do I." Bethany lifted her skirts and headed toward the door.

Just as she opened it, the earl's luxurious carriage, pulled by the team of perfectly matched white horses, came to a halt. Huntley, seated beside the driver, stepped down and stood at attention.

"Come along, ladies," Geoffrey Lambert called.

Bethany led the way, stopping to smile at the butler. "Good evening, Huntley."

"Good evening, Miss Lambert."

"I'd like you to meet my family. My grandfather, Captain Geoffrey Lambert. My sister, Darcy. Our nursemaid Miss Mellon, our housekeeper, Mistress Coffey, and I believe you know our friend, Newton Findlay."

He nodded stiffly to each and helped the women into the carriage, then offered a hand to the men.

The old sailor looked uncomfortable in a shirt and dark waistcoat. The wooden peg that served as a leg tapped nervously on the floor of the carriage as Huntley climbed to the driver's seat.

"Would you rather ride up front, Newt?" Bethany asked.

"Ye know I would, lass."

"Then go ahead. I'm sure Huntley would enjoy your

company. Huntley,'' she called. ''Newt wishes to join you and our driver.''

The old man shot her a look of gratitude and climbed out, then hauled himself up beside the butler. With a flick of the reins, they took off.

The late-afternoon air was gentle, with just a touch of a breeze that carried the tang of ocean and a hint of summer flowers.

As they moved into the forest, Geoffrey Lambert gazed up at the tall timbers. ''Thanks to the generosity of the earl, our ship can now be repaired.''

''You realize, Grandpapa—'' Bethany lowered her voice ''—once the *Undaunted* is repaired, the earl will demand his right to sail on her.'' She glanced at the others. ''When do you propose we tell him the truth about what we do?''

Geoffrey shrugged. ''The right time will present itself, Bethany. Until then, I wouldn't worry about such things.''

''But I do worry, Grandpapa. I don't believe two people should harbor secrets when they're courting. After all, the next step will be...'' She couldn't bring herself to speak the word. A formal pledge of betrothal was too final. Too frightening.

Seeing her reluctance, her old nursemaid patted her hand. ''I know you're concerned, Bethany. But I hope you won't let your nerves prevent you from enjoying this occasion.''

She swallowed. ''Of course not, Winnie. It's just...'' She glanced across the seat at her grandfather, who looked so proud. She couldn't bear the thought of disappointing him. ''Everything's happening so quickly.''

''That's the way of life,'' the old woman said with a sigh. ''For the longest time it seems that nothing's happening. And then suddenly it all speeds up, and we have all we can do to catch our breath and hang on as life hauls us along in its wake.''

Bethany turned to watch the passing scenery. It was better than looking at the others, and seeing them all looking so pleased when she felt… She didn't know what she felt. Numb. Dizzy. And afraid that this whole thing had too quickly gotten out of hand. How had it happened? All she'd wanted was some timber. And now, days later, she was being courted. By a man she didn't know.

As the carriage rolled up the long curving drive, she heard the gasps from the others, and remembered her own sense of astonishment at the extent of the earl's holdings.

''Sweet heaven.'' Beside her, Miss Mellon couldn't seem to find her voice. ''I'd never dreamed anyone but the king could have such gardens. And look, Geoffrey.'' She pointed to a fountain, gleaming in the late-afternoon sunlight. ''Isn't it spectacular?''

''Quite.'' Geoffrey Lambert surveyed the house in the distance as one might study a palace.

As they rolled to the courtyard, the entire family fell silent. Standing to one side, waiting to greet them, was the earl, looking splendid in dark breeches and waistcoat. At his feet was Storm. Behind him stood his housekeeper and several servants, prepared to assist them.

''Welcome,'' Kane called as he walked toward them. And though he smiled at everyone, his gaze remained locked on Bethany.

While Newt and Huntley stepped down, the others were assisted from the carriage.

''What a magnificent estate,'' Geoffrey remarked as he shook Kane's outstretched hand.

''Thank you. There won't be time to show you everything tonight. But I hope, in the weeks to come, you and your family will have an opportunity to see all of Pen-hollow Abbey.'' He turned. ''This is my housekeeper, Mistress Dove. She and the servants have been at work all day hoping to make your first visit with us as comfortable as possible.''

Bethany thought the poor woman looked completely frazzled. But she managed a weak smile before returning to the house to oversee the work in the kitchens.

''I thought we'd begin with a stroll in the rose garden, and then retire to the main parlor for ale before we dine.'' Kane allowed the women to precede him, then walked beside Geoffrey and Newt. Storm moved silently behind them.

While Kane made small talk with the men, he couldn't keep his eyes off the young woman in green, who was unnaturally silent while her sister and the two old women chattered away.

''Oh, this is lovely, your lordship.'' Miss Mellon paused to admire a bed of white roses, surrounding a small fountain.

''It was my mother's favorite.''

''I can see why.'' The old woman smiled in appreciation and the others gathered around, listening to the sound of the water splashing and birds trilling.

''I imagine you spend many happy hours here, your lordship.'' Mistress Coffey bent to inhale the perfume of one perfect rose.

''Not nearly as much as I'd like. But perhaps all that will change now.'' He smiled at Bethany and she could feel the others watching her.

He led them farther along the paths, pointing out the red roses, the pink ones, and the allowing them to pause and rest on benches set here and there in shaded spaces.

When they returned to the house, he led the way to the parlor, where a servant stood waiting beside a silver tray on which rested crystal glasses and decanters. As soon as they were settled around the fire the servant passed among them with goblets of ale.

As Kane sipped he asked, "How are the repairs to your ship coming along, Captain Lambert?"

"They're moving smoothly now, thanks to your generosity, your lordship."

"How soon before you can take to sea again?"

"Perhaps a week if the weather holds. Two at the most."

"So soon? I'm delighted, since I'll be the one to benefit. I'm eager to go to sea again."

"You'll soon have your wish, your lordship. Newt chose a fine crew of workers from the docks of Land's End."

"Then I'm in your debt, Newt." The earl offered his hand to the old sailor, who looked surprised and more than a little pleased.

"Ye might not want to thank me yet, yer lordship. Life aboard the *Undaunted* is nothing like the life ye lead here."

"Nor would I expect it to be." Kane smiled when his butler paused in the doorway.

"Mistress Dove wishes to inform you that dinner is ready, your lordship."

"Thank you, Huntley." Kane turned to the others. "Shall we see what my housekeeper has prepared for us tonight?"

He offered his arm, and Bethany had no choice but to accept. As they led the others toward the dining hall, she wondered at the strange heat that curled along her spine. It was, after all, nothing more than a touch of his hand.

Nerves, she thought miserably. Something so alien to her, she didn't know how to deal with them. Why was it that this man had such a troubling effect on her? After a lifetime of knowing absolutely no fear, she was trembling at the thought of what she'd agreed to. Courtship. With a stranger.

It must have been a moment of madness.

Huntley showed them to their places at the table, where servants waited behind each chair to assist. The earl sat at the head of the table, with Bethany on his right, and Darcy on his left. Old Newt sat between the two older women, with Geoffrey at the other end.

Mistress Dove entered, followed by a line of serving wenches, each bearing a covered tray. As before, each dish was presented to the earl for his approval, then offered to the others.

While the others began to eat, Kane glanced at Bethany. He kept his tone low, for her ears alone. "You've lost your appetite. Is there something wrong?"

"Nay." She stared at her plate, avoiding his eyes. "Too much excitement, I suppose."

Kane continued to study her and when she looked up saw something in her eyes that had him nearly smiling. "What's this? Nerves? I thought you were fearless, Miss Lambert?"

"I thought so, too. But it appears there are still things that can send me into a panic, your lordship."

"Such as?"

"Look around you. How can my family help but be impressed by such a display of wealth?"

"Do you wish I were poor?"

She almost smiled. "Of course not. But we're...so ordinary."

He had to choke back his laughter. "Miss Lambert, I defy anyone to call your family ordinary."

"All right. Not ordinary. But...simple. We've never been exposed to such grand surroundings."

At that very moment Mistress Coffey looked up. "Your lordship, this lovely meal puts me in mind of our time spent with His Majesty at Hampton Court."

"Hampton Court?" He glanced over at the housekeeper. "I'm afraid Miss Lambert hasn't told me about such an adventure. How did you happen to spend time with the king?"

"We were—" she glanced at the others and realized she'd revealed a family secret better left alone "—in London with Ambrosia's new husband, Riordan Spencer. He's a good friend of the king."

"Aye. I'm aware of that." He glanced at Bethany. "Just another tale of your ordinary family?"

She groaned inwardly, while managing a weak smile. "It seems I'd forgotten that one."

"I'll remind you to tell me about it some time, Miss Lambert."

"Aye, your lordship. I'm sure you will."

In an aside he muttered, "You can depend upon it." Then he turned and gave his full attention to her younger sister. "Tell me about yourself, Darcy. Do you love to ride and sail as much as your sister?"

"Aye. Sailing is my passion. And though I ride, I haven't the love for it that Bethany has. My heart and soul belong to the sea."

"And to Graham Barton," Bethany said.

"Aye. To Gray." At the mere mention of his name, Darcy beamed. "I've known him since I was five. And loved him nearly as long."

"Then he's a most fortunate young man." Kane turned

to their grandfather, who had finished second helpings of everything. "How did one man manage to have two such beautiful granddaughters?"

"Actually there are three." The old man shared a laugh with the others. "And I consider myself a lucky man indeed to have them. They filled my life after an accident aboard ship forced me to give up my command."

"You appear to have recovered from your accident."

Geoffrey nodded. "I lost a good bit of my hearing when a cannon misfired aboard deck. But it hasn't slowed me down much."

The earl turned to the old nursemaid. "And you, Miss Mellon. I understand you've been with the Lambert family for many years."

"Aye, your lordship. Since they were just motherless children."

"A bit of a handful, I'd wager." He smiled.

She shared his smile. "More than a bit. I'd never known such active children. Instead of learning to sew and knit, they were always jumping off rocks into the ocean, or racing around the bay in their little boat. I thought they'd be the death of me."

"And we may yet, Winnie," Darcy said with a laugh.

The old woman shook her head. "Don't you believe her, your lordship. They welcomed me into their home as one of the family. I don't know what would have become of me if they hadn't insisted I stay on long after they had need of me."

"We still have need of you, Winnie." Darcy shared a smile with her sister. "Who else would drag us off to her sewing circle when we'd rather be sailing? And who sees to it that we go to Psalm readings when we'd prefer to stay home and beat Grandpapa at chess?"

"Aye. Who indeed?" she said with a perfectly straight face. "It's my duty to see to your complete education. Even if you do fight me every step of the way."

Seeing that they'd finished their meal, the housekeeper presented a tray of pastries for the earl's approval.

"They look lovely, Mistress Dove. But I believe my guests and I will take our desserts in the parlor."

She nodded and sent the servants scurrying from the dining hall. A short time later, when they had assembled in the parlor, servants passed around trays of pastries while the housekeeper poured tea for the ladies. Huntley filled tumblers with ale for the men.

Geoffrey Lambert held his glass aloft and said, "Your lordship. My family and I wish to thank you for your generosity. This has been a lovely evening."

Kane smiled and lifted his own glass. "I assure you, Captain Lambert, your generosity far exceeds mine." He glanced at Bethany. "What you are giving me is priceless."

Winnie gave an audible sigh. She couldn't think of anything more romantic than this. Mistress Coffey nodded her approval as well.

Geoffrey emptied his glass, then set it down. "I do believe, your lordship, we should be leaving. We've a long day ahead of us, if we're to get the *Undaunted* seaworthy."

A short time later they made their way to the courtyard, where they were helped into the waiting carriage. As Bethany offered her hand, Kane caught it in both of his and brought it to his lips. "Good night, my lady. A safe and pleasant journey home."

She felt the thrill and wondered again at her reaction to his mere touch. "Thank you, your lordship. There is..." She cursed this nervousness that had her stumbling over words. "There is something I must tell you."

"And you shall. But not tonight. I'll send my carriage for you on the morrow." He turned to her nursemaid. "I hope, Miss Mellon, that you'll accompany Bethany here to Penhollow Abbey."

The old woman smiled her pleasure. This proper gentleman was taking no chances on creating a scandal. "I'd be most happy to, your lordship."

As the team started forward, Bethany turned for a quick glance. Kane was standing alone in the courtyard, his dog at his feet, watching their departure. When she turned back, Darcy leaned over to whisper, "Why didn't you tell me the earl was so handsome and worldly?"

Overhearing, their nursemaid nodded. "He may be worldly, but I'm pleased with his sense of propriety."

Their housekeeper agreed. "And I was touched by his kindness."

"So." Bethany couldn't help laughing. "Does this mean you've discounted Edwina's dark tales?"

"That silly young woman." Mistress Coffey dismissed her with a wave of her hand. "I should think she'll likely faint when she hears that you're being courted by the earl of Alsmeeth."

Bethany sucked in a breath. She hadn't thought about Edwina and her petty gossip. When she heard the news, she was bound to repeat every sordid thing she could think of. It was simply her nature to do so. As they neared MaryCastle, Bethany tried to calm the butterflies in her stomach. It was true that the more she got to know the earl, the more she began to see something other than the stern face he showed the world. And, though he was nearly as cautious around her as the deacon, there was a certain pleasure in his touch. But it was so brief. So careful. So tightly controlled. As though he feared doing anything that might invite…more. If only she hadn't been introduced to passion by the Lord of the Night. His kisses could make her pulse race and her blood heat until she was burning for more. All she had to do was close her eyes, and the feelings washed over her. Feelings that had absolutely no place in the life of a woman being courted by another man. Perhaps that was what frightened her the most. That she was being unfair to the earl, allowing him to think that her heart had been untouched. Tomorrow she would tell him about the Lord of the Night, even though to do so would be to invite his wrath. But to hold her silence seemed somehow dishonest. And so she would confess her little indiscretion.

Oh, why did life have to be so complicated? She couldn't wait to take herself off to her bed, where she could hide under the covers and try to sort out her jumbled thoughts.

Chapter Nine

"Are you certain you ought to wear that, Bethany?" Miss Mellon wrinkled her nose at the simple shirtwaist, buttoned clear to her throat, and over it, a long navy skirt. "Don't you think the earl might want to see you in something a bit more...elegant?"

"He probably won't even notice what I'm wearing, Winnie. If today is like all the others, he'll lock himself away in his room and spend his time going over his ledgers. It seems to be the only thing that truly interests him."

"If that were true, he wouldn't have approached your grandfather seeking permission to court you." The old woman was rewarded with the sight of a flush on Bethany's cheeks, proof that she'd hit a nerve.

Bethany had spent a miserable night, agonizing over how to tell the earl about the highwayman. She owed it to him to be completely honest, no matter what the outcome. Though she feared he might demand an immediate end to their courtship, which, when known, would bring disgrace to her family, it seemed her only choice.

They looked up at the sound of the arriving carriage. "Ah, well." The old woman gave a sigh. "At least fetch a pretty bonnet and shawl."

When she was seated in the earl's sumptuous carriage, she looked over and gave a sound of disgust. Bethany had snatched up a simple white shawl, and had neglected to bring a bonnet, leaving her hair to blow in the breeze.

As Huntley was assisting her into the carriage, Bethany pulled back. "Do you think the driver would allow me to handle the team?"

Huntley actually shuddered. "Miss Lambert, please don't press. If his lordship were to see, the poor young lad might lose his position at Penhollow Abbey. Would you want such a thing on your conscience?"

"Would his lordship actually do such a cruel thing?"

The butler showed absolutely no emotion. "It's quite within his realm as earl of Alsmeeth."

"But would he do such a thing, Huntley? I need to know."

The older man's voice lowered. "I've not witnessed such a thing since the present earl assumed the title. Though, in truth, his ancestors were known to be harsh masters."

She released the breath she'd been unconsciously holding. "Thank you, Huntley." She took her place across from Miss Mellon in the back of the carriage, deep in thought. She couldn't hold the present earl responsible for what his ancestors had done. Still, as Winnie was fond of saying, the apple rarely fell far from the tree.

When they arrived at Penhollow Abbey, they were greeted in the courtyard by the housekeeper, who seemed, as always, a bundle of nerves.

"His lordship sends his regrets. He had an unexpected visit from his cousin, and bids you to make yourselves comfortable in the parlor. Will I fetch you ladies some tea?"

"That would be lovely." Bethany followed Miss Mellon inside.

As they made their way toward the parlor, they heard footsteps on the stairs and looked up to see Oswald Preston striding toward them. His face was contorted with anger. He stopped, his hand on the banister. "What's this? Miss Lambert, isn't it?"

"Aye." She smiled. "Bethany Lambert. And my nursemaid and friend, Miss Mellon."

He barely acknowledged the older woman. "Are you here to beg also, Miss Lambert?"

"Beg? I'm afraid I don't understand." She looked from him to the earl, who stood at the top of the stairs, watching and listening in silence.

Following the direction of her gaze Oswald glanced up. His tone rang with contempt. "Aye. My cousin enjoys keeping a firm grasp on the family purse. It pleases him to make me beg for every little scrap of food from his table." He descended the rest of the stairs and brushed past Bethany. As he did he said loudly, "Beware, Miss Lambert. Make your visit a brief one. For you're in the presence of one who enjoys wielding power over others."

He slammed out of the house. Minutes later they heard the sound of hoofbeats racing across the courtyard. And then there was only silence.

Kane descended the stairs and Bethany had a quick impression of heated anger in his eyes before he composed himself and came to a halt in front of her.

"Good morrow, Miss Lambert. Miss Mellon."

"Your lordship."

Bethany tried a shaky smile. It occurred to her that he was in no mood to hear her explanation about the highwayman. Still, she had to try.

As he lifted her hand to his lips in greeting, he studied her. It was clear that she'd been badly shaken by his cousin's words.

"There's...something I wish to tell you, your lordship."

"I hope it can wait until later. Forgive me, but I have some pressing work this morrow. I hope you and Miss Mellon will feel free to explore Penhollow Abbey. Perhaps, if I'm fortunate, I'll be able to join you for a midday meal."

"Of course." Feeling oddly deflated, Bethany watched him turn away and climb the stairs. It would seem that he didn't even have time to listen to something so important it had robbed her of a night's sleep.

So be it. She would tell him in her own good time. Having decided that, her good nature prevailed and she looped her arm through Miss Mellon's. "Come on, Winnie. I've always wondered how many rooms are in Penhollow Abbey. Now we're free to explore at will."

The old woman allowed herself to be led along the hallway, where they peered into dusty rooms, admired portraits, and explored to their hearts' content.

"Did you know that there are three-score and six rooms, not counting the tower?" Bethany was seated at Kane's right hand, Miss Mellon on his left, as they enjoyed their midday meal.

"You counted them?" Kane seemed more relaxed now that the morning had passed. He even paused to touch a hand to the dog that lay at his feet.

"Aye. And explored as many as looked interesting. We found trunks filled with gowns. And a gallery of fascinating portraits, though I must confess, none of them looked like you."

A quick little frown tugged at his lips before he composed himself and turned to her chaperon. "What do you think of Penhollow Abbey, Miss Mellon?"

"It's simply the loveliest home I've ever visited. I hope you don't mind that we invited ourselves into the various rooms."

"Not at all. I want you to be comfortable here. And I want Bethany to learn to love it as I do." He turned to the young woman beside him. "I hope you don't mind if I call you Bethany?"

She flushed, liking the sound of her name on his lips, though she wasn't certain why. "Not at all, your lordship."

"I wonder if you would do me a favor, Bethany. I'd like you to call me by my given name. It's Kane."

"I couldn't possibly. It...wouldn't be proper."

"Not proper? I'll remind you I've been granted permission to court you now."

That word again. A word that always sent her into a panic.

He persisted. "Will you at least consider it?"

"Aye, your lordship."

That damnable title again, he thought with a trace of frustration. She couldn't seem to get past it. Still, he managed to keep his tone light. "Since you ladies spent the morning touring the house, I think you might enjoy a tour of my estate, as well." The thought hadn't occurred to him until just this moment. But without waiting for a chance to change his mind, he rang for Huntley. "Have Richmond prepare a horse and rig."

"A horse and rig, your lordship?" The butler caught himself and nodded. "Very good, your lordship."

When he was gone, Kane finished his tea and turned. "Are you ladies ready?"

Winnie tore her attention from the endless parade of

servants, which fascinated her. She and Bethany moved beside Kane down the stairs and out into the courtyard, where a stable lad stood holding the reins of a horse and small rig.

"I thought we'd dispense with the carriage." Kane helped the two ladies up to the seat, then climbed up between them and took the reins from the lad. At once Storm leapt up to sit beside his master. "This is the perfect way to see the land."

As they took off at a easy pace, Bethany had to agree. She drank in the sight of colorful rose gardens, formal hedges, and grand sloping lawns. They rolled across fields that housed tenant farms, with neat cottages and carefully tended vegetable gardens. There were green hills that seemed to fold into one another, and undulating flocks of slow-moving sheep. The sky was a brilliant blue, with soft white clouds rolling in from the Atlantic.

Bethany brushed at a wisp of hair that had pulled loose from the neat knot at her nape. "Where do you live when you aren't here in Cornwall?"

He held the horse to a walk and watched the way the sunlight turned her hair to flame. He itched to touch it. "I have an estate outside of London."

She wrinkled her nose. "After London, it must stir your heart to see all of this."

"Aye. I take it you've been to London?"

"Once or twice."

"You didn't like it?"

"I found it...interesting." She lifted her face to the sun. "But I could never bear to think of living anywhere but here."

Kane studied her, loving the play of sunlight on her face. It occurred to him that her skin was fascinating. Far from the cool, pale English beauty he was accustomed to, her sun-kissed skin gave her the look of a tawny angel. "I must admit that my preference lies here as well. But I can't always do as I please. There is a great deal of responsibility that goes with my title."

She turned to him. "You seem to have so many obligations."

"It wasn't meant as a complaint." He slowed the horse to a walk. "I realize that I'm more fortunate than many in this land. My father's name and title have opened doors that would have otherwise been closed. But at the same time it requires a great deal of work, much of it bookish and tedious, that makes me yearn to be free of it."

"Can't your bankers and solicitors see to the book work?"

"They could. But then, who would be looking over their shoulders? If it's my business, I'd best see to it, or others will relieve me of it."

Bethany thought of the adventures she and her sisters had enjoyed aboard the *Undaunted*. She wouldn't trade them for any amount of wealth and security, and the dull responsibilities that went with it.

"And," Kane continued, "for every door that is opened to me because of my title, others are closed. Once people know who I am, they embrace me or reject me for the wrong reasons. They judge me, not by what I do and how I live my life, but by how vast my holdings. How large my purse."

Bethany bit her lip, deep in thought. Wasn't that what she had been doing? She had decided, before ever meeting him, that she wouldn't like him.

"I think it best that we turn back now." He slowed the horse, then eased horse and cart into a wide turn.

Bethany watched as he handled the reins. She thought

she sensed a sadness in him. Or was she reading too much into this strange, aloof man's moods? By the time they returned to the courtyard, the sun had begun its westward arc. Kane handed the reins to a stable lad and helped the two ladies down. Winnie pressed a hand to the small of her back.

"You look weary, Miss Mellon. Perhaps you'd like to rest in the garden and enjoy some tea?"

"Aye. That sounds pleasant, your lordship."

He led the way to the gardens, where a servant hurried over with a tray laden with a silver tea service.

As they sat on stone benches sipping tea, Bethany glanced at the ruins in the distance. "What can you tell me about them?"

"That was the original abbey that gave Penhollow its name." He glanced at Miss Mellon. "Would the two of you care to explore them?"

"Aye." Bethany was up in a flash. "Winnie? Will you come along?"

The older woman shook her head. "I don't think I could bear to leave this lovely spot. Would you mind going without me?"

Bethany thought she caught a glimpse of laughter in Kane's eyes. But his tone was solemn enough. "You don't mind?"

"Nay." Winnie waved a hand. "You two go along now."

Leaving her to rest in the garden, they walked across an expanse of lawn, with the dog running ahead of them. As they walked, Bethany took a deep breath and decided to risk all on the truth.

"There is something I've been trying to tell you, your lordship. Something which I think is of the utmost importance."

He sighed. "All right, Bethany. We're alone here. Why don't you tell me?"

"I...lied when I said that the highwayman's kiss meant nothing to me."

He stopped in his tracks and stared at her. Her head was lowered. Her cheeks suffused with color.

"It meant something to you?"

"It did. Aye. It...deeply affected me."

"Was there anything more than a kiss?"

"Your lordship!" She took a step back and stiffened her spine as though he'd slapped her. "It was nothing more than a kiss. Actually, several kisses. Still, I think, since you have asked to court me, you deserve to know."

"I appreciate your honesty, Bethany." He struggled not to smile, since she looked so serious. "At least now I know who my rival is."

"He is not your rival. That is—" she chewed her lower lip "—he told me he was leaving forever."

"Is that why you agreed to allow me to court you?"

His question caught her off guard. "Perhaps." She looked away. "I know not. If you wish to end this courtship, I'll understand."

"End it?" He folded his hands behind his back, to keep from touching a hand to the lock of her hair that dipped over one eye. "You were kissed by a bold outlaw, and his kiss affected you. That's hardly worth ending a courtship, Bethany. I care not—" he snapped his finger "—this much about you and the Lord of the Night. Come." He swept his hand, indicating that she should lead the way once more. "Let's continue our exploration."

Was that it? she wondered. Was he so sure of himself that he was able to dismiss the highwayman's affect on her with a mere snap of his fingers?

When they reached the ruins, Kane caught Bethany's hand and helped her over a pile of stones. There it was again, she realized. That quick rush of heat, the moment they touched. And that throbbing in her temples. Had he felt it too? She glanced over, but could read nothing in his eyes.

"We're standing in the section that had once held the altar." He seemed absolutely determined to keep both their minds off their earlier subject as he pointed to a column of rock that stood amid the debris. "When I was a boy, I used to come here often. I swore I could hear the sound of a choir singing, but my mother insisted it was only the sighing of the wind."

Something in his tone caused Bethany to turn and look at him.

"I wanted to believe her." He shook his head. "But I couldn't. I knew what I heard. And some days, I could even hear the words quite clearly."

"What were they singing?"

"Hymns." He paused, considering, then went on. "One day an old woman came by, hunting pheasant eggs. She told me that in her grandmother's day Cornwall had been invaded by a roving band of pirates. The residents of the nearby villages had sought sanctuary here in the chapel, and the invading army killed them while they sang hymns for courage."

Bethany felt a shiver along her spine. "Did you tell your mother?"

He nodded. "She seemed uneasy, and asked me not to speak about it with anyone, not even my father."

"Why?"

He frowned. "She was afraid, and rightly so, that I would be shunned if others knew. Or considered, at best, an odd little boy." He turned away, amazed that he had shared this with her. It was the first time in his life he'd mentioned it to anyone. "She considered such a thing a curse."

"A curse?" Seeing his pain Bethany touched a hand to his arm. "What you were given was a gift, Kane."

For the space of a heartbeat he froze, before turning to her. "Say that again."

"What you were given—"

"Nay." He touched a finger to her lips. Just the merest touch, but it sent a rush of heat through her system, as though she'd just stepped into a blazing fire. "Say my name again. I want to hear you say it."

"I didn't—"

"Aye. You did. Now say it again, Bethany."

"I couldn't. It isn't proper."

"When did you ever care about such things as propriety? Say it."

She wondered if she could speak over the dryness in her throat. "Kane."

"Again." He framed her face with his hands. His eyes, staring into hers, were hot and fierce.

"Kane." The word was little more than a whisper.

"Oh." His face lowered to hers. His lips hovered above hers, sending another flare of heat along her spine. "You've made me wait so long. Too long."

She tensed, waiting for his kiss. Without realizing it, she lifted her face in invitation. Instead, as though realizing his mistake, he suddenly released her and took a step back. She watched as the heated expression in his eyes cooled, degree by degree, and he slowly composed himself.

He turned away and casually locked his hands behind his back, in order to keep from touching her. "But the waiting has only added to the pleasure. Like you, Bethany. Having you here gives me so much pleasure.'' He glanced over his shoulder. "Have you noticed?''

She swallowed, wondering why she felt such keen disappointment. He had intended to kiss her. Of that she was certain. And she'd wanted him to. Desperately. "Noticed what?''

"We're alone. No servants. No housekeeper. No Huntley. And no Miss Mellon.''

"Aye, I'd noticed.''

"I'll see that it doesn't happen again.''

"Why?'' She struggled with a wave of frustration.

"Because.'' He circled a pile of stones, giving himself time to think. To breathe. To fight for control. "The next time we're together, I'll see that we stay in the company of others. I doubt that your grandfather would want you to be alone with me.''

He stayed where he was, unwilling to get too close. The need for her was still too strong.

Because she was embarrassed and more than a little annoyed at the strange longing that betrayed her, she turned away and stumbled over a pile of stones. Up ahead she was relieved to see Winnie just walking toward them.

"Well, now. Isn't this lovely?'' the old woman called. "I had a little rest in the garden, and I'm feeling quite refreshed.''

In the courtyard, they could see the earl's carriage waiting, with a driver holding the reins.

Kane caught up with them and moved along beside Bethany. In an aside he murmured, "It would seem you've just been given a reprieve until the morrow. Perhaps when you arrive, you'll speak my name again.''

She paused. "Perhaps.''

As she started forward, he trailed slowly behind her, feeling a fresh rush of heat at the sway of her hips. He couldn't wait for tomorrow. For the sound of her voice. For the touch of her hand. But he would definitely see that they weren't alone. Now, more than ever, it was far too dangerous.

Bethany started down the stairs, then paused at the sound of Edwina's grating voice drifting up from the parlor. Before she could duck out of sight, Edwina peered up the stairs and screeched, "There you are. You must come at once. I have the most wonderful news."

Unable to contain her excitement, she raced up the steps and latched on to Bethany's arm. "Stop holding back. The others are waiting."

"The others?"

"The rest of your family." She hauled Bethany along, then urged her into the parlor and turned to the Lamberts, her face flushed with pleasure. "I'm to be wed."

"Bed?" Geoffrey Lambert cupped a hand to his ear and bellowed, "Of course we're just fresh out of bed. It's too early for visitors."

"Nay, Captain Lambert. Wed. I'm to be wed."

Mistress Coffey looked from Bethany to Darcy. "Who's the lucky gentleman this time?"

Edwina was too excited to note the trace of sarcasm. "Oswald Preston." She flashed a smile of triumph. "He's cousin to the earl of Alsmeeth, you know."

"Aye. We know him." Miss Mellon frowned, recalling the surly man who'd confronted them at Penhollow Abbey.

"That's grand news, Edwina." Bethany struggled to put some enthusiasm into her words. "But you've hardly had time to know Oswald."

"I know all I need to. He's handsome and charming.

And such fun. Mama says he's exactly what I need to forget my heartache over poor Silas.''

"Rile us? Nay, you didn't rile us, lass.'' Geoffrey shook his head from side to side. "It's just a bit early, though.''

"Nay, Captain Lambert. Silas. Oswald will help me get over him.''

"Another handsome and charming fellow,'' Geoffrey said in an aside that had the others grinning.

"Have you set a date for the wedding?'' Mistress Coffey asked.

"Nay. Oswald said he needs some time to put his affairs in order. He'll likely go up to London soon. He has a lovely estate there, and several tenants who have been negligent in their finances. Mama and I may go along.''

"I should think that would stir up all sorts of unpleasant memories for you.'' Mistress Coffey's voice held a note of impatience. Cook would be wondering what was keeping them.

"Aye. I'm sure I'll mourn Silas while I'm there. But I do so want to see Oswald's estate. It will, after all, be mine when we're wed.''

"Along with his debts,'' the housekeeper muttered.

"There will be no debts, Mistress Coffey. Oswald told me he's to come into great wealth soon.''

"And how is he to do that?''

"Apparently it's an inheritance of some sort. He is, after all, the cousin of an earl. I wouldn't be surprised if he inherits a king's ransom.''

"Handsome?'' Geoffrey nodded vigorously. "I'd say, if he's caught your eye, Edwina, he'd have to be one of those pretty boys.''

"Not pretty, exactly.'' She dimpled. "But so charming, Captain Lambert.''

"Thank you, lass. I try my best." He turned to the housekeeper. "What about our morning meal, Mistress Coffey? Or do we live on Edwina's tasty news for the day?"

The old woman turned away to hide her laughter. "I can see you awoke with a hearty appetite, as usual. I'll tell Cook you're ready, Captain."

"Aye. More than ready." He strolled past Edwina and patted her arm. "I should think you'll be wanting to leave for town now, to spread your happy news to all of Land's End."

"I will indeed, Captain Lambert." She shot a look of triumph Bethany's way. "Can you just imagine me the wife of a cousin to the earl of Alsmeeth?"

"I can indeed." Bethany walked her to the door, eager to be rid of her.

When the door closed, she leaned against it a moment, then squared her shoulders and headed for the dining room. Another minute and Edwina might have spotted the earl's carriage pulling up to their door. Then tongues would surely wag.

She ought to be grateful for Edwina's sudden betrothal. That should keep the gossips out of her business for at least a little longer.

"What's this?"

Kane greeted Bethany and Miss Mellon as they stepped from the carriage in the courtyard of Penhollow Abbey. Bethany's arms were laden with linen-wrapped packages.

"I asked Cook to make some of her bread pudding."

"So much? I know your housekeeper wanted me to try it. But it looks like enough to feed an entire village."

She blushed. "Actually, I thought we might take it to Miss Pike and the children at her home."

Though his expression never changed, she saw a look of surprise in his eyes, and then a slow smile of pleasure tug at his lips. "I'm sure the children would love it. And what are these others?" He pointed to the packages in Huntley's arms.

"Some gifts for the children. Newt whittled several wooden ships. Grandpapa made a rocking horse. Mistress Coffey and Miss Mellon have been working all week on little rag dolls." She blushed and looked away. "Darcy and I even tried our hand at a few of them, though they're not as fine. We've never been gifted with the womanly arts of sewing and handwork."

He had to break his self-imposed rule about touching her. He caught her chin and lifted her face for his inspection. "You have an even finer gift, Bethany. That of a good and generous heart."

She couldn't speak. All she could do was stare into those opaque eyes and wonder at the feelings that pulsed through her.

Beside them, Miss Mellon cleared her throat.

At once he took a step back and looked at Huntley. "You can return those things to the carriage. These gifts are far too fine to wait even another hour."

He turned to the housekeeper. "What has Cook planned for our midday meal?"

"Pheasant, your lordship. And fresh salmon."

"Have a servant fetch them, Mistress Dove. We'll add them to our treasures."

A short time later a serving wench hurried forward, holding aloft several linen-wrapped parcels. Huntley set them in the back of the carriage with the other packages.

"I'll be gone for a few hours, Mistress Dove." Kane

dismissed her with a wave of his hand. "My guests and I are going to the village of Mead."

"Aye, your lordship."

He helped Bethany and her nursemaid into the carriage, then took the seat across from them. At once Storm joined them, resting his head in Bethany's lap.

As they rolled along the country paths, Kane seemed content to remain silent while Bethany described the village of Mead and the residents of the Mead Foundling Home to the old woman beside her. It occurred to him that the mere sound of her voice had a strange calming effect on him. If he could, he'd listen to her all day and all night. In a lifetime or two he would never tire of hearing her speak.

The older woman drew her shawl around her shoulders as the carriage bounced over ruts. "What do you know of Miss Jenna Pike?"

"Only that she is truly beautiful." Bethany smiled. "You'll soon see for yourself, Winnie. She has generously dedicated herself to caring for these children who have no one else to see to their needs."

"But how does she survive with no one to keep them in food and clothing?"

Bethany shrugged. "They live in an abandoned vicarage. They bake bread and sell it in the village. I suppose some in Mead share their bounty with them."

"Still—" Miss Mellon looked doubtful "—it would take a great deal more than that to feed and clothe so many."

"That's why we must do our share." Bethany gave a laugh. "And why I nagged all of you into helping, Winnie."

"You didn't nag." Her nursemaid patted her her hand. "You merely asked, and we agreed."

"Whatever the reason," Kane interrupted, "I'm certain Miss Pike and the children will be delighted."

As they rolled through the tiny village, the wharf was nearly deserted. At this time of the morning the fishing boats could be seen far out to sea. Women tended their small gardens, or shook bedlinens from upper windows, while children hauled buckets of milk from thatched-roof sheds. They passed the crumbling church and came to a stop in front of the tidy vicarage. Almost at once a shout went up from inside and children tumbled out the door, circling the fine carriage.

"Welcome, your lordship," they shouted. "Welcome, Miss Lambert."

When Jenna Pike stepped out, the children fell into a respectful silence.

Wiping her hands on a towel she strode forward. "What a lovely surprise, your lordship. Miss Lambert. I was just baking bread. Won't you come inside?"

Kane helped the women down before saying, "Miss Pike, I'd like you to meet Miss Winifred Mellon. She was a nursemaid to Miss Lambert and her sisters when they were young."

"Miss Mellon. Welcome to our home."

"Thank you, my dear. I've been hearing such lovely things about you and these children."

Kane saw the children eyeing the packages. With a mysterious smile he said, "Let's go inside and leave these things in the capable hands of my butler."

The children reluctantly trailed the adults into the house. Inside, the air was perfumed with the wonderful fragrance of baking bread.

Miss Mellon stared around with a look of approval, noting the freshly swept floors, the spotless windows. When they reached the kitchen, the children gathered around the large wooden table and watched as Huntley began depositing the packages in a corner of the room.

"What is all this?" Jenna Pike asked.

"Gifts from my family." Bethany settled herself comfortably at the table and picked up a curly-haired toddler. "Our cook sent her bread pudding."

"Oh, my." Jenna unwrapped an enormous bowl of pudding. "There's enough for all of us."

"I should hope so." Bethany laughed.

"And this?" Jenna studied the brace of pheasants and freshly caught salmon.

"Gifts from his lordship."

"You are too kind." She gave him a grateful smile.

"What about these?" Young Noah was nearly twitching with excitement at the sight of so many packages still unopened.

"Something to fill your hours when you're not helping Miss Pike." Bethany set the toddler on her feet. "Perhaps each of you ought to open one."

The children stared in wonder at the treasures. And as the wrappings were torn away, they revealed several wooden boats that would sail across a pond or puddle. Rag dolls with button eyes and bits of yarn and ribbon to dress them up. And a wooden rocking horse that brought squeals of delight.

"Oh, my." Jenna looked dazed and delighted. "I can't believe all this."

"Is it Christmas, Miss Pike?" Noah looked up from the boat he held lovingly in his hands.

"Nay, lad." She crossed the room to hug him. "It's even better."

For the next hour, while sipping tea and nibbling warm bread in the cozy kitchen, the grown-ups laughed at the antics of the children as they enjoyed their new toys.

Even Huntley, who had been coaxed to relax and enjoy a cup of tea, was smiling as the children took turns on the wooden horse, and little girls toddled around, hugging their rag dolls. In the midst of it all, Storm lay wagging his tail, his tongue lolling happily.

Jenna circled the table, filling their cups with fresh tea. She paused beside Kane's chair. "I almost forgot, your lordship. More than half a dozen people have come from across Cornwall to claim treasures left here by the Lord of the Night."

At the mention of the highwayman, Bethany felt a quick tug at her heart.

Would she never be able to put away his memory?

"They were extremely grateful to have their valuables returned to them. So grateful that one of the gentlemen, a Lord Farley from Craigshead, pressed a score of gold pieces upon me. I nearly wept, for it means the children will all have boots and warm coats by the time winter is upon us."

"That's good news indeed." Kane was smiling, and watching the antics of a little boy who, with Bethany's help, was climbing aboard the wooden rocking horse.

Noah tugged on Bethany's skirts and whispered, "If only he'd done so a few days earlier."

"What do you mean, Noah?" Bethany paused.

"Miss Pike was so desperate to provide us clothes for the coming winter, she sold her harp. And I know for a fact it nearly broke her heart, for she played like an angel."

It occurred to Bethany that Noah, as the eldest of the children, took a special, proprietary interest in their teacher. "How sad. Did she weep?"

"Not our Miss Pike. But sometimes, when she thinks

no one is looking, I see a sadness in her eyes and she glances at the corner, where her harp always stood.''

Bethany turned toward the young woman, who was chatting with Kane.

''I had another visitor yesterday, your lordship.''

''Aye?'' Kane tore his gaze from Bethany and the child.

''Your cousin, Oswald Preston, paid me a visit.'' Jenna steeled herself not to shiver, though he had made her feel extremely uneasy. ''He had been here earlier with Miss Cannon and her mother.''

''Did he say what he wanted?'' Though Kane's tone remained even, there was a chilling look in his eyes.

''He offered to return the rest of the gold and jewelry to the rightful owners.''

''For what reason?''

''To spare them the long trek here to Mead, he claimed. But, though I thanked him for his kind offer, I told him that it was too late. All of the treasures have now been claimed.''

Kane visibly relaxed.

Hearing this, Bethany looked up. ''In all the excitement of coming here, I nearly forgot. Edwina Cannon told us that your cousin has asked for her hand in marriage.''

Kane looked thunderstruck before he composed himself. ''Has she accepted?''

Miss Mellon nodded. ''If you knew Edwina Cannon, you'd have no need to ask that. Not that I mean to imply that she's a loose or wicked woman. But she's so easily flattered by the attentions of a man. Any man. By now, the entire town of Land's End has heard her news, and she's preparing to tell the rest of Cornwall, as well.''

Deep in thought, Kane drained his tea. Minutes later

he shoved back his chair and got to his feet. "I fear we must take our leave now."

As he and the women walked to the door, the children made no move to follow. They were too entranced by their toys.

"Children," Jenna called. "What have you to say to our guests?"

"Thank you," they shouted in unison.

"Come back again," Noah called.

"Oh. We will, Noah. Often, I hope." Bethany paused to hug him before stepping out the door.

As she followed the others to the carriage, Jenna turned to Bethany. "How can we ever thank you, Miss Lambert?"

"I need no thanks, Miss Pike. Seeing all that you do, you're the one who has my thanks and admiration."

The young women embraced. Then, stepping apart, Bethany was helped into the carriage, where she took a seat beside Miss Mellon.

As the driver lifted the reins, Jenna stepped closer to the carriage. "Thank you, your lordship. And you, lovely ladies. Please come back soon."

They waved as the carriage started forward.

Miss Mellon continued waving, then turned away. "You were right, Bethany. What a lovely person Miss Pike is. I don't believe I've ever seen a more generous, kind heart."

"I knew you'd like her, Winnie." Pleased, she linked her arm through that of her old nurse, while rubbing the head of the contented Storm. "Now we must think of more ways to help her and those children. She needs more willing hands. Women from the village, perhaps, who might help mend some of the clothes. Think how large her mending basket must be. And an occasional meal so that she doesn't have to spend so much time in her kitchen. And perhaps even some men and lads who might help with the gardens. So much work for one woman. And yet she does it all without complaint.''

The old nursemaid was already nodding in agreement. ''Just another pair of arms at times, to hold a frightened child, or soothe a sick one, would mean the difference between a night's sleep and a sleepless one. When I think how much energy I needed to keep up with you and your sisters, I marvel that this young woman can take on the care of so many.''

''But, as his lordship pointed out to me, at great personal sacrifice. Young Noah confided to me that Miss Pike was forced to sell her beloved harp in order to secure clothes for all the children for the coming winter.''

''How sad. And yet how noble of her.''

Bethany glanced over at Kane and saw that he hadn't heard a word, but was, instead, deep in thought. Wherever he had gone in his mind, it wasn't a pleasant place, judging by the look on his face. She was reminded again of how little she knew him. He could be gallant and kind. But there was another side to him. One that puzzled her, and at times, frightened her. He was still a mystery. And there were dark places inside him. Places she wasn't at all certain she wanted to explore.

Chapter Ten

"**W**asn't it sweet of the earl to invite your sister along today?" Miss Mellon had become accustomed to her daily ride to Penhollow Abbey in the fancy carriage. For the past weeks they had explored the house and grounds, and had even traveled to several nearby villages.

True to his word, Kane had seen that he was never alone with Bethany. Whether in his library, or enjoying a walk in the gardens, they were always accompanied by her nursemaid or sister, or a battery of servants trailing at a discreet distance. Their meals had become family affairs, which often included their housekeeper and old Newton, who traveled to the estate in the late afternoon, after his chores aboard the *Undaunted* were finished for the day.

Bethany glanced at Darcy. Both sisters were clad in their riding clothes. "Aye. I'm glad for your company."

Darcy could hardly contain her excitement. "It was kind of the earl to offer his horses for our enjoyment. He said I may ride any horse in the stables, except his stallion."

Bethany wrinkled her nose. "I'd prefer to ride Lacey, but Kane didn't want me to ride her such a distance."

"And rightly so," Miss Mellon said. "He feels a sense of responsibility for you now, Bethany. You never know what might happen between home and Penhollow Abbey."

Bethany bristled at the very thought. "I've sailed in dangerous seas and battled bloodthirsty pirates, yet you side with Kane."

"I don't side with anyone. I merely agree that it's wiser to ride in the carriage, and then avail yourself of the earl's fine stable of horses."

Bethany shrugged. "In truth, there's a big bay mare in one of the stalls that I've been wanting to try. And I must admit, I'm eager to ride across the rolling hills of Penhollow Abbey. I can't think of a lovelier way to spend a day. Unless it's aboard ship."

"Aye." Darcy nodded. "Newt says the repairs are almost completed."

"I can hardly wait to set foot aboard the *Undaunted*." Bethany brushed a stray lock of hair behind her ear. "Though I do think Kane deserves a warning before sailing with a family of privateers."

"You know what Grandpapa said. The time isn't right."

"And when will the time be right?" Bethany's eyes flashed. "He spends all his time in his library, lost in his ledgers."

"He also manages to spend a good deal of time with us," Miss Mellon scolded. "Mistress Dove told me just yesterday that she's never seen the earl so relaxed at mealtime."

"Perhaps he'll relax even more today and join us on a ride." Bethany leaned back, watching as Penhollow Abbey came into view.

She had mixed emotions about all of this. It was a

strange courtship. Kane seemed warm and considerate at times. But there were other times when he seemed distracted and distant. And though he had begun to win the confidence of her entire family, she still knew nothing more about him than she had when they'd first met. He was a stranger to her. A handsome, wealthy and, at times, aloof stranger, who rarely touched and never kissed her.

As their carriage entered the courtyard she struggled to put aside her worries. It was a lovely day. She would make an attempt to enjoy it.

"Ah. Here you are Miss Lambert." The housekeeper stood back as Huntley helped the women from the carriage. "His lordship awaits you in—"

"The library," Bethany finished.

"Nay, Miss Lambert. He awaits you down at the stables."

Bethany glanced from her sister to their nursemaid. This change in routine sounded hopeful. Perhaps Kane was to be free of his burdensome duties for the day.

She and the others walked through the gardens, then farther along until they came to the stables, where several horses were already saddled and waiting. Bethany experienced that odd little stirring she always felt at the first sight of Kane, standing with the stable master. This day he wore black riding breeches tucked into tall boots and a soft, full-sleeved shirt of white lawn. His dark hair was ruffled by the wind. When he turned and caught sight of her, she saw the way his words trailed off and his face became animated.

He hurried forward. "Good morrow, Bethany. Darcy. Miss Mellon."

"Kane." She saw the pleasure in his eyes at the use of his given name. By now it fell as easily from her lips as her name from his. "Does this mean you intend to ride with us today?"

"Aye. I worked late into the night so that I might put aside my book work and join you." He turned to their nursemaid. "Will you ride with us, Miss Mellon?"

The old woman shook her head. "If you don't mind, I'll just walk in your gardens a bit, your lordship, and then perhaps join Mistress Dove and the others inside for a bit of tea."

"Be assured the servants will see to your every comfort, Miss Mellon." He turned to Bethany. "I've saddled the bay mare for you."

She flushed with pleasure. "How could you possibly know she'd be my favorite?"

"Richmond told me you've been admiring her every time you visit the stables. Here. Let me help you up."

As his hand brushed her elbow, she felt the quick flutter of nerves. Even after he'd turned away to help her sister, she could feel the warmth, and found herself wondering at it. What was this strange reaction to his simplest touch? And why this sense of excitement at the prospect of being in his company for an entire day?

She glanced over at the chestnut gelding as he pulled himself into the saddle. "Where is your stallion?"

"He pulled up lame. Richmond is tending to him in his stall."

"I've yet to see your horse. Each time I visit the stables, he seems to be out in a pasture, or being rubbed down with blankets for some illness or other. Is he sickly?"

"I prefer to think of Midnight as high-strung. Come." He started along a grassy path, turning in the saddle as he did to assure that the two young women were following. "It's time you saw more of Penhollow Abbey."

Bethany and Darcy needed no coaxing. As the path grew wider, they caught up to his mount and rode three abreast, drinking in the beauty of the dew-freshened countryside. As they crested a hill, a doe and her fawn leapt gracefully across the field and disappeared into the darkness of the forest.

Kane slowed his mount to a walk. "On my nightly rides I've been watching those two. I saw the fawn take its first steps. And now, just weeks later, it can run and leap."

"You ride here every night?"

"Most nights. It allows me to free my mind from the tedious rows of numbers in the ledgers."

Darcy reined in her mount. "Do you hunt, your lordship?"

Kane nodded. "Every year, when the crops were harvested, my father invited our tenant farmers to a hunt. From the time I was old enough to sit a horse, I was allowed to join them."

"How kind of your father."

"It was also prudent. It helps thin the herds, and fills larders for the coming winter. I'm looking forward to continuing the tradition."

Bethany smiled. "I'm sure your tenants will be grateful for the meat."

"And I'm grateful for their labors on my behalf. Look." He pointed and Bethany and Darcy turned in time to see a herd of perhaps a dozen or more deer crossing a distant hill and fading into the forest. "If I were riding Midnight, he'd be quivering at the prospect of giving chase."

"He's a hunter?" Bethany lifted her head.

"Aye. But then, I suspect all the males of the species

are." He was looking at her in a way that had her throat going dry and her heart speeding up.

Uncomfortable under that dark gaze she nudged her mare into a trot. Kane and Darcy did the same.

Oh, it felt so good to be astride a horse and skimming over green fields. Nearly as good as sailing aboard the *Undaunted*. She'd missed this. Missed this feeling of freedom. She urged her horse faster until she felt as if she were flying.

She chanced a look over her shoulder, and could see Darcy and Kane moving up behind her.

When they pulled even with her mount she shouted, "Let's race."

"How far?" Darcy called.

"To the edge of the forest."

When she saw them nod in agreement, she dug in her heels and the mare bolted ahead, with the others in hot pursuit. As they crested a rise she pulled ahead. Sensing victory, she urged her mare even faster. Suddenly the ground beneath them seemed to open up. The mare stumbled, and then horse and rider were tumbling into an abyss.

Bethany was thrown from the saddle and tossed about like one of the rag dolls she'd made for the children at Jenna Pike's home. She landed on hard earth, and lay perfectly still, struggling for breath. Beside her the mare lay on her side and thrashed about, unable to stand.

"Bethany. God in heaven." Seeing her as still as death, Kane was out of the saddle and scrambling down into the pit. He knelt beside her, his face etched with concern.

"I'm...alive."

At her words he let out a sigh of relief and cradled her in his arms, pressing his lips to a tangle of hair at her temple. Then, digging his booted feet into the soft earth, he carried her out of the pit and lay her in the grass.

"Oh, Bethany." Darcy knelt beside her sister and grasped her hand in both of hers. "I was so frightened when you disappeared. Did you not see the pit?"

"Nay. It must have been covered with weeds and branches. We came upon it so quickly, there was no time to stop."

Kane touched a finger to her lips. "Hush, Bethany. Don't move until I ascertain if you've broken any bones."

She felt the quick rush of heat, and then the slow curling sensation deep inside as he began probing her flesh. With a gentleness she would have never believed possible, he moved her legs, her arms, even each of her fingers. It occurred to her that, despite her fall, she'd felt a powerful surge of emotion when he'd pressed his lips to her temple. It was, she thought, the closest they'd come to a kiss.

Satisfied, he sat back and watched as the color slowly returned to her cheeks. Even Storm seemed animated as he licked her face and rested one paw on her arm.

"Can you sit up, Bethany?"

"Aye." With Kane's arm beneath her head she sat up and waited until the dizziness passed. Then she looked beyond him to the gaping hole in the earth. "Whatever could that be? Do you think it was dug by a hunter, to fool the deer?"

He followed her gaze, his eyes narrowed in thought. "I know not. But I intend to find out."

"What about the mare?"

He shook his head. "I'll send Richmond out to see to her."

"Is she...?" Bethany couldn't bear to speak the word.

He was grim-faced as he lifted her into his arms. "We'll know more later, when Richmond's had a chance to examine her."

As he pulled himself into the saddle and cradled her against his chest, he could feel his hands shaking. When he'd seen her lying there, his heart had nearly stopped. He'd realized, in that one brief moment, just how important she had become to him. He spoke not a word all the way back to Penhollow Abbey. But his thoughts centered on the freshly dug pit. Just last night he'd ridden this very trail. There had been no hole in the earth. That meant that whoever did this, had worked in the small hours of the morning.

This was no accident. It was a deliberate act.

Bethany had suggested it might be the work of a hunter. Aye. A hunter stalking prey. Except that the prey was human. And the hunter had evil on his mind. And what was worse, this deadly game had almost claimed the life of an innocent. By selfishly drawing Bethany into his life, he'd made her vulnerable.

He would do whatever necessary to see that she was kept safe.

Their return to Penhollow Abbey caused quite a stir. As soon as word filtered through the line of servants that only two horses were approaching, Huntley and Mistress Dove sought to restrain Miss Mellon, who came racing across the courtyard.

"What is it? What has happened to our Bethany?"

"Here now, Winnie. There's no cause for alarm. My horse took a tumble. But I'm fine now. Truly I am."

"Oh, praise heaven." The old woman stood by while Kane dismounted, still holding Bethany in his arms. "Have you twisted an ankle?"

"Nay. I can stand." She glanced up at Kane, and was staggered by the way he was watching her. There was a look in his eyes that she'd never seen before. "You must set me on my feet to assure poor old Winnie that I can walk."

"Inside perhaps." He swept past her nursemaid and his servants, who stood by with looks of stunned surprise.

Darcy had to run to keep up with his brisk strides.

"Fetch some ale, Huntley."

"Aye, your lordship."

"And Mistress Dove, have Cook prepare some broth."

"I'm not ill, Kane."

"And an opiate, in case there's pain."

"There's no pain."

He completely ignored her protests as he strode along the hallway and deposited her on a chaise in the parlor.

"Let's get those boots off and see if there's any swelling."

As he slipped off the first boot she touched a hand to his. At once he stilled his movements and looked up at her through a haze of impatience.

"I said I'm fine, Kane." Her tone was softer now. What she'd seen in his eyes had touched her deeply. "I was caught by surprise. And a bit shaken up. But other than that, I have no injuries."

"Truly?"

"Aye." She smiled. "Truly."

They both looked up when Darcy charged in, followed by Miss Mellon, who was wringing her hands in distress.

"I should have gone along."

"Whatever for, Winnie? You know you don't ride. Do you think you could have spared me this fall?"

"I don't know. I only know that your grandfather trusts me to see to your safety. And I failed him."

"Nonsense. I'm responsible for myself. As you are for yourself. Your presence would have made no difference at all."

Not entirely convinced, the old woman sank down in a chair, watching as Huntley entered carrying a silver tray. When he offered her ale, she accepted gratefully. As did all the others.

Kane downed the liquid in one long swallow, then handed the tumbler back to his butler.

"Will you have another, your lordship?"

"Aye." He took the glass, this time sipping more slowly as his nerves began to settle.

When Mistress Dove entered the parlor with an opiate, she was pleased to see that it was unnecessary. "You're in no pain, Miss Lambert?"

"None, Mistress Dove. But I thank you for your concern."

The old woman took a deep breath and began to take her leave. But at the doorway she turned, as a thought struck. "Forgive me, your lordship. In all the confusion, I forgot to tell you that a message was delivered from the Lambert family." She hurried away, then returned bearing a small silver tray on which resided a scroll.

Kane unrolled it and read, then looked up with a smile. "I believe this will help erase any lingering discomfort you may have, Bethany. Newton informs me that the repairs to the *Undaunted* have been completed. She is, even now, taking a quick voyage along the coast, to determine her seaworthiness. I am invited to sail aboard her on the morrow."

"The morrow." Bethany sipped her ale, hoping to erase the dryness that had suddenly appeared in her throat.

Kane looked extremely pleased as he turned to Huntley. "Prepare my carriage. Our guests will desire to leave early, so that they can rest for tomorrow's adventure."

Bethany swallowed. "Perhaps, before I take my leave, we could speak privately."

"Of course."

Kane looked up as Mistress Dove paused in the doorway. "You have a visitor, your lordship. Your cousin."

His expression never changed. And yet Bethany knew him well enough now to note the sudden coolness in his tone. "I'll meet with him in the library." Kane lifted Bethany's hand to his lips. "Forgive me. We'll have that talk another time. I give you my word. For now, Huntley will accompany you to your home. And I'll be at the beach by sunup." He gave her a mysterious smile. "Until the morrow, Bethany. I can't wait to sail with you aboard the *Undaunted*."

As he walked away, she thought of how easily he had accepted her first confession, regarding the highwayman. At the time she'd wondered if he was merely putting a good face on his disappointment. But as the days went by and the matter was never mentioned again, she began to think that he truly didn't mind that she'd enjoyed being kissed by the Lord of the Night.

Now she wondered whether he would take the fact that she and her family were privateers as lightly. Or would this be more than a man in his position could possibly accept? If so, theirs might be the briefest courtship in history.

She didn't know why that thought should disturb her so. After all, she'd known from the beginning that they were completely mismatched. He was the earl of Alsmeeth, and she was Bethany Lambert, the daughter of a ship's captain.

Still, though he seemed reluctant to display any affection, she was more convinced than ever that he cared for her. The look in his eyes after her fall, and the gentle manner in which he'd touched her, told her more than any words that she was beginning to mean as much to him as he now meant to her.

And that was a great deal indeed. A fact that continued to puzzle her. When had this cool, aristocratic man begun to matter so much to her?

Dawn was just beginning to paint ribbons of light across the horizon when Bethany awoke. For a moment she lay very still and listened to the familiar sounds of seabirds crying, of surf slapping gently against the shore.

She decided not to wait for the others. She desperately needed to go aboard the *Undaunted*. To feel again the deck beneath her feet, rolling and tilting in the pull of water. To breathe the salt air into her lungs, and hear the slap of waves against the hull.

She slid from her bed and dressed quickly in a simple gown, tying her hair back with ribbons. If only, she thought wistfully, she could slip into the breeches, shirt and boots which she usually wore aboard ship. Instead she stuffed them into her seabag, along with her pistol and knife, which she intended to secrete below deck. These would have to wait until the morrow. Today she would pretend to be a proper lady, out for a day's sail. Tomorrow would be soon enough to resume her family business of hauling cargo, while also keeping an eye out for enemies of England.

She was too impatient to think about eating. Knowing Cook would send along a basket of food for their day's voyage, she avoided the kitchen and slipped out the back door. With her seabag in one hand, she used the other to lift her skirts as she raced across the sand. When she reached the beached skiff, she tossed in her seabag, then climbed in and began rowing toward the *Undaunted*. Anchored some distance from shore, it loomed like a darkened fortress against the backdrop of sky and water.

Once there she worked quickly to tie the skiff, then hauled herself and her seabag up the rope ladder. She climbed over the rail and dropped the seabag at her feet, then turned. And froze. Standing in the middle of the deck was a man, who appeared to be dressed all in black. Black breeches and coat, black boots, black hat. To stifle her gasp of surprise, she covered her mouth with her hand. For a moment she couldn't breathe. Then the fear evaporated as quickly as it had come. Though his back was to her, she would know him anywhere. He hadn't left her forever. He'd been watching and waiting. And now, for whatever reason, he'd come back.

"You're here." She started toward him at a run. Even in her own ears her voice sounded too breathless.

He turned. "Aye. I couldn't wait for dawn. I see you couldn't, either."

"Kane." She halted. His name came out on a whoosh of air.

He stepped closer. "I believe that's disappointment I see in your eyes, Bethany. Were you expecting someone else?"

"Nay. Of course not. You merely...caught me off guard." She turned away, and busied herself with her seabag, hoping to keep her feelings hidden from view. "How did you get out here?"

"I swam."

She straightened. "But your clothes aren't wet."

"Like you, I stuffed them in a seabag and hauled it with me."

He would have to be, she realized, a powerful swimmer to manage such a thing. She knew seasoned sailors who couldn't accomplish such a feat. "How long have you been here?"

"An hour or more." He nodded toward her bag. "Would you like me to take that below deck?"

"Nay. I'll manage." She hefted it over her shoulder and hurried away, eager to keep him from discovering the clothes and weapons inside it. Below deck she stowed her bag, then climbed topside where the sea and sky were just beginning to lighten. Kane was standing at the rail, staring out to sea. Bethany joined him and lifted her face to the sky. Bands of gold and pink and rose threaded the clouds, and were reflected in the waves. She stood very still, staring around her with a look of hunger. "Oh, how I've missed this."

"I can tell." He turned to study her, seeing the reflections of the pinks and golds on her burnished skin. "You know, you have a most expressive face, Bethany."

She turned away, and was surprised when he touched a hand to her shoulder. Just a touch, but it sent heat blazing through her veins.

"That's why I could tell, after just one look at you, that you thought I was someone else when you first caught sight of me on deck."

She flinched. He was too close to the truth. Still, she tossed her head in a gesture of denial. "For all I knew, you could have been a thief, hoping to loot our ship while no one was aboard."

His voice was gruff. Whether from impatience or humor, she couldn't tell. "Admit it, Bethany. You and I both admire honesty too much to deceive. You were hoping I was the Lord of the Night, back to claim another kiss."

Her head came up defiantly. "I thought you said you didn't care that much about the highwayman."

"Nor do I."

"Now who is trying to deceive?" She turned to face him. "Is the outlaw the reason you haven't tried to kiss me? Have you decided that since I enjoyed his kisses, I might not enjoy yours as well?"

His smile was quick and dangerous. "Are you asking to be kissed?"

"Are you afraid to comply?"

It might have been the seductive pull of her eyes. Or the gentle pitch and roll of the ship beneath his feet. Whatever the reason, he forgot, for the moment, all the promises he'd made to himself. His hands grasped her shoulders and he dragged her roughly into his arms. She felt a quick flash of fear at the heated look in his eyes. And then the fear was replaced with a blaze of desire.

She had such a hunger to be kissed by him. A hunger laced with frustration. She hoped, the moment his lips met hers, that she would be able to forget the passion that had been uncovered by the highwayman. She wanted, needed, to put that part of her life behind her, and feel the same desperate desire for this man.

She lifted her face to his. "Kiss me, Kane." She could feel his muscles straining, and knew that he was exerting an almost superhuman effort to hold back. That only made her bolder. "Or are you afraid?"

"You're a witch, you know." His hands moved along her shoulders, down her arms, as he stared into her eyes. "A witch who knows me well enough to realize that I can never resist a challenge." His fingers tightened, and he drew her fractionally closer.

"I was hoping as much." Her heart began a wild hammering inside her chest and she waited, waited, for the touch of his lips on hers.

"Bethany, lass." Old Newton's voice carried across the water and broke the morning stillness.

Both Bethany and Kane lifted their heads to the sound.

"Are ye out at the ship, lass? If so, I need the skiff to bring the crew aboard."

Disappointment washed over Bethany as Kane lowered his hands and stepped back. With that simple distraction, the spell had been broken. And once again she was left feeling as though she were standing on the very edge of the unknown. One step and she might have tasted heaven. Or possibly hell. Either way, she would have had her first taste of Kane Preston.

Instead, she was left with only emptiness and frustration.

"You stay here." Kane turned away and headed toward the opposite rail, eager to escape. "I'll fetch Newt and the crew." He slipped over the rail and climbed down the rope ladder.

Bethany remained where she was, hearing the sound of oars skimming the water as he rowed back to shore.

Kane had actually seemed relieved by the distraction. As though old Newton had just saved him from a fate worse than death. But if that was the case, why had he asked permission to court her? She rubbed a hand to her temple as if to erase these troubling thoughts. All she ever got in answer to a question was another question.

By the time Kane returned with Newton and the crew, she was below deck in the captain's cabin, busily studying the charts and maps in anticipation of their voyage.

She looked up as the old sailor knocked and entered. "Where are Miss Mellon and the others, Newt?"

"None could come today, lass. But yer nursemaid was

persuaded that I could keep an eye on ye and yer earl and see that ye behaved yerselves.''

"I assure you, Newt, we don't need to be watched and worried over. In fact, I doubt the earl has ever stooped so low as to indulge himself in a single ungentlemanly act in his entire life.''

As she flounced away, she saw Kane standing in the doorway, holding a basket of food. On his face was a look of frustration and fury that matched her own. So be it. It was just as well that he overheard her complaint. Without a word she brushed past him and hurried up the steps.

The old sailor noted the fire in Kane's eyes as he turned to watch her departure. The tension between these two was as thick as the fog that often blanketed the sea. Something had happened this morrow. And if he was any judge of character, he'd wager it was Bethany who'd goaded, and the earl who'd resisted. He nearly chuckled at the thought, and found himself wondering just when the next firestorm would erupt.

When Kane spoke, his tone was carefully controlled. "Where would you like this food, Newt?''

"The galley's just beyond this cabin, yer lordship. But I can handle it.''

"I thank you, but I'd rather do it myself. And then I'd like to find something a bit more taxing than this, if I'm to get a certain female off my mind.''

The old man nearly laughed aloud before he managed to control himself. "Perhaps ye'd care to swab the decks, yer lordship?''

Kane shot him a dark look. "Do you think it would help?''

"When it comes to our Bethany, I doubt a week of swabbing would be enough. But I'm afraid Captain Lambert would have my hide if I allowed ye to handle the duties of the sailors. If ye'd like, yer lordship, ye can take the wheel.''

"Thanks, Newt." Kane found himself smiling as he deposited the basket and made his way up the stairs to the deck. An hour or two of fresh air might be just the thing to sweep away this burning need. A need to throttle Miss Bethany Lambert within an inch of her life. Or kiss her until she couldn't hold a single coherent thought in that infuriatingly independent mind of hers.

His smile grew. Maybe, if pushed hard enough, he just might give in to both. Still, as he took the wheel from a sailor and studied the foaming sea, he found himself doubting that anything would eliminate the needs churning inside him like a whirlpool. Needs that, once released, might take them both down to the depths.

Bethany sat on deck sipping her tea. In her other hand was a parasol to shield her from the sun. The streamers of her bonnet danced in the breeze. She tilted her head and watched as two sailors climbed the rigging and unfurled the sails. She was itching to climb with them. She and her sisters had been handling such chores since they were lasses, and were by far the best sailors aboard the *Undaunted*. But here she sat, unable to do the things she loved. The effort of trying to behave like a proper lady was getting to her. She crossed her feet at the ankles and jiggled one foot nervously. It wasn't fair. At least Kane was allowed to steer the ship. And the sailors, after their initial awe of him wore off, had begun talking and laughing with him as easily as if he were one of the crew. But they studiously avoided Bethany. Probably, she thought, because it was the first time they'd ever seen her in a gown. They didn't know how to treat her. She was no longer a sailor, but a female. And so they kept their distance.

She finished her tea and wished she could fling the cup into the ocean. Or better yet, against the railing, and watch it smash into pieces. Instead she continued to hold it in her hand, tapping it against her knee in rhythm to the movement of her foot.

Kane turned the wheel over to Newton and joined her on the afterdeck. "Are you enjoying yourself, Bethany?"

"Aye." Her word lacked conviction. "And you?"

"Indeed." He leaned against the rail, as comfortable as though he'd been doing this all his life. "Newt tells me we'll soon be stopping at the Isles of Scilly."

She nodded. "Just at St. Mary's. My family thought, since we were taking a simple voyage along the coast, we could make a quick stop to deposit goods from Land's End. I hope you don't mind."

"Not at all. It was never my intention to disrupt your means of business with my little voyage. I merely desired to feel a ship beneath my feet. A real ship, that is, and not some sleek pleasure craft."

"Is that why you didn't use one of your own ships?"

"Aye." He stepped away from the rail and took the seat beside her. Up close, her eyes were a deep, fathomless green. Greener than the ocean. And her skin, despite the parasol, held the blush of the sun.

He thought about the way she'd felt in his arms for that brief moment before they'd been interrupted, and felt again the purely sexual tug. What was he going to do about it? About her?

One of the sailors shouted from high in the rigging. "Shallows dead ahead, Newt."

"Aye, lad." Newton held the wheel steady and maneuvered the ship toward the tidy harbor of St. Mary's.

When they'd lowered the anchor, the men began carrying the small cargo from the hold and loading it aboard the skiff.

"Would you care to go ashore, yer lordship?" Newt asked.

Kane considered for a moment. "Are you going, Bethany?"

She nodded. "I wouldn't mind."

As she descended the rope ladder to the skiff, she found herself once again cursing the heavy skirt and petticoat that made such movements clumsy. How much more fortunate were the men, who could manipulate the ladder with ease.

She and Kane sat in the bow of the skiff while the sailors rowed to shore. Once there, they were met by men with horses and carts, who would transport the cargo to its final destination.

Newton turned to Kane and Bethany. "This shouldn't take more than an hour. If ye'd care to ride into the village, ye might find a tavern that would serve a midday meal."

"That sounds fine." Kane approached a driver, and soon he and Bethany were seated in a rig, heading toward the nearby village.

At a tavern they were treated to ale and hot crusty bread, as well as thick slices of roasted mutton. As he ate and sipped his ale, Kane watched the way the light flowing through the high, narrow windows played over Bethany's face.

He'd never had a woman affect him like this. Even now, relaxed and content, he wanted her. And the thought of taking her above stairs to one of the little rooms had him aching with desire.

"What do you think?"

He blinked. "Think of what?"

She shot him a puzzled look. "I was talking about..." She paused. "Where was your mind?"

He gave her a lazy smile. "You don't really want an answer to that."

"Why not?"

"If I were to tell you, you'd blush." He threw back his head and laughed as color flooded her cheeks. "You see?"

It was the oddest sensation, to feel herself growing warm simply because he was looking at her. And yet, she couldn't help herself.

"Now, what were you talking about, Bethany?"

"I'd—" she struggled to compose herself "—I'd suggested a walk around the village before we return to the *Undaunted.*"

"A fine idea." It would get him out of this place, and would hopefully cool his desire. He paid the tavern owner, then followed Bethany out into the sunshine.

As they walked along the village street, she paused at a small shop. "Look, Kane. Isn't that lovely?"

He stopped beside her and studied the tiny miniature in the window. "Aye. Probably the shopkeeper's wife and children..." His words trailed off, and then he swore. Loudly. Fiercely.

At her gasp of surprise he turned to her. "Excuse me, Bethany. Wait here a moment."

He opened the door to the shop and strode inside. Puzzled, Bethany watched as Kane and the shopkeeper exchanged words. Moments later the shopkeeper removed a piece of jewelry from the window. It appeared to be a man's stickpin, adorned with a single glittering diamond and a circlet of emeralds. While she continued to watch, Kane counted out a handful of gold and tucked the piece of jewelry into his pocket. Why in the world, she wondered, should a lovely piece of jewelry cause such anger? Surely he could afford to purchase it if it appealed to him. Apparently it did appeal to his vanity, since he'd readily paid the price. But he'd seemed more angry than surprised. Almost as though he'd stumbled upon some hidden horror, rather than a simple stickpin.

He stepped from the shop and took hold of her arm, moving quickly toward the docks. As they walked, Bethany turned to study him. His profile was a hard, tight line of repressed fury. He offered not a word of explanation for his strange behavior.

When they arrived at the docks, she was relieved to find Newton waiting. As the sailors rowed them toward the waiting ship, she found herself hoping that the return voyage might bring at least a little relief from the anger that seemed to weigh so heavily on Kane's mind.

She was mystified. Whatever had transpired in that shop, it had turned their simple voyage into something quite different. Whatever pleasure he'd taken in this day was now erased.

She thought again about the layers of mystery that surrounded him. Perhaps she shouldn't be so quick to discount the rumors. They took on added meaning, now that she'd seen his sudden changes of mood.

From the look of him, Bethany could imagine that anyone who dared to cross swords with the earl of Alsmeeth would pay dearly for such a deed. And would surely rue the day they'd taken on such a determined opponent.

Chapter Eleven

The sun had long ago burned off all traces of the mist that had earlier hugged the shore. A fresh breeze filled the sails and sent the *Undaunted* skimming across the waves. Except for the incident in port, the day would have seemed idyllic. Now, however, there seemed no way to salvage it.

Bethany sat on deck, holding the hated parasol and wishing she could work off her restless energy. She glanced at Kane, who was standing by the rail, staring morosely into the distance. Since their return from St. Mary's, he'd been sullen and distracted. She wisely kept her silence, giving him time to work through his anger. Lifting a hand to her eyes to shield the sunlight, she watched a sailor high in the rigging. Suddenly his shout had everyone looking up.

"A ship with no flag, bearing down hard on our port side."

"Sweet heaven." The parasol slipped from Bethany's fingers as she got to her feet. She raced to the rail. "Come, Kane. You must go below deck at once."

"Aye. In a minute. You go ahead, Bethany. See to your safety. I need to speak with Newt."

''Not now.'' She caught Kane's hand. ''He knows what he must do. And what you must do is get out of his way.''

Already the sailors moved with a purpose, sweeping aside the trappings of comfort and tugging a cannon from its place of concealment. Another sailor moved among them, handing out weapons.

As she led him across the deck, Bethany realized that the time for lies was well past. ''You must forgive our deception, Kane. We thought to keep our identities secret. But now, of course, you can see for yourself that the *Undaunted* is more than a cargo ship, and my sisters and I are much more than mere daughters of a ship's captain.''

''Aye. And what exactly are you?'' Seeing her agitation, Kane allowed himself to be led below deck.

''We are privateers, in service to King Charles.'' Bethany indicated the captain's cabin. ''I wish I had time to tell you more. For now, you're to wait in there, for your own protection. There's a bolt which can be thrown from the inside. That way no one can get to you unless they break down the door.''

He paused in the doorway. If she hadn't been so distracted, she might have realized that his frown was gone now, replaced by a look of eager anticipation. ''Pirates are about to attack, and you worry for my safety? What about you, Bethany? Don't you intend to join me?''

''Nay. My place is with my men.'' She gave him a shove and turned away, missing the smile that touched his lips.

Once in the galley she hauled out her seabag and began stripping off her gown. Minutes later, dressed in her shirt, breeches and boots, she tucked a knife at her waist and picked up her pistol. Then she raced up the steps and emerged on deck to join the crew.

The pirate ship was already close enough that she could see the ragged men leaning against the rail and hanging from the rigging. As always the sight of them brought a sudden rush of energy, sending her heartbeat racing. It wasn't fear, she realized, but anticipation of the coming battle. She'd missed this. The action. The excitement. She'd been like a fish out of water. And now, having admitted the truth to Kane, she was free to be herself.

''Watch for cannon fire,'' Newt shouted as they caught sight of a plume of smoke trailing from the pirate ship's cannon.

A moment later there was a terrible explosion, and the *Undaunted* shuddered with the force of the cannonball that glanced off the bow. Though it tore a jagged hole, it was high enough that they weren't taking in water, and were in no danger of sinking.

At the same time, the crew of the *Undaunted* returned their own cannon fire, and the pirate ship took a hit that ripped apart the hold and sent flames spewing into the air. At once the pirate ship began listing as it rapidly filled with water.

''Good one, lads.'' Newt drew his sword as the first of the pirates tossed their ropes and began to swing, hand over hand, toward the deck of the *Undaunted*. Within minutes there were a dozen more, screaming and cursing, filling the air with obscenities.

Bethany braced herself for the attack. She was no longer aware of the pounding of her heart, or of the feelings that curled along her spine. She stood, feet apart, pistol in hand, prepared to defend the *Undaunted* at all cost.

''Look, mates,'' one of the pirates shouted as he

landed on their deck. "A female. Just waiting to greet us. Come on, lass. Give us a kiss. I'll make you forget every man you've ever seen."

Bethany cursed the fact that she'd had no time to cover her hair, and realized that she'd be targeted by the pirates as an easy mark. She gritted her teeth, more determined than ever to prove them wrong.

As the first man raced toward her, sword raised, she took careful aim with her pistol and fired. The man looked astonished as he realized he'd been hit. With a cry, he fell to the deck, clutching his chest.

It took her precious moments to add fresh gunpowder to her pistol. In those few seconds, another pirate advanced, cursing loudly and brandishing his weapon. Just as he was about to run her through, she calmly took aim and fired again.

She turned and watched as old Newton battled three pirates. "I'll lend a hand, Newt." Leaping into the fray, she managed to drop another man, evening the odds.

The old man shot her a look of gratitude. "Thanks, lass. I can manage these others."

She was already racing across the deck, where a cluster of pirates had engaged in a fierce battle with several of the *Undaunted*'s sailors.

As she fired her pistol, she saw, out of the corner of her eye, a strange figure dueling with three screaming pirates. Having no time to reload, she drew her knife from her waist and tossed it, sending one of the pirates to his knees.

As she added gunpowder to her pistol, she looked up and realized that the stranger was Kane. He had removed his jacket and hat, and anything that might set him apart as a man of wealth and title. Instead he wore only his black breeches, tucked into tall boots, and his white shirt, the sleeves billowing as he wielded his sword and pistol. She felt a sudden rush of fear, mingled with anger.

At once she was beside him. "I ordered you below deck."

"You ordered?" He shot her an incredulous look, then turned to defend himself against a swordsman. It was several minutes before he managed to dispatch the pirate. Then he looked up in time to see Bethany calmly take aim and fire. Another pirate dropped to the deck in a pool of his own blood.

While she replenished her gunpowder she fixed him with a dark look. "I'll remind you that you're a guest aboard my ship, Kane. My family and I are responsible for your safety. I order you to go below at once."

He would have laughed if it weren't for the pirate advancing upon her with bloodlust in his eyes. Without a word Kane took aim and fired, dropping the man just as he was about to strike with his sword.

Bethany whirled, then turned back with a look of admiration at his skill with a pistol. "I thank you. But that changes nothing. As I said before—"

There was no time to finish. Four more pirates, screaming like banshees, came racing across the bloody deck, aiming swords, knives and pistols. Bethany and Kane were forced to stand back-to-back, fighting them off.

As he stopped the first man in his tracks, and took aim at the second, Kane was keenly aware of Bethany calmly fighting alongside him. She was, he realized, as magnificent as that first time he'd seen her.

Hadn't he always known that they were fated to be together like this? Hadn't he sensed, that first time he'd spotted the flame-haired marksman, that he would have this opportunity to fight in her company? He'd schemed and plotted, and all but forced her to this point, so that he could feel again the thrill he'd felt that day. And now, he could see that he'd been right. They were perfectly matched.

"Behind you, Kane."

At her words he turned and dodged the sword tip aimed at his heart. In one smooth motion he dropped the pirate, then picked up the man's sword and began backing a second pirate toward the rail. Behind him he heard the report of Bethany's pistol and nearly smiled. Aye. She was a scrapper. A brave, daring, defiant fighter. And the only woman who would ever make his blood run this hot. And when this battle was over, he would tell her so.

This pirate was more determined than the others. Kane found himself having to dodge and swerve to avoid feeling the sting of his blade. He was sweating profusely by the time he'd managed to run the man through. For good measure he tossed the man's body overboard, where the swirling water was littered with charred wood, as the pirate ship began breaking apart. Floating amid the debris were the bodies of the hapless pirates.

Aboard the *Undaunted,* the fighting seemed to have ended. There were no more fierce screams. No savage oaths. In fact, the sailors had fallen strangely silent.

Kane turned and surveyed the damage. Bodies littered the deck of the *Undaunted.* A deck that ran red with blood. And then he absorbed the first sickening jolt as he realized that Bethany wasn't among those standing.

He heard a hoarse voice shouting, and dimly realized it was his own, as he stumbled among the bodies until he came to her. She lay crumpled on deck, three dead pirates around her. Her pistol had fallen beside her. Her hand was pressed to her upper arm. Her shirt showed a torn and jagged hole, pierced by a sword tip. The flesh beneath oozed a pool of crimson. Her fingers were stained with it.

Newt and the others gathered around as Kane dropped to his knees beside her. As he probed the wound, he looked puzzled.

"It isn't a serious wound. But..." He felt a swelling at the back of her head, and his hand came away stained with her blood. "Ah. Sweet heaven. She's taken a terrible blow to the head."

Her eyes were closed, her body so still, his own heart ceased to beat as he felt for a pulse.

From a great distance he seemed to hear the old sailor's voice, trembling with fear. "Not our lass. Not our Bethany. Tell me, yer lordship. Is she...?"

He felt the faintest sign of life. Feeble. Thready. But it was enough to keep him from despair. "There's a pulse, Newt. Not much of one. But it's at least something. We have to get her to shore at once."

"Aye, sir." Newton was shouting orders at the sailors, who were scrambling to hoist the sails and turn the ship toward land.

"Where is the closest port?" Kane demanded.

Newt squinted at the shore. "We're not that far from Penhollow Abbey, yer lordship. But ye'll have a terrible distance from shore to yer home."

"I'll make it." Kane gathered her against his chest, and pressed his lips to her temple, willing her his strength. "Take us in, Newt. And pray we're not too late."

Kane carried Bethany, as she drifted in and out of consciousness, through the shallows and across the beach toward Penhollow Abbey in the distance. There would be miles of forest to traverse before he reached home.

The crew of the *Undaunted* had already hauled anchor and set a course for the little cove at MaryCastle, where old Newton would have the painful task of telling her family the news.

As he drew near the house, Kane saw Huntley throw open the door and start across the courtyard in that stiff-backed, military gait. Racing after him was Storm.

"What is it, your lordship? What has happened?"

"Bethany has been wounded."

"But how?" The old butler was staring at her odd clothing, soaked with her blood.

"Not now, Huntley. Notify Mistress Dove to prepare my bed. I'll need hot water and clean linens. And opiates for her pain."

"Aye, your lordship."

The old man turned and fled inside. Minutes later, as Kane carried Bethany up the stairs, most of the household staff had assembled in the hallway to watch in grim silence.

"I've turned down the bedlinens in your chambers, your lordship." Huntley stood aside as Kane strode across the room and lay her gently on the bed.

When Mistress Dove came scurrying into the room, she took one look at the bloody clothes and swayed as though she might faint. For a moment her face lost all its color. With a fierce oath Kane took the basin of water from her hands and set it on a bedside table. Then, ignoring propriety, he stripped aside Bethany's shirt and began to bathe away the blood. When he saw how the jagged wound marred her unblemished flesh, he had to bite down hard to keep his composure.

Though Mistress Dove's hands shook, she stepped up beside him and assisted, disinfecting the wound, then dressing it with clean linen. Afterward, at her insistence, Bethany was dressed in a modest white nightshift.

"What's this?" she asked as she probed Bethany's head.

"She took a blow when she fell to the deck. It's far more serious than this wound."

The old woman sucked in a breath as he gently bathed away the blood from the swelling at the back of her head.

Through it all, Bethany lay as still as death. That was what frightened Kane the most.

From the time he'd first seen her, this woman had been a whirlwind of activity. To see her like this, still and silent, her face as pale as the bedlinens, caused an ache around his heart unlike anything he'd ever known.

As Mistress Dove stepped aside, Kane dropped to his knees and clasped Bethany's hands in his. With his lips pressed to her temple he whispered fiercely, "You cannot leave me, Bethany. Do you hear me? I couldn't bear it if you left me now."

He lifted his head to study her face. To the untrained eye, she might appear to be merely asleep. But it was much deeper than sleep. Her skin had lost its tawny sheen. It now appeared as luminous as pearls in water. Behind her eyelids there wasn't even the merest flicker of movement. Her chest barely rose and fell with each slight breath.

She was slipping away from him. And he was helpless to keep her here.

He brushed his lips over her hands and whispered, "Stay with me, Bethany. Please stay with me."

Alarmed, Huntley exchanged a look with the house-keeper. Neither of them had ever witnessed such emotion in the earl before.

They backed out of the room, leaving him alone with

his grief. And hoping with all their hearts that this lonely man would not have to face the loss of another loved one. For this time, they feared, his poor heart would surely be shattered beyond repair.

The servants gathered around the open door of the chamber, peering inside without a word. With every opportunity they paused in their chores to view the scene, before moving on.

The earl was on his knees beside the bed, his hands still grasping Bethany's. His clothes still bore the stains of her blood. All efforts to have him change had been resisted. He refused to leave her side for even a moment.

Storm had settled himself on the bed beside Bethany's still form, his head on his paws, his eyes watching her every breath.

Mistress Dove, moving like a ghost, had brought a tray of supper. It sat forgotten on a night table.

Huntley climbed the stairs, and though he spoke not a word, he sent the servants scathing looks, which had them scattering. When they were gone he peered inside and took a deep breath before shoving the door open and stepping inside.

"Your lordship."

Kane didn't bother to acknowledge him.

Huntley stepped closer. "The Lambert family has arrived from MaryCastle, your lordship."

Kane lifted his head.

"They will want to see Miss Bethany."

"Aye."

"May I bring them up?"

Kane gave a curt nod of his head.

Huntley hurried away. Minutes later he returned, followed by the entire family.

"Oh, sweet heaven." Miss Mellon stopped in the doorway, her hand to her mouth to stifle her little cry.

The housekeeper bumped into her, then stood to one side, too upset to come into the room.

"Bethany." Darcy brushed past them and hurried to the bedside. She stood staring down at the still form of her sister. Tears filled her eyes and she blinked them away. Leaning close she touched a hand to Bethany's shoulder and shook her gently. "Bethany, wake up. We're all here now. You must wake up."

Seeing no response she turned to her grandfather, who crossed the room and stood beside her. "Oh, Grandpapa." She fell into his arms and the old man gathered her close, all the while peering down at the still figure in the bed.

He turned to Kane. "How bad is it, your lordship?"

Kane tore his gaze from Bethany long enough to whisper, "The wound itself was minor, Captain. The sword missed her chest, and merely pierced the fleshy part of her arm. But the blow to her head is what has me concerned. I don't know how to reach her." He forced himself to stand and face the older man. "But your granddaughter is a fighter."

"Aye. That she is, lad." Seeing the pain in the younger man's eyes, and the bloodstains on his rumpled clothing, Geoffrey clamped a hand on his shoulder. "How long have you been here?"

"I know not. Since I carried her from the ship."

"Then you'd best see to your own needs while we stay with her."

"Nay, sir." Kane dropped to his knees and caught Bethany's hands in his. He had a desperate need to touch her. To hold her. Afraid that if he left, she might give up the fight. "I can't leave her."

Mistress Coffey and Miss Mellon inched near and stared down at the pale, still face of the young woman who had always been so vibrant. So alive. Both women were weeping softly as they moved around the bed, smoothing the bedlinens, and brushing a strand of hair from her cheek.

"She's so hot." Miss Mellon touched a hand to her forehead.

"Aye, Winnie." Mistress Coffey followed suit. "She's burning with fever."

Geoffrey Lambert kept an arm around Darcy, holding her as she wept against his chest. "Your housekeeper has been good enough to invite us to stay, your lordship."

"Of course. I would have invited you myself, if I'd had my wits about me. I insist that all of you stay. For as long as you wish." He glanced over. "Have you had time to eat?"

"Nay. We left as soon as we heard."

Kane turned to his butler. "Tell Mistress Dove to prepare a meal for our company."

"That isn't necessary," Geoffrey was saying.

But the butler had already anticipated their protest. "A meal was already prepared for his lordship, but he refused to eat. Please follow me."

Reluctantly the others trailed from the room. When they looked back, Kane had already forgotten them, and returned his attention to the young woman in the bed.

"More salmon, Captain Lambert?" Mistress Dove directed the servants, who circled the table offering trays of salmon and beef.

"Nay, thank you." Like the others, Geoffrey had no appetite. He'd barely touched his meal.

Mistress Coffey was fretting at the care being given to

Bethany. "What if the wound wasn't properly cleaned and disinfected?"

Taking offense at her suggestion, Mistress Dove lifted her chin. "I saw to it myself. Along with the earl."

"But the slightest bit of carelessness, and our Bethany would be the one to pay the price."

Mistress Dove's chin quivered. Her nerves were reaching the breaking point. "I can assure you that we weren't the least bit careless with Miss Lambert. Why, I'd stake my life on it."

"No one's accusing you." Winifred Mellon patted the housekeeper's hand. "We're just upset is all."

"As are we. We've come to care a great deal for Miss Lambert. As has the master. You could see that he is overwrought by all this." Mistress Dove turned to Huntley for assurance.

"Quite right." He stood stiffly beside her, determined to defend her. "I don't believe I've ever seen his lordship so distraught."

"Speaking of which…" Geoffrey drained his goblet of ale and looked around at his family. "I believe we should get back to Bethany's bedside. Perhaps if we offer to sit with her, the earl will take himself away to change his bloody clothes."

"I hope you can persuade him." The housekeeper poured tea for the ladies. "But be warned. His lordship hasn't left the young lady's side since he carried her here."

"He's probably feeling guilty, because it was at his request that the *Undaunted* set sail," Mistress Coffey said.

"But that's foolish." Darcy, ever the practical one, shook her head. "The *Undaunted* would have set sail today whether he'd commissioned her or not."

"Aye. But that won't stop his guilt." Mistress Coffey turned. "Don't you agree, Winnie?"

The old nursemaid nodded in agreement. "It's the nature of man to assume guilt for everything that goes wrong with a woman while in his company."

"That does it, then." Geoffrey pushed away from the table. "We must disabuse him of such guilt at once. Who'd care to go with me?"

Darcy and the two older women got to their feet. Only old Newton remained seated at the table. When they turned to him he merely smiled. "I'll be along. But don't be surprised if the earl refuses yer offer to see to his own needs."

"Do you know something we don't, Newt?"

The old sailor shook his head. "Only that I doubt he'll leave our lass's side until she's herself again."

As the others hurried away, the earl's housekeeper exchanged a look with the butler. They had seen for themselves that the old sailor was correct. And if the young lady didn't recover, neither would his lordship. Of that they were quite certain.

Kane remained by the bedside while Bethany's family fluttered around her like chattering birds. The old women had to remove the dressings from her wound and examine it, to satisfy themselves that it had been properly cleaned and disinfected. Afterward, they'd fussed over the bedlinens, opened the windows to chase any lingering poisons, pressed cool, moist cloths to her forehead, brushed locks of hair from her face, anything that would make them feel that they'd done everything possible for her.

At last, when they found themselves dropping into chairs, stifling yawns, and even nodding off, they allowed themselves to be led off to guest chambers.

Darcy was the last to leave. She continued standing over her sister, staring intently at her face for any sign that she might be getting stronger. At last, with her grandfather's arm around her shoulders, she was led away in tears.

Grateful for the precious sounds of silence, Kane knelt beside the bed and lifted Bethany's fingers to his lips, kissing each of them with a sort of reverence. When he sensed a presence beside him, he looked up to see Newton standing beside him. The old sailor's gaze was fixed on Bethany's pale face.

"Has she awakened yet, yer lordship?"

"Nay."

There was such sadness in that single word.

"It's not so unusual after a blow such as our Bethany sustained."

"But she's so still. So quiet, Newt."

"Remember, our Bethany's young and strong." The old man studied the desperation in the earl's eyes as he clung to her.

"I've bathed and disinfected her wound. Dressed it. Slipped a few drops of opiates down her throat. But she hasn't responded at all. Not even the simplest of movements. I don't know what more I can do, Newt."

"There's nothing more to be done except wait and pray."

"But I need more. I feel so helpless. I need...I must do something."

The old man took pity on him. "Ye might try telling her what's in yer heart, yer lordship."

Thunderstruck, Kane looked up. "Do you think she might hear?"

The old sailor shrugged. "I know not. But whether she stays in this world, or must go to that other, ye can take comfort in the knowledge that she'll carry yer words with her.''

Kane grew thoughtful before nodding. ''Thank you, Newt.''

The old sailor paused in the doorway and turned back. The earl was already seated on the edge of the bed, bent low over Bethany, his lips pressed almost hungrily to hers, his voice low and deep with feeling.

Chapter Twelve

"**I**'ve long wanted to tell you this, Bethany, my love, even though I have no right." Kane's voice was a fierce whisper as he brushed her lips with his. "But now I must bare my heart and soul to you. If you never awaken, at least you'll know how deeply, how desperately you were loved."

He paused a moment to take her hands in his. He studied the long, tapered fingers. "Who would believe that such hands could calmly hold a pistol, and fire it with such accuracy? Do you know, you are the fiercest privateer I've ever had the good fortune to sail with?" He brought both of her hands to his mouth and pressed kisses into each palm. "Knowing you, being with you, has fulfilled my every fantasy. You are the woman of all my dreams." A sigh welled up from deep inside and broke free. "And now, just as I've found you, I may have lost you forever. Oh, Bethany. Don't leave me. Please don't leave me. I couldn't bear to lose you now that I've found you."

He framed her face with his hands and stared down into that pale face. So perfect. So serene. Not a trace of pain marred her features. It frightened him to realize that she'd gone beyond pain. She'd slipped deep into a sleep from which she might never awaken.

He bent close and touched his mouth to hers. As he did he whispered, "The first time I saw you, I knew I had to have you. That's why I forced you into this unhappy bargain. But I never meant you any harm. If I could, I would give up everything, even my chance to see you again, if it would bring you back from the brink of eternal sleep. Oh Bethany. Bethany. You have captured my heart and soul."

He heard a sound. Just a small sigh. But it was enough to have him clutching her against his chest in a fierce embrace as he whispered words of endearment against her temple.

Bethany thought she must surely be dead. Earlier she'd heard a chorus of chattering, as of birds. High-pitched, they were, and drifting in and out, as though carried aloft on the breeze. Angels, she supposed, come to greet her. But then they'd faded away, and all she'd known was silence. Then the cloud returned, dark and pain-filled, and she'd realized she couldn't possibly be dead. How could she feel pain if she were dead? This had to mean that she was alive. But if that was true, why couldn't she open her eyes?

The pain grew, threatening to take her. But then suddenly she heard the whispered voice. She would know that voice anywhere. That fierce, lovely whisper. Then she felt the brush of warm, firm lips over hers. Oh, such lips. And she knew with certainty that it was the Lord of the Night. He'd returned to claim her heart.

No one else would ever kiss her the way he did. Gently, like a drop of rain, falling into the cool, clear Atlantic. Then more firmly, sending little ripples that grew ever wider, spreading through her, easing all the pain.

It was his voice, his kiss, that roused her, lifted her from the depths of hell, until she gradually surfaced.

At first, all Kane heard was that soft sigh. So soft, he thought he'd only dreamed it. But then he heard it again. And felt her breath, warm against his lips as she whispered, "You've…come…back. "

Astonished, he held her a little away and saw her lids flutter, then open.

He watched as she struggled to focus.

Despite the blurred image, she managed a smile. "I…knew…you'd…come."

"Did you?" He touched a finger to her cheek. Just the gentlest touch, but he saw her smile grow.

"Aye. And…now…you're…here." She blinked, once, twice, and struggled to touch his face. When she did, she could feel the tingling that began in her fingertips and slowly pulsed through her veins.

"I was so afraid, Bethany. So afraid I'd lose you."

"Never…lose…me…again."

"Nay. I couldn't bear it." He gathered her close and pressed his lips to hers.

As he drew away she peered at him, then blinked and stared as hard as she could, until he came into sharp focus. "You're not—" she ran her tongue over her dry lips "—not the Lord of the Night."

"Nay. I'm Kane."

"Kane." She smiled, then gave another sigh. "Nay. Though your face says one thing, your voice says another. I know that whisper. More, I know the taste of those lips."

She saw his quick frown. That only made her lips part

in a smile. "Of course. Now I know why you...never kissed me all these long weeks. You knew if you did, I would recognize you."

"Aye. But it doesn't matter now, love. Nothing matters except that you've come back from the brink. You're safe now, Bethany."

"Aye. Safe with you. Kane Preston. The earl of Alsmeeth. My Lord of the Night. Please don't leave me. Promise me."

"I promise." He watched as her lids fluttered closed and she drifted into sleep.

Exhilarated, exhausted, he ordered Storm to the floor, then lay down on the bed beside her and gathered her into his arms, reluctant to let her go for even one minute. It no longer mattered that she'd uncovered his secret. Nothing mattered except that she'd come through this crisis unharmed.

Drained, he fell asleep holding her.

It was the middle of the night when Bethany awoke and found herself lying in Kane's arms. He was staring at her so intently, all her thoughts scrambled. But gradually, as she studied him by the light of the fire, it began to make sense.

"You saved me." She touched a finger to his lips.

"Nay, Bethany. It was your own strength that saved you. All I could do was stand by helplessly and watch."

"Hardly helpless." She smiled. "As I recall, you carried me from the ship, through miles of forest, and here to your home."

"You remember?"

"Aye. I remember feeling safe and secure as long as you were holding me. And I remember the pain when you lay me in the bed and your arms left me. But then I heard your voice. That wonderful whisper that touched my heart. And I knew that I couldn't leave you. Couldn't leave this world, as long as you were in it.''

''Oh, God in heaven, Bethany.'' He pressed his lips to her temple and felt the wild rush of heat. ''I had no right to speak those things that were in my heart. But I couldn't bear the thought of losing you without at least sharing them.''

''And now that you have—'' her smile grew ''—I know your secret.''

''At least one of my secrets.'' He touched a fingertip to her lips, tracing their fullness, while he stared down into her eyes. ''Promise you'll stay now, and not slip back into that other world?''

''Aye. If you'll promise me something.''

''Anything.''

''Will you kiss me?''

He pulled back. ''I'll remind you that you've just returned from the brink. You very nearly died.''

''And may again, if you don't kiss me right this minute.''

He smiled. And then he brushed his lips over hers. The merest whisper of a kiss, but all the love, all the longing he'd kept locked inside poured through him into her, igniting fires that had them both pulling apart.

Her eyes widened. ''Now I know I didn't dream your kiss.''

''Nay, love.''

Love. She thought it the most wonderful word she'd ever heard. She wound her arms around his neck and lifted her face to him. ''I'm so relieved to know the reason why you wouldn't kiss me before.''

''And now that you know my secret, what are we to do about it?''

She gave him a sly smile. "You might try finishing what you started that night when, as my bold highwayman, you left me forever."

"I dare not."

"Why?" At his refusal, she felt a wave of bitter disappointment.

"Because I gave my word as a gentleman to your grandfather that I would protect your virtue."

She snuggled against him, and saw the way his eyes narrowed on her. "I gave no such word."

"Little witch." He tried to pull away, and she only drew him closer, until every part of her body was brushing his.

"Nor did the Lord of the Night make such a promise."

With the merest touch, he was thoroughly aroused. This flame-haired stranger he'd viewed from afar. This creature in men's clothing, calmly fighting a pack of wild-eyed pirates. This woman who had fueled all his fantasies, was here in the flesh, offering herself to him.

He'd always considered himself a man of strength and integrity. But in Bethany, he'd met his match. His hands were in her hair before he even realized he'd reached for her. He dragged her against him, even as he told himself this was all wrong.

"Kiss me, Kane. Please."

He struggled for some shred of decency. "If I do, I'll never be able to stop."

"I don't want you to stop."

"You don't know what you're saying." Determined to be strong for both of them, he pushed away and stalked to the balcony, hoping the chill night air would restore his sanity.

When he turned, she had followed, to stand behind

him. With a lazy smile she wound her arms around his neck. "I know this much, Kane. I love you."

Love. The word did strange things to his heart. Of all the arguments she could have given him, this was the only one that mattered. He had no armor against it. Still, he had to try. For her sake. "It isn't me you want, Bethany. The earl of Alsmeeth. Tell the truth. Isn't it the Lord of the Night you love?"

"Does it matter?"

"Aye." His eyes narrowed on her with such intensity, she felt a little thrill of fear. "I need to know."

In the glow of firelight her eyes gleamed like emeralds. Her hair tumbled wildly around her face and shoulders. "It's true that I was intrigued first by the Lord of the Night. But then, when I met the earl of Alsmeeth, it was the same. Don't you see? Both men are mysteries to me. One gives back all that he steals, without explanation. The other seems unable or unwilling to enjoy his wealth and position, and instead lives like a recluse. Both men touch my heart deeply, though I know not why." She pressed a hand to his cheek in an achingly sweet gesture. "Newt told me that love has a way of sneaking up on a person, without any warning. And that's what has happened to me. I don't know how or when or why. But I simply love you, Kane. Without rhyme or reason."

"Oh, Bethany." He closed his eyes a moment. "Do you know how long I've waited to hear you say that?" Her simple honesty shattered all his defenses. He gathered her into his arms and kissed her until they were both breathless.

"I love you, Kane. Please love me back."

He was making a valiant effort to hold back. Drawing her a little away, he studied her in the glow of the fire, his eyes hot and fierce. "Surely you've heard the rumors and whispers about me. Aren't you afraid?"

This was the first time he'd made mention of his past. And though she could have pursued it, she merely shook her head. "I've heard. But the man I've come to know could never do or be what the rumors imply. The only thing I know is that I want you to lie with me and love me."

His tone roughened. "Do you know what it is you ask? Do you have any idea what I would do to you? I can't be a gentle lover. It won't be just sweet kisses and whispered words of love. I'll want to do things you can't even fathom. And once this thing is done, it can never be undone. What is even worse, I can make you no promises. There are too many...unsettling things in my life."

She touched a fingertip to his lips. "I'll ask nothing more of you than that you love me, Kane. I'll not rest until you do."

"Then God help us, Bethany. For I already do love you." He dragged her close. His hands were no longer gentle. His mouth on hers was eager, avid. "And have from the first moment I saw you."

She was caught in an explosion of feeling that was unlike anything she'd ever known. This kiss wasn't like any of the others. All the need, all the flash and fire and fury that had been building up through the long days and weeks, came spilling over into one breathless mating of mouth to mouth. She hadn't known a man could kiss like that. With lips and teeth and tongue. Teasing and tormenting, daring and demanding, he took her higher than she'd ever been.

She responded, kissing him in ways she'd never dreamed. Experimenting until his sighs matched hers.

For Kane, there was no turning back. He'd crossed the

line, and all his careful control was gone. He would touch her in all the ways he'd dreamed of. He would do all the things he'd fantasized on long, lonely nights. He would take and give and fill all the empty places inside himself with her. Only her.

He let his hands move over her. The thin fabric of her nightshift, as gossamer as angel wings, only added to his excitement. Impatient with the row of tiny buttons that ran from throat to waist, he tore them in his haste to find her flesh. As the bodice parted, he found her skin, as smooth and pale as milk. For the space of a heartbeat he merely stared at her, drinking in the sight of that lush body. Then he lowered his mouth to taste.

His lips covered one erect nipple, and he nibbled and suckled until she felt her knees buckle. He lowered her to the floor, then moved to the other breast, feasting until her sighs became murmurs, and her murmurs became urgent moans laced with both pleasure and need.

She thought he would take her then, and end this desperate hunger. She reached a tentative hand to his blood-stained shirt and slid it from his shoulders, needing to touch him as he was touching her. But before she could do more, he tore aside her nightshift and uncovered another secret. She tensed, about to protest. Too late, her body reacted, and she shuddered as she reached the first glorious peak.

For Kane, the journey of love had just begun. He felt his own pulse speed up as he watched her reaction. This was how he'd wanted her. Dazed with desire. Weak with pleasure. And his. Only his.

He could hear his own voice, rough with need, as he tore his mouth from hers and let it roam over her body. Hers was the sweetest taste. Hot and wild and sweet. So incredibly sweet.

He slowed his movements, giving her time to savor. To relax. To slow her racing heartbeat.

Bethany lay steeped in pleasure. Though all of this was new to her, it was also familiar. This man. His touch. His taste. The scent of him filled her lungs, and she breathed him in, feeling as though she'd come home. She'd been born for him alone. And he was the only one who would ever touch her like this. Love her like this.

The fire on the hearth had burned to embers, and their glow was reflected in his eyes. They gleamed like silver in the darkness as he trailed his clever mouth down the length of her body until she shuddered and moaned. Then, giving her no time to collect her thoughts, he drove her even higher, until she cried out in desperation.

Now there was no hesitancy as she reached for him. He helped her undress him, until they were lying together, flesh to flesh. They came together in a frenzy of need, and as he entered her, she let out a strangled cry.

"Oh, I'm such a brute." Alarmed, he went very still, struggling to hold on to the last thread of his control. "How could I forget that you're a maiden? Oh, sweet Bethany, I've hurt you." As he started to pull away she tangled her fingers in his hair and dragged his face down until their mouths met.

"Nay, Kane. Don't stop now."

She arched herself to him and began to move.

Stunned, half-mad with desire, he tore his mouth from hers and let it roam over her face and throat. And then there was only this desperate need for her, growing like a rage inside him until it was clawing to break free.

He could wait no longer.

He took her hard and fast, and was amazed when she wrapped herself around him, matching her strength to his. Their hearts were racing in perfect rhythm.

He whispered her name a moment before they reached the first shuddering crest. And then they were caught in a hurricane. Flying, soaring, before shattering into tiny pieces and drifting slowly back to earth.

Kane expected regrets. He braced himself for tears, for recriminations. Instead, Bethany lay snuggled in his arms, as though she'd always been there. The strange thing was, he felt the same way. As though she'd always been here in his arms, loving him with wild abandon.

He stared down at her face, covered with sheen. "You aren't sorry, Bethany?"

"Sorry?" She looked into his eyes. "Are you?"

"Of course not. But…you were a maiden. And I've sullied your virtue."

"Sullied it?" She sat up, indignant. "If it's sullied, why do I feel so alive? So…cherished?"

Why indeed? He merely stared at her, before throwing back his head and laughing. "Oh, Bethany. You constantly amaze me. Do you know, you're unlike any woman I've ever known?"

"I should hope so." She snuggled again, loving the feel of those powerful arms around her. "I have a confession to make, Kane."

He waited, wondering what other surprises lay in store for him.

"Since the first time the Lord of the Night kissed me, I was hopelessly lost."

"What about Kane Preston?"

"I didn't know him then." Nor did she now, she realized.

"Now I'll make a confession of my own. The first time I saw you, you were but a flame-haired stranger viewed from afar."

"A stranger?"

"Aye. A woman dressed in men's clothes, fighting a pack of wild-eyed pirates, when your ship interceded on behalf of mine."

"Your ship?"

"It was a small gentleman ship flying an English flag as it made toward Land's End and was attacked by pirates."

She sat back, staring at him in surprise. "That was your ship?"

"I'm pleased to see that I can still catch you off guard." He grinned. "I was watching through my spy glass. I thought you the most magnificent woman I'd ever seen. And I vowed there and then I'd have you."

"And when you kissed me as Lord of the Night?"

"I didn't plan that. It just happened. I knew you were the woman I'd seen aboard ship. The same hair. The same fearlessness. And a tart tongue to go with it. I must say, you left a…lasting impression, my lady. And I knew I'd have to taste those lips again."

"I felt the same, though I tried to deny it. But that night you took your leave of me, I was filled with despair. I thought the Lord of the Night had gone from my life forever."

His tone roughened. "He has, Bethany. The Lord of the Night is dead. He died that night, never to return. He will never again ride alone in the dark of night, challenging the wealthy to look beyond their gold and jewels." He ran his finger over her lips, fascinated by the shape of them. "Do you mind?"

"I suppose I don't mind. As long as I can still have Kane Preston." She shot him a mysterious, woman's smile. "Of course, I really ought to be given a sample of Kane Preston's charms before I decide."

"You're a greedy woman, Bethany Lambert."

"Aye." She leaned close and pressed her lips to his throat. At his little intake of breath she thrilled to her newly discovered power. "Greedy to learn all there is to know about the mysterious earl of Alsmeeth."

As she brought her mouth lower, she felt his muscles contract on a moan of pleasure.

"Not only greedy, but heartless, my lady. Have you no pity?"

"None, unless you agree to cooperate." She looked up and fluttered her lashes. "Or would you rather I retire to one of the guest chambers, your lordship?"

"You drive a hard bargain, Bethany Lambert." He dragged her into his arms and kissed her until she was gasping for air. "We'll soon see who…cooperates more fully."

She gave a delighted laugh, which soon turned into a moan of pleasure, as his hands and mouth began to weave their magic once more.

The first faint ribbons of dawn light found their way across the balcony, and spilled over the two figures snuggled comfortably under the bedlinens, which were now tangled around them. All night they had loved, then dozed, only to awaken and love again. Now they lay, sated, content.

Kane's arm was wrapped possessively around her waist.

He looked down at the figure in his arms, loving the way her hair fell across his arm and tickled his chest.

She woke slowly. Her cheek was pressed firmly against his chest. The steady sound of his heartbeat was more soothing than any lullaby. Her lids fluttered, then opened as she gazed up at Kane.

He stared into those green depths and couldn't help smiling.

"What are you thinking?" She lifted a finger to his lips.

"I'm wondering how I've lived all these years without you."

She'd been wondering that very thing herself. In the space of a few hours, her entire life had changed, because of this man who filled her heart as no one else ever could.

"And I'm wondering how I'll explain all this to your grandfather. Last night when he went off to his bed, he feared his granddaughter might not live until morning. Now, I must tell him that I couldn't keep my promise made as a gentleman."

She snuggled close. "How can you say that? I thought you were a perfect gentleman."

He laughed at her remark. "If you believe that, then I haven't expressed myself completely." With his eyes steady on hers, he began a long, lazy exploration of her body. As his fingers worked their magic, his lips began burning a trail of fire down her body until she gasped and clutched the bedlinens.

When her breathing was shallow, and her heart was pounding like a runaway carriage, he brought his mouth over hers in a savage kiss. Against her lips he whispered, "Now, Bethany, do you still think I'm behaving like a proper gentleman?"

With her breath burning her lungs, and her throat so dry she couldn't form a single word, all she could do was shake her head.

He gave her a dangerous smile. "Nor will I ever be able to behave like one with you."

With her pulse thundering in her temples, she gave herself up completely.

And as he lost himself in the pleasure of her love, Kane realized that if he was truly a gentleman, he would have left her as he'd found her. For his reputation would surely sully hers as well. But now, there was no turning back. She was his destiny. He was hers.

There would be time enough for regrets on the morrow. For now, this was all that mattered.

Together they slipped over the edge of madness, into a world of dark, sensuous delight.

Chapter Thirteen

Kane stood on the balcony, watching as the sun climbed above the horizon. What he wanted, more than anything, was to lie in bed with Bethany and make slow, delicious love to her all day. But what a man wanted was often in direct conflict to his obligations.

He took the small stickpin from his pocket and studied the winking jewels in the morning light. For a moment he had to close his eyes against the pain. Then he swallowed back the bitter bile of fury that rose up to choke him.

Who would have believed that a day trip to a tiny island would change the course of his life? But it had been a turning point, in more ways than one. Hearing the sounds of movement in his bed, he tucked the pin in his pocket before turning.

Bethany watched as he walked toward her. For a moment she thought she detected sadness in his eyes. Or perhaps anger. But then he blinked and the look was gone, replaced with a smile.

It was still difficult for her to believe that the distant, aloof earl she had feared, and the dark, dangerous highwayman who had fueled her dreams, was the same man who had loved her so tenderly through the night.

"Will you answer me something, Kane?" She opened her arms to him as he sat on the edge of the bed.

He kissed the tip of her nose. "What would you like to know, my love?"

Love. It was the sweetest word she'd ever known. For a moment the sound of his voice, the touch of his hands, stole her voice. When at last she found it she whispered, "Why did an earl become a highwayman?"

He frowned. "It wasn't my intention. At least in the beginning. When I was younger, I simply dressed in black to ride about the countryside undetected after dark. In my youth, with tutors and servants constantly surrounding me, it was the only way I could have some time to myself. But then something happened that changed my life. And when I returned to Cornwall, I was dismayed at the disparity between the wealthy and the poor. What was worse, there seemed no way to make the wealthy aware of the poor among them. And so I decided to take their most cherished possessions, so that they could realize that their lives, their safety, was much more important than mere things."

"But why did you give their possessions to Jenna Pike?"

"It was something you said."

"I?"

He nodded. "I'd been mulling how to return the bounty I'd collected. And you said that if people never saw how others lived, they couldn't possibly know that their own land was paradise."

"But we were talking about the weather."

"Aye. But you see, it suddenly made perfect sense to me. If the wealthy and titled were given a glimpse of

Miss Pike's life, they might be jolted out of their complacency and actually begin to see others who are in need. And in doing so, might also offer to make such lives better.''

''As you do.''

He shook his head. ''I don't do nearly enough. There have been so many…complications in my life.''

Bethany waited, hoping he might share some of those complications. But before he could say more there was a brisk knock on the door, followed by Huntley's voice. ''Your lordship.''

Kane saw the flush on Bethany's cheeks and couldn't help laughing. ''As I recall, you were the one who insisted that we share this bed, my lady.''

''Aye. But I didn't think I'd have to share that knowledge with your butler.'' She put a hand to her mouth. ''Oh, Kane. I don't think I could bear to face him.''

Seeing her embarrassment, he took pity on her. In a stern voice he called, ''I have no need of your assistance this morrow, Huntley. Tell Mistress Dove that Miss Lambert is much improved. I'll break my fast with the others below stairs.''

''Aye, your lordship.''

As the butler's footsteps retreated, Kane took a look at Bethany's face and burst into laughter. ''A word of advice, my love. See that you never play cards with my London friends.'' He tipped up her chin and kissed her full on the mouth. ''All your emotions are right there in those lovely green eyes for everyone to see.''

''If that's true, then what am I feeling now?''

He stared down into her eyes. ''Relief, that Huntley has gone. Hmmm.'' His eyes narrowed. ''I believe I see passion, as well.'' He kissed her, long and slow and deep, then whispered against her mouth, ''Aye. Passion. And a hunger which I feel it is my duty to fill before we leave this bed.''

She started to laugh, but it was cut off by his mouth possessing hers as they came together in a storm of passion.

''Praise heaven you've recovered.'' Mistress Coffey took both Bethany's hands in hers and squeezed. ''I hardly slept the entire night, worrying over you.''

''I had little enough sleep myself.'' Bethany saw Kane's quick smile as he entered the room and took his seat at the head of the table. He was dressed, as always, in black breeches and boots, and a proper black waistcoat. But she'd been privileged to see, to touch, to explore the muscled body beneath the proper clothes. The mere thought brought a blush to her cheeks.

They had all assembled in the dining hall, where Mistress Dove fluttered around the table directing the servants. In the space of a single day she'd begun to take a cue from Mistress Coffey, her voice stronger, her directions clear and without any trace of nerves.

''I'd call it no less than a miracle,'' Miss Mellon said from across the table. ''Why, look at you, Bethany. You're the picture of health. Don't you agree, Geoffrey?''

The old man studied his granddaughter, then turned to the man beside her. ''I'd say both of you look far better than you did last night.''.

Kane and Bethany shared a quick glance, then looked away.

From his place at the table, old Newton kept his thoughts to himself. But there was no denying the glow that seemed to radiate around both the earl and the lass. If he had to hazard a guess, he'd say the two of them had discovered something more precious than sleep last night. And about time, he thought.

"Will we be going back to MaryCastle today, Grandpapa?" Darcy sat beside her sister, feeling as though the weight of the world had been removed from her shoulders now that Bethany had recovered.

Bethany glanced at Kane, hoping he would insist that they remain a while longer.

Instead, he surprised her by nodding his agreement. "I'm certain Bethany would be more comfortable in her own home."

"What say you, lass?" Geoffrey turned to her. "The decision is yours. I want to be certain you're strong enough for the carriage ride."

She could feel everyone watching her. But the only one who mattered was Kane. And he was studiously avoiding her, staring intently at the food on his plate.

Had he already tired of her? Was he regretting what they'd shared last night? She had, after all, practically forced herself on him.

She gave a sigh. "I'm fine, Grandpapa. There's no reason for me to stay."

No reason, unless Kane should state one. When he offered no objection, she ducked her head, afraid the others might see the tears that threatened.

"It's settled, then." Geoffrey heaped his plate with thin slices of roast beef and the lightest biscuits he'd ever tasted. If they didn't leave this elegant estate today, Winnie would need to let out the buttons on his waistcoat. He smiled at the housekeeper and old nursemaid. "We'll be back at MaryCastle in time for a midday meal."

Mistress Dove exchanged a glance with the butler. Though she'd initially resented the intrusion of these noisy people, she'd actually come to enjoy their company. Especially that of Miss Lambert. In her presence the earl had, for at least a little while, put aside his private grief and had begun to emerge from his self-imposed confinement. Though her duties would be reduced, the old housekeeper wasn't certain she wanted things to return to the way they'd been, when the earl had hidden himself away for days at a time, and the servants had cringed whenever he was near.

"If you're going to venture out in the cold air, Bethany, you'll need a warm shawl." Miss Mellon sipped her tea. "Perhaps we could borrow several blankets as well, your lordship."

"Of course."

At his cool, controlled tone, Bethany bristled. "I don't need a shawl or blankets, Winnie. It's quite warm."

"But you might take a chill."

"I'm not an invalid. I merely suffered a tiny cut, and a bump on my head. I'm feeling as strong as ever. Stronger, in fact."

"Winnie's right, of course. Wear your shawl, Bethany." Mistress Coffey held up her steaming cup. "And you should drink lots of tea before we leave. It'll warm your blood."

"My blood is warm enough, thank you." It was so hot, it was steaming, and growing hotter by the minute.

"Don't take that tone, young lady." Mistress Coffey shot her a look that she'd perfected through the years. "Drink your tea."

Realizing it was useless to argue, Bethany drained her cup and glared around at the others. But she simply couldn't hold on to her anger. Not at these sweet old dears, who only meant well. "Perhaps we should go now."

"Not yet." Geoffrey tucked into another biscuit. "Take a moment to build up your strength, lass."

"I don't need a moment, Grandpapa. I'm as good as new."

"Nonsense." Miss Mellon shook her head. "You don't take a blow such as that and recover the next day. Why, it might take weeks, months even, before you're fully recovered."

"You must stop this." Bethany nearly stomped her foot with impatience. "I feel strong enough to sail aboard the *Undaunted,* and take on an entire company of pirates single-handed."

Mistress Coffey looked around, relieved that Huntley and Mistress Dove weren't close enough to overhear. "You must contain yourself, Bethany. You wouldn't want strangers to know about our business."

"It's a little late for that. Kane was aboard ship. He saw our cannon. Watched our crew arm themselves. Why, he even joined in the battle. And I've told him the truth about what we do." She looked around at her family. "I owed him that much, after the way he came to my rescue."

"Indeed you did, lass." The old man smiled at Kane. "What do you think of our news?"

Kane bit back a smile. "I have to admit that I'm not the least surprised."

Miss Mellon lowered her voice. "Newton told us you were an accomplished swordsman. I wish I'd been there to see it."

"Aye." Bethany nodded. "And did you know that he can fire a pistol with as much accuracy as I can, Winnie?"

Her grandfather wondered if Bethany was aware of the note of pride in her voice. He cleared his throat. "Well, if you're certain you're up to the journey home, lass, I think it best if we take our leave now.''

Kane pushed away from the table. ''Before you do, Captain Lambert, I'd like to meet with you in the library.''

''Right you are.'' Geoffrey winked at his granddaughter as he followed Kane from the room.

As he walked away, Bethany stared after him, wondering about this matter Kane wanted to discuss. Could it be…? She had to swallow several times to dislodge the lump in her throat. Kane had said he could make her no promises. Still, the fact that he wanted to speak with her grandfather had her heart beating faster than ever.

A short time later, as they awaited the arrival of the earl's carriage, Huntley approached them in the parlor. ''You have visitors, Miss Lambert. A Miss Edwina Cannon is here, along with Deacon Ian Welland.''

''Thank you, Huntley.'' Bethany smiled as the two approached. ''Whatever are you doing here?''

''Miss Lambert.'' The young deacon took her hands in his. ''We heard that you'd sustained a serious injury during a voyage aboard your ship. We had to come and see for ourselves.''

Bethany laughed. ''I did take a nasty fall. But as you can see, I'm feeling fine now.''

''What a relief.'' Edwina stepped between them, to draw attention to herself. ''I persuaded Deacon Welland that you might be in need of his prayers.''

''I'm most grateful.'' It occurred to Bethany that Edwina had cleverly used this injury as the perfect excuse to see the earl's estate. She would, when she returned to town, hold all her friends spellbound as she described everything, down to the smallest detail.

Over Edwina's shoulder, Bethany caught sight of Oswald Preston striding toward them. "I didn't know you'd brought the earl's cousin, as well."

"Did I neglect to mention Oswald? No matter. He assures me that as family he's come often to Penhollow Abbey." Edwina turned and linked her arm with his in an intimate gesture.

He caught Bethany's hand in his and lifted it to his lips. "When we heard the news of your injury in the company of my cousin, Miss Lambert, we all feared the worst." He looked around to include the others. His voice lowered conspiratorially. "Especially in light of my cousin's…history."

"History?"

"I'm sure you've heard the rumors, Miss Lambert. There is a…dark side to my cousin. So many who were close to him have died in most unusual circumstances."

Annoyed, Bethany snatched her hand away. Her tone was pure ice. "I don't believe in indulging in petty gossip."

He merely smiled. "Nor do I, Miss Lambert. But this is much more than mere gossip. It is considered fact in most circles."

The young deacon seemed equally disturbed by Oswald's words. "I quite agree with Miss Lambert. Such things ought not to be repeated in polite company, sir."

"As you wish." With a thin smile, Oswald inclined his head. "I merely meant it as a warning to anyone who might get too close to my cousin."

"Well. What have we here?" Geoffrey Lambert came strolling into the parlor, followed by Kane.

Bethany handled the introductions. "I don't believe you've met Edwina Cannon and Deacon Ian Welland. This is the earl of Alsmeeth."

Edwina flushed and bowed, while the deacon offered his hand.

"Your lordship."

"Deacon Welland. Miss Cannon. Welcome to Penhollow Abbey." Kane glanced at his cousin. His tone was carefully controlled. "Oswald."

"Cousin." Oswald chose to ignore the less-than-cordial welcome. In fact, his smile grew. "We came because we'd heard of Miss Lambert's injuries. I was just telling her how fortunate she is to have survived, when so many others haven't fared as well."

Embarrassed by his suggestion, the young deacon was quick to interrupt. "Imagine our joy at finding Miss Lambert feeling so strong."

Edwina had been standing back, thoroughly dismayed at the thought of Bethany getting all the attention. She turned to Oswald with a sudden radiant smile. "Shall we tell them our news, my dearest?"

He gave a negligent shrug of his shoulders. "If you wish."

She stared around at the others, nearly trembling with excitement. "Oswald and I are to be wed next month in London, at his estate."

"So soon?" Mistress Coffey arched a brow. "What does your mother think of such a thing, Edwina?"

"Mama is delighted. Of course she'll go up for the ceremony. Oswald has assured us that there is plenty of room for guests." She turned to the earl. "I'm sure you'll want to be there for the wedding of your cousin, as well, your lordship."

Kane glanced at Oswald. "I don't know if I'll still be there a month from now, since I'm going up to London this very day."

"London?" Bethany felt her heart stop. "When...did you decide?

"Just this morning."

This morning. Yet, when they'd been alone in his chambers, he hadn't said a word about his intentions. The realization that he'd kept such news from her cut deeply.

She struggled to keep her voice steady. "When will you be returning to Cornwall?"

He forced himself to look at her. The pain and confusion in her eyes tore at his heart. But he managed to reveal absolutely no emotion. "I know not. For as long as my business takes, I suppose."

He saw her lips tremble and hated himself. He wished more than anything in the world that he could take her into his confidence. But there was no time.

Time. He hated the fact that it seemed always to work against him.

When Huntley announced that the carriage was ready, he led the way to the courtyard.

The young deacon and Oswald settled into Edwina's carriage, while Huntley assisted the Lambert family into the earl's carriage.

Bethany stood to one side, struggling with so many emotions, she could hardly hold herself together.

Kane took her hand in his, absorbing a jolt to his heart. And because he knew the others were watching, he merely brushed his lips over her knuckles, before taking a step back. "There's so much I wish I could tell you, Bethany. For now, I bid you safe journey home."

"Thank you, your lordship."

He acknowledged her use of his formal title and knew that something rare and precious between them had been shattered. But there was nothing to do now but get through this. He stepped aside as Huntley helped her into the carriage. The driver flicked the reins.

Bethany stared straight ahead, refusing to turn and look at him. She feared if she did, she might break down and weep. And she would never, never allow that. At least not until she reached the privacy of her own room.

As for Kane, he waited until both carriages disappeared down the long curving ribbon of drive. Then he turned and gave last-minute instructions to his staff, before taking his leave of Penhollow Abbey.

Chapter Fourteen

For Bethany, the days since Kane had left for London went by in a blur of work. As always, her cure for anything painful was to engage in a whirlwind of activity. She took Darcy's place aboard the *Undaunted,* hauling cargo up the coast to Wales, where she managed to engage a boatload of pirates, sending them retreating in fear when they realized they'd met their match. On the voyage back the *Undaunted* endured a storm and picked up sailors who'd survived a shipwreck. Now, sadly, the *Undaunted* was anchored just offshore, until a request for more cargo was forthcoming.

Eager to find another activity to fill the hours, Bethany had decided to haul a wagonload of goods to Mead, for Jenna Pike and her children. It was just the thing to soothe an aching heart.

"Bethany." Darcy knocked, then stepped into her sister's room. "Winnie says you must be back in time to accompany her to the weekly Psalm reading at the vicarage tonight."

Bethany frowned. "I believe I'm going to have a headache tonight, Darcy."

"If you tell Winnie that, she'll think you've had a

relapse and will be sending Newt to the apothecary for
one of her powders. You know how she's been hovering
over you.''

''Aye.'' Bethany sighed as she picked up her shawl
and headed toward the stairs. Then she had a sudden
thought. ''I believe I'll go to the vicarage right now.''

''Are you daft?'' Darcy trailed behind her, eyes wide
with disbelief. ''Whatever for?''

Bethany merely smiled. And as she walked out the
door, she paused at the threshold to press a kiss to their
old nursemaid's cheek.

''What was that for?'' Charmed, Miss Mellon lifted
her hand to the spot.

''For reminding me of something I'd nearly forgotten.'' Bethany danced down the steps and climbed up on
the hard seat of the wagon. As she flicked the reins, she
called, ''Tell Mistress Coffey not to wait supper for me.
I'll take a meal with Miss Pike and the children.''

''How fortunate that you caught me at the vicarage,
Miss Lambert.'' The young deacon sat beside Bethany
looking slightly dazed. It wasn't every day that a beautiful young woman stopped by and asked him to go for
a ride. Especially one of the beautiful Lambert sisters.

He'd long been dazzled by them, especially Bethany.
Not just by her beauty, but by her boundless energy, as
well. But though he'd entertained an occasional thought
about pursuing her, he'd long ago realized they were
completely unsuitable for one another. A woman like
Bethany Lambert would never be content to be the wife
of a simple village vicar. There was a spark in her. A
spark that, once ignited, would blaze across the heavens.

Bethany gave him a sideways glance as she handled

the reins. "Has Vicar Goodwin given you any indication when you might expect to be ordained?"

He flushed. "I'd hoped by now to have that behind me, and perhaps be assigned to a parish somewhere here in Cornwall. But Vicar Goodwin feels that I'm much more useful in Land's End, as his assistant. He suggested, since he won't be ready to retire for another decade or more, that there is plenty of time for my ordination in the years to come. He hasn't even seen fit to recommend me to the bishop yet."

"Doesn't that bother you?"

He smiled at her huff of impatience. "It is not for me to question. It will all come about in God's good time, Miss Lambert."

"But what if there was a poor, small village in need of a vicar? Would you ask to move up the time of your ordination, in order to serve the needs of such people?"

He spread his hands. "I suppose I might. But I believe in placing all my needs in the very capable care of our Creator, Miss Lambert. If I'm meant to leave Land's End, it will surely happen. If not, I'm prepared to live out my life here as a humble assistant."

"What about a wife and family? Are they part of your hope for the future?" The words were out of her mouth before she could stop them.

He paused and looked over. A flush spread across his face and neck. "Are you...asking for yourself, Miss Lambert?"

She nearly laughed aloud at his discomfort. But she managed to swallow it back. "Nay. Forgive my boldness, Deacon Welland. I just meant that it would be difficult for you to consider your future as a man, until your future as a vicar is decided."

"I realize that there are some women who might be

hesitant to consider marriage to a man of the church. Especially one who had no desire to direct one of the splendid cathedrals, but would rather remain vicar in a poor village. As churchmen we are, after all, dependant upon the charity of our parishioners. But I must follow my heart, Miss Lambert, and trust that there is a woman somewhere whose heart will beat in harmony with mine.''

She fell silent for long minutes, digesting what he'd said. Oh, how she wished she had his faith. Though she managed to fill her days with activities, the nights were almost unbearable. Thoughts of Kane came unbidden to her mind, tormenting her with visions of his life in London, surrounded by exotic, sophisticated women who would know how to tease and please a man. They certainly wouldn't throw themselves at an unwilling partner and practically beg him to take them. Every time she thought about the way she'd behaved, she cringed. No wonder he'd fled Cornwall in haste, and returned to the life he knew best in London.

Without a word of explanation.

That was what hurt the most. He'd left her without a word.

''I don't believe I've ever gone in this direction before, Miss Lambert. Where are we headed?''

She pulled herself back from her troubling thoughts. ''Mead. It's a little fishing village.'' As they crested a hill she pointed, and in the distance could be seen the harbor, with its fleet of boats.

As they drew near, they could make out the fishermen sitting in the sun, mending their nets, while women and children sorted through their catch.

''How did you come to know this place?'' Ian turned

to watch as she guided the horse and wagon along the narrow path that wound through the town.

"A...friend brought me."

"Will that friend be here today?"

"Nay. But I've made some new friends. And I'm bringing them a few gifts."

He glanced over at the parcels in the wagon. "I've been meaning to ask you about them. Is this a special occasion?"

"Nay. Although every day spent in their company is special." She smiled. "I don't mean to be mysterious. You'll see soon enough." As she guided the horse and cart past the ancient church, she saw Ian's attention shift.

"What's this?"

"The church of Mead. It's been so long without a vicar, it has fallen into disrepair."

He looked beyond it, up the winding path. "But how can that be? There seems to be someone living in the vicarage."

"Aye. My friends." She brought the horse to a halt and heard the shouts from inside.

Minutes later the door was thrown open and the children came tumbling out, followed by Jenna Pike.

"Miss Lambert." She was drying her hands on an apron that spanned her slender waist. It was clear that she'd been baking bread, for there were traces of flour on her cheek and the tip of her nose. Little wisps of her hair had fallen from the knot at her nape to fall in damp tendrils around her face.

"Miss Pike." Bethany leapt to the ground and was instantly surrounded by the children who were wriggling about like puppies. She hugged and kissed them before saying, "I'd like you to meet Deacon Ian Welland. Ian, this is Miss Jenna Pike."

"Miss Pike." Ian climbed down from the rig and offered his hand. Then he glanced around at the cluster of children, who were climbing into the back of the wagon, staring excitedly at the parcels. "Are these all yours?"

"Aye."

"But how can that be? Surely you can't be more than ten and six."

She laughed. "Actually I'm nearly a score. And they aren't mine by birth. But they're mine all the same. This is the Mead Foundling Home. It was begun by my mother, and I am the current proprietor."

He blinked, then realized his mistake and began to smile.

Jenna turned to the children. "Here, now. Mind your manners."

"But look, Miss Pike." Noah held up a bucket of fish. "There are so many I can hardly count them all."

Bethany laughed. "My sister and I caught them this morrow. They'll make a tasty supper. And our housekeeper sent some jars of fruit conserve to go with them. And some lovely bread pudding. And Miss Mellon is knitting sweaters for all of you. I brought only five so far, but she said not to worry, the rest of them will be ready before the first cold winds of winter."

"Oh, Miss Lambert." Jenna walked over to take her hand. "That's far too formal a title, when you have become such a good friend. Do you mind if I call you Bethany?"

"I'd like that. And I'll call you Jenna."

"Bethany, how can we ever thank you?"

"I don't want your thanks. I just want to see the children's faces when they see what else I've brought."

"What? What?" The children danced around her until she began laughing. "All right. I can't make you wait any longer." She pointed to a mysterious parcel, wrapped in a blanket and an old sail. "Let's bring that inside, and perhaps you can all take turns opening it."

It took all of the children working together to haul it from the cart and carry it inside, while the adults followed behind.

As they strode through the house, Ian took the time to study the sparkling windows, the freshly swept floors, softened with handmade rugs scattered here and there.

In the big fragrant kitchen Jenna said, "Please sit. I'll make tea and we'll enjoy some bread and conserve."

As they sat around the wooden table, the older children stood back and allowed the youngest ones to unwrap the mysterious object. When it was finally uncovered, the children merely stared in silence, while Jenna Pike walked over and touched a hand to it almost reverently.

"Oh, Bethany. A harp."

"Aye. It was my mother's. But she died before she could teach any of us to play. And so it's gathered dust upstairs all these years. When I heard that you could play, I thought how happy it would make my mother, to know that someone would love it the way she did."

"But how could you have known?"

"Noah told me of your sacrifice."

Jenna's eyes filled as she reached out a hand to tentatively pluck the strings. Then, blinking back her tears, she sat and cradled the harp in her arms. and began to play. The children gathered around her, listening to the lovely music that flowed through her fingers. When the song ended, they clapped their hands and called for more.

"It sounded like angels," Noah said with a trace of awe.

"Aye. Angels." The other children danced around Jenna, urging her to play another song.

She played more than half a dozen songs, mostly hymns and lullabys, while the children and her guests sat enthralled. Bethany glanced at Ian's face, and could see that he was absolutely fascinated by this lovely creature.

At last Jenna held up her hands. "All right. No more until after we've had our tea." She walked to the kettle and filled three cups, then returned to the table and sat beside Bethany, her eyes glistening. "I don't know how to repay you."

Bethany shook her head. "Don't say such things. You do so much. I'm just glad to see that my little gift makes you happy."

"Little gift?" Jenna shook her head. "This is the finest thing anyone's ever done for me."

"Nay. What you do for these children is finer than anything I'll ever do." Bethany sipped her tea until a little toddler tugged at her skirt. Then she lifted her up and snuggled her against her chest, all the while feeding her bits of bread and fruit conserve, and allowing her sips of tea as it cooled.

Ian turned to Jenna. "Would you mind if I walked to the church, Miss Pike?"

"Not at all. The door sticks a bit, but if you put your shoulder to it, it will yield."

Bethany looked up. "Why don't you go with him, Jenna. I'll stay here with the children."

"You don't mind?"

"Not at all."

As the pair walked away, she gathered the children around her. "All right. Now that I've finished my tea, why don't we play a game of hide-and-seek. I'll stay here until you've had a chance to hide. Then I'll call out when I'm ready to search."

With squeals of laughter the children dashed from the

room. As she waited for them to find hiding places, Bethany strolled to the window and watched the figures of Ian and Jenna disappear inside the old church.

She turned away to begin searching for the children. On her face was a contented, knowing smile.

"Thank you for this day, Miss Lambert." When they reached the vicarage, Ian climbed down from the wagon, then stood looking up at Bethany while shading the setting sun from his eyes. "Miss Pike is a truly remarkable young woman."

"Aye. The moment I met her I knew she was special. And I felt certain you would share my feelings."

"I do. And I find Mead a truly appealing little village. I can't get that intriguing old church out of my mind." He stared at her before smiling. "You know, Miss Lambert, you're quite remarkable yourself."

She merely laughed.

As she lifted the reins he called, "Will I see you tonight at the Psalm reading?"

"No doubt," she called over her shoulder. At least, if Miss Mellon had her way.

Her only comfort lay in the fact that, as soon as she returned from the vicarage, she would take Lacey for a long midnight ride along the beach in an effort to exorcise a certain man from her mind. A man whose mere image had the power to break her heart.

Kane stood alone at the bow of his ship, staring at the canopy of stars overhead. The days and nights spent in London had run together in a blur of official meetings. His bankers. His solicitors. Even the lord mayor of London, whose men were accompanying him to Cornwall, with orders to return with Oswald Preston.

Kane knew that this matter was far from resolved. But at least it was a start toward clearing his good name, and punishing the one responsible for so much pain and heartache.

As he caught sight of the Cornish coast, Kane felt his spirits rise. He'd left in such a rush. Poor Bethany. She must think him mad. And perhaps he had gone a bit mad. But now he felt as though he were coming out of a fog. He would find a way to make it up to her.

The ship slowed as it reached port. Kane and the men stepped into the little skiff and were rowed to the dock. Once there, they spoke quietly, then shook hands and went their separate ways. The men to the home of Miss Edwina Cannon, in search of Oswald Preston. Kane to MaryCastle, where he would beg Bethany's forgiveness and try to make amends.

Bethany pulled on the faded gown she used for her night rides. The Psalm reading had been mercifully brief. Several of the ladies remarked that the young deacon had seemed especially dramatic while reading from the Songs of Solomon. Almost as though, they'd suggested, he was speaking to a lover. But afterward, during the discussion period, he'd been called away to speak with some strangers. When he returned, he'd seemed distracted, and had shortly thereafter abruptly dismissed them. All except for Edwina and her mother. He'd asked them to stay and speak with the strangers, as well.

Bethany hadn't waited around to see what they wanted. She'd been too eager to return home. Now she was free, she thought with a smile. Free to ride Lacey across the beach and lose herself in the night. She paused as she tied her hair back with a ribbon. Would she ever be able to look out at the darkening sky and not think about her Lord of the Night?

"Oh, Kane." The words came out on a sigh.

She knelt at the window and leaned her chin on her hands, feeling the familiar pain around her heart. Suddenly her head jerked up. Could it be? She blinked and stared out at the gathering shadows.

A horse and rider were moving along the beach. In the swirling mist rolling in from the sea they seemed little more than ghostly specters.

The horseman lifted his head, as though searching the windows of MaryCastle for a glimpse of someone.

"You've come back." With a laugh of delight she ran from her room and raced down the stairs. At the stable she didn't bother to saddle her horse. She pulled herself onto Lacey's back and dug her hands into the mare's mane.

"Come, girl. Let's fly."

Her mount, sensing her agitation, danced to one side, then took off like an arrow fired from a bowstring. Within minutes they were racing across the beach in the direction of the horseman.

"Kane." Bethany cupped her hands to her mouth and shouted into the darkness. "Wait for me."

She saw the rider bring his mount to a halt, then turn and watch her approach.

She was laughing as she leaned low over her horse's neck and held on. When she came alongside she shouted, "I knew you'd return to Cornwall. You love it as much as I. Admit it. You simply couldn't stay away."

"Aye, my sweet Bethany. I'll admit, I couldn't stay away. I came looking for you. But I never dreamed you'd make it so easy."

A hand snaked out, imprisoning her wrist when she tried to pull away.

"What...?" It wasn't fear, she told herself. It was merely surprise. She moistened her dry lips and tried again. "What are you doing here, Oswald?"

"I've come to ride with you, Bethany."

She tried to pull herself free of his grasp, and was stunned when he tightened his grip. Her tone became frosty. "I...don't wish to ride with you. Let me go at once."

His smile was chilling. "I'm afraid I can't do that." He withdrew something from his pocket and held it up.

Bethany's eyes widened when she recognized the blade of a knife.

"You won't need your horse, Bethany. You and I are going to ride together only as far as your skiff."

"Skiff?"

"Aye." He threw back his head and laughed. "I need a means of escape from Land's End. And you have the perfect answer. Your ship."

"But why take me along?"

"Because I feel certain my cousin will follow. And when he does, you'll be my armor."

"Armor?"

"I'll have this knife at your throat, my sweet. When Kane sees it, he'll be more than willing to lay down his own weapons and do as I say."

"You would use me to trap Kane? Nay." She lashed out with her other hand, at the same moment digging her heels into Lacey's sides. The mare responded instantly, breaking into a run.

She heard the sound of Oswald's vicious oaths as he urged his mount into a gallop. As the two horses raced through the surf, Bethany chanced a quick look over her shoulder and saw that Oswald's horse was gaining.

She veered away from the beach, all the while clinging to Lacey's mane. But as they came up over a rise, she felt something heavy slam against her. Oswald had leapt from his horse to hers. It took all her skill to keep from being knocked to the ground. But then an arm came around her throat, and she felt the press of a blade against her flesh.

"Rein in your horse, my sweet. Or I'll slit your pretty throat."

"I'll never yield to you."

"Oh, but you will." He pressed until she felt the sharp pain, and the warmth of her blood trickling down the bodice of her gown. "Now rein in your horse."

"L-Lacey." She could barely get the word out over the pressure of his knife. At her command the horse slowed, then halted.

Oswald yanked her head back with such force, she felt tears sting her eyes. "Now, woman, you'll do as you're told."

"I'll not." Defiantly she brought back her elbow with such force, she heard him grunt in pain. But instead of knocking him down, it merely enraged him.

With a string of oaths he sliced the knife across her arm, causing her to hiss in pain. Blood streamed from the cut, and she was helpless to stem the flow as he yanked her head back and pressed the knife to her throat. "I wanted you to know that my blade is honed to a razor-edge. The next time, I won't hold back. Unless you stop fighting me at once, I'll sever your head from your body and toss it into the sea. It'll make a tasty meal for the sharks."

Bethany knew, from the way he ground out each word,

that he was now blind with fury. There would be no stopping him. When she went very still, he hauled her from her horse and dragged her across the sand to where his own mount stood, blowing and snorting. After tying her hands, he climbed into the saddle and lifted her into his arms. She shuddered when his hand came into contact with her breast. He merely laughed, then nudged his horse into the surf.

As they headed toward the beached skiff in the distance, he said against her temple, "Now will I have my revenge against my hated cousin, Kane Preston. And you, my sweet Bethany, will be the one to assure me of success."

Kane approached MaryCastle warily, noting that there were few lights showing in the windows. Apparently this seagoing family retired early. He regretted that he would have to disturb their sleep. But this couldn't keep until the morrow. He had to see Bethany tonight, and explain his actions. He dismounted and hurried up the steps. At the door he knocked, then waited until he heard the sound of approaching footsteps.

"Your lordship." Mistress Coffey, dressed in a robe hastily tossed over her nightshift, looked startled. "We...weren't expecting company. We'd heard you were in London."

"Aye. I was. Please forgive this intrusion, Mistress Coffey. There was no time to send a proper missive. But I must speak with Bethany at once."

"I'm afraid that isn't possible." The old woman drew herself up stiffly, determined to strive for propriety, despite the circumstances. "She retired to her chambers right after returning from the vicarage. And the rest of the household has retired to their beds as well."

"I realize it's quite late. But I need to explain some things to her. They are...matters of the utmost importance." Seeing that the housekeeper was wavering, he pressed his advantage. "I departed so abruptly, she may think it was something she said or did. But I assure you, Mistress Coffey, when she hears my explanation, it will ease her troubles considerably."

While the old woman continued to dither, he looked up to see Darcy standing on the stairs, trailed by her grandfather and Miss Mellon. "Please, Darcy. I beg of you. Wake your sister and tell her that I must speak with her at once."

Darcy glanced at her grandfather, then back at the man who had caused her sister such turmoil these past days. It took her less than a moment to decide. "Aye, your lordship." She spun away before her grandfather could issue a protest. Minutes later she raced down the stairs. "She isn't in her room." While the others looked around uncertainly she added, "Bethany often rides along the beach at night, your lordship."

"Aye. Of course." He was just starting out the door when he heard Newton's voice, shouting loud enough to wake the entire household.

Kane raced ahead, with the others following. When they reached the stables, Kane came to a sudden, shocking halt when he caught sight of the old sailor, trying to soothe a quivering, trembling Lacey. "What is it, Newt?" Kane demanded. "What's happened here?"

The old sailor's face was contorted in fear and anger. "I was just returning from the village tavern where I heard a most distressing tale. It seems several gentlemen from Land's End were accosted and robbed by the Lord of the Night."

Kane's eyes narrowed. "How do they know it was the outlaw?"

"He told them his name as he relieved them of their gold. And when one of them tried to resist, he shot him."

"Is the man...dead?" Kane felt his heart stop.

"Nay, yer lordship. He'll live. But the outlaw seemed in a great hurry to be on his way. And now that I've found this, I fear the worst for our lass." The old man pointed. "Look here, yer lordship."

Kane reached up and rubbed his hand through the horse's mane, then stared at the blood staining his flesh. At the sight of it the others gasped.

"She's fallen," Geoffrey shouted.

Kane shook his head. "If that were true, the blood wouldn't be on the horse's back, but rather in the sand. Did you see which direction the horse came from, Newt?"

The old man turned and pointed along the beach. "From there, yer lordship."

"Do you think the Lord of the Night has her?" Darcy demanded.

Kane felt a band tighten around his heart as he raced toward his stallion, still tethered at the front porch. "I know not. But I give you my word. I'll do everything in my power to bring her home safely."

Minutes later, as horse and rider churned up the sand and headed out across the beach, the others stared after them. Then Geoffrey turned and started toward the house.

"Where are you going, Grandpapa?"

"To dress. I suggest the rest of you do the same."

"Then we're going after Bethany?"

The old man didn't even break stride. "Aye. Whether it be land or sea, the rule's the same. When one of our own is in trouble, we'll not back away from a fight.

Newt,'' he called over his shoulder, ''saddle a couple of horses. And you'd best hitch up a rig for Mistress Coffey and Winnie, as well.''

''Aye, Cap'n.'' The old sailor tucked a knife in his waist and another in his boot, then began leading the horses from their stalls and saddling them as quickly as possible.

Bethany lay on the deck of the *Undaunted,* struggling against the ropes that bound her wrists and ankles. All the while, Oswald was busy hoisting anchor and unfurling the sails. The sight of them, pure white against the darkness, filled her with a sense of calm. This was, after all, her ship. She knew every inch of it. Sooner or later she would find a way to use her knowledge against this madman.

To delay his actions, she realized she needed to get him to talk. ''What makes you think your cousin will come to my rescue?''

''Don't pretend you don't know how Kane feels about you. He's far too noble to stand by and watch the woman he loves die.''

''The woman he loves? What a farce. Even now Kane is in London, determined to be as far away from me as he can get.''

''If you believe that, you're a fool. My cousin went to London because he discovered the funds that are missing from his accounts. But now he's come back, with soldiers commissioned by the lord mayor himself.''

''He's come back?'' Her heart started racing, and she had to swallow back the tears that sprang to her eyes. ''How would you know this?''

''The lord mayor's soldiers came looking for me at

Edwina Cannon's estate. But her maid, who had only recently left my bed, told them I was not there.''

Poor Edwina. The thought flashed through Bethany's mind. She seemed always attracted to black-hearted villains.

Oswald watched as the sails began to fill. Waves slapped against the hull as they began to slip through the shallows. He took the wheel. ''They were too close, like hounds to the scent. I knew I needed a means of escape. But I wanted an assurance that my esteemed cousin would follow, so that I can finally have my revenge against him. Which is where you come in, lovely Bethany. I've begun to realize that where you go, Kane follows. Once he finds your horse, he'll move heaven and earth to save you.''

Oh, if only it were true. But she wasn't sure she could believe that. What she did believe was that her family would come after her. And she had to delay the voyage of this ship as long as possible, to give them time to reach her. ''Why do you hate Kane so?'' She could feel her wrists beginning to bleed as she twisted mercilessly against her bonds.

''Because he took what is rightfully mine.''

She paused in her efforts. ''And what would that be?''

He spun the wheel, avoiding the rocks that threatened. When they slipped safely past, he turned to glance at her. ''Kane Preston stole my title and my inheritance.''

Chapter Fifteen

Kane pushed his mount to the limit as they raced along the shore, following the trail of hoofprints. It suddenly occurred to him that Oswald had left a very clear path to follow. If he'd wanted to escape undetected, he could have raced through the surf, where the waves would have washed away all the evidence of his passing.

Kane reined in his stallion as the truth dawned. Oswald wanted him to follow. Was, in fact, daring him to. As he approached the cove where the *Undaunted* was anchored, he saw a lone horse standing by the water's edge. When he drew close, he realized the horse was tethered to a rock at shore.

Oswald's horse? But why would he leave it? And where had he gone?

Kane saw that the skiff was missing. And far out in the cove, he caught sight of the sails of the *Undaunted,* billowing in the breeze. Could actually hear the anchor being lifted.

He slid from the saddle and began tearing off his coat and boots as he waded into the water. He was forced to discard his sword. The weight of it would slow him down. As for his pistol, it, too, was tossed aside. The gunpowder would be soaked and useless. His only weapon was a knife, which he tucked into his waist.

The ship was nearly a thousand yards from shore, and already beginning to move away. He was a powerful swimmer. But it would take a superhuman effort to catch up to the *Undaunted* now. And even if he did, there would most likely be no strength left to fight Oswald. It mattered not. All that mattered now was Bethany. As long as he could exchange his life for hers, he would die a happy man. He dove beneath the waves and began to swim with a strength born of desperation.

"Look, Grandpapa." Darcy reined in her mount and pointed to the two horses standing by the shore.

They'd wasted precious time racing along the beach, following the path taken by Kane's stallion. Now, as they drew closer, they were puzzled.

"Where the devil...?" Geoffrey turned to the two old women who sat alongside Newton in the cart. "Forgive my rough language. But where has everyone gone?"

"Look, Cap'n." Newt pointed toward the white sails of their ship, moving through the shallows.

"By heaven. Is that the *Undaunted*?"

"Aye, Cap'n."

Geoffrey Lambert looked thunderstruck. "We must find a way to follow."

"Leave that to me, Cap'n." Old Newt stepped down from the cart and pulled himself into the saddle of Darcy's horse. While the others watched, he disappeared into the darkness.

With her cheek pressed to the deck, Bethany could hear the groaning and creaking of the wood as it strained against the waves. Though they were still inching through the shallows, she could feel the boat begin to pick up speed as the wind filled the sails.

"A word of caution. It takes a seasoned seaman to navigate these waters."

Oswald sneered. "Is this some feeble attempt to have you freed from your bonds? Would you have me believe that you know how to navigate these waters?"

She held her silence, aware that he was in no mood to believe her. Minutes later he had to work frantically to keep the ship from hitting a half-submerged shelf of boulders.

Bethany watched as Oswald struggled to hold the wheel steady. As they threaded their way between rocky outcroppings, they heard a grinding sound. For a moment the ship shuddered, before continuing on its path.

"What was that?" Oswald's eyes were wide with sudden fear.

"We nearly ran aground. I warned you, but you chose to disregard my words. These shallows are some of the most perilous on this entire coast. My sisters and I have been navigating them since we were children."

He caught her roughly by the arms and hauled her across the deck until she was standing in front of the wheel. Taking a knife from his waist he cut the ropes that bound her wrists. "Here, now. See that we make it through." He lifted his pistol to her head. "And if you try to escape, I'll send you to swim with the sharks."

"I'll need my ankles free as well. Otherwise I'll never be able to keep my balance."

He dug the pistol into her flesh. "I've made all the concessions I intend to make. See that you remain upright and get us through these shallows, or we'll both perish. And know this. If you run us aground, I'll see you're dead before I abandon ship."

Bethany clung to the wheel, fighting to remain standing while maneuvering the ship through the maze of hidden dangers. And as the moon struggled to break through the mist-shrouded night, she waited for an opportunity to overpower this brute. It was her only hope for survival.

Kane heard the grinding of wood against stone, and knew that he was gaining on the *Undaunted*. His eyes burned from the seawater, and his arms felt as heavy as boulders. But one thought kept him going. Bethany. Sweet Bethany. In the hands of his hated cousin. He propelled himself through the waves that rolled over him, kicking legs he could no longer feel. And though at times it felt as if he must surely be losing ground with every stroke, he finally saw the hull of the ship looming directly before him.

Calling on every ounce of energy left, he continued swimming until he saw the rope ladder just beyond his grasp. He reached out, only to watch it slip away. Desperate, he was forced to push himself to the limits until he was alongside the ladder. This time when he reached up, he caught hold of the bottom rung and began to climb. When he reached the top, he waited, struggling for breath. Then, peering over the edge of the rail, he caught sight of Bethany at the wheel.

She was alone.

A voice came from just beside him. "Looking for me, cousin?"

He turned his head and saw Oswald standing at the rail, the pistol pointed at his head.

"I'll take that knife at your waist."

Kane slipped it free and handed it over.

"Now come aboard, your lordship." Oswald was smiling as Kane climbed over the rail and stood dripping water. "It took you long enough to catch up."

"You didn't make it easy." Kane turned to study Bethany. The sight of blood staining her gown had his own running hot. He clenched his hands into fists at his sides. "Untie the woman and set her free."

"Don't use that tone with me, cousin. Why should I want to free the woman?"

"Because this is between us. She has nothing to do with it."

"So you say. But she has everything to do with this. You see, cousin, your feelings are there in your eyes. The woman is special to you. That makes her perfect for my vengeance. For if I merely wanted you dead, I'd have shot you before you reached the top of the ladder. But just so you understand that I have the power…" He took aim and shot Kane through the arm.

A cry was torn from Bethany's lips, but she could do nothing more than watch helplessly. The force of the blow sent Kane to his knees, where he clutched his arm and watched blood ooze between his fingers.

Oswald stood over him, gloating. "I rather like having you kneel before me, cousin. It's where you belong. Like a dog, begging for scraps."

Through gritted teeth Kane asked, "What do you want, Oswald?"

"Everything. Everything that should have been mine in the first place."

"According to my solicitors, you've already stolen enough from my father's estate to live like royalty."

"And why not? If it weren't for you, I'd have been the heir. All your estates, and especially Penhollow Abbey, would be mine."

"Are you saying you hate him just for being born?" Bethany demanded.

Oswald looked over at her. "Aye. That's exactly it. I hate him for being born. And worse, for being taken in by a childless couple and given all that should have rightfully been mine."

"I don't understand." Bethany looked from Oswald to Kane.

"I see. You didn't bother telling her the truth, did you?"

"I would have. Given enough time."

"Oh, aye. Perhaps on your wedding night, cousin?" Oswald roared with laughter. He turned to Bethany. "Did you know, he never bothered to tell his high-born bride about the fact that he'd been born to some unwed slut, and that my uncle took him from a foundling home and made him his son and heir? An heir to a fortune that was rightfully mine, since I am blood related."

Bethany found herself speechless. A foundling. Now, it all made sense. His love and devotion to Jenna Pike and the children at the Mead Foundling Home. His disdain for wealth and titles. His yearning to be free to live his life as he chose. She glanced at Kane's face, hard and tight with pain and anger. Her heart nearly broke for him.

His gaze was fixed on his cousin. "But you told her, didn't you, Oswald? You enjoyed telling Caroline the truth about my birth."

"Aye. And you should have seen her face, Kane, when she learned that she'd just given herself in marriage to a bastard."

"Why didn't you just plunge the knife yourself?"

Oswald laughed. "I didn't need to. She was only too happy to oblige. Caroline considered death a far more acceptable alternative than being tied for a lifetime to a man who had been an...accident of birth. A mongrel. Actually I did you a favor. She only married you for your wealth and title.''

''And now you'll kill me, too. But it won't get you the wealth and title you so desperately want, will it?''

''Nay.'' Oswald's eyes narrowed. ''Even with you out of the way, they're all lost to me now. But to make up for that little fact, I'll see that you suffer before you die.''

''You don't think killing my father was enough suffering?''

Oswald blanched. ''So. You know. How did you find out?''

''The stickpin. He was wearing it the night he was killed. When I came upon his body, the stickpin was gone. I knew the killer must have taken it. In time the authorities agreed, and gave me my freedom from Fleet Prison, since the servants swore I was in the house when the shot was fired. Despite that fact, there are some who still believe I was the killer. If you hadn't sold my father's stickpin to that shop owner, I'd have never known who actually did the deed. But then, you probably never thought I'd visit a little shop in the Scilly Islands, did you?''

''Nay. But no matter. It's done now. I needed money.''

''You've always needed money. No amount was ever enough for you, Oswald.''

His cousin waved the pistol. ''I've heard enough from you. Lie down here on the deck, where I can keep an eye on you.''

''Nay. No more. Just kill me.'' He glanced beyond Oswald to where Bethany stood holding the wheel. ''And when you toss my body overboard...'' He looked meaningfully toward the rail, hoping she would understand his intention. While his cousin was busy shooting him, she would have time to make her escape. "You'll finally be rid of me, cousin."

Oswald stood over him, sneering. "You'd like that, wouldn't you? You'd like me to end your pain? Do you know, if you'd fallen into that pit I dug, I'd intended to leave you there, bloody and broken, for days before 'happening' upon your body. It was my intention that your death would be slow and painful. But since that failed, I've come up with an even better way." He walked over to where Bethany stood at the wheel. "Isn't this cozy? I have my own ship, just like you, Kane. My own captain. Oh, and a pretty thing she is. Don't you agree, cousin?"

When Kane refused to answer he pressed the pistol to Bethany's cheek. "I've decided that the best way to make you suffer is to let you know that I intend to take my pleasure with your woman. If she pleases me, I may keep her alive until we reach Spain. I have a friend who runs a house of pleasure. He may have some use for her. As for you, I'll dump your body in the Atlantic." He smiled. "A pity you had to find out what I was doing. A little while longer and I've had put enough away to live like...like my cousin, the earl."

"It was your greed that was your undoing, Oswald. If you'd stolen only a little, it may have gone undetected by the solicitors. But you took such enormous sums, they were bound to find out. What amazes me is how quickly you've gone through it. Have you set nothing aside?"

"And do without my pleasures? Unlike you, cousin, I'm still able to attract beautiful, high-born women, who will be more than happy to pay for my few...vices, so long as I keep them happy." He glanced at Bethany. "I assure you, my sweet, you'll be more than pleased with my...manly ability." He laughed, a high, shrill sound that sent tremors along Bethany's spine.

He was mad. Absolutely mad. She was certain of it.

He looked over at Kane, then fisted a hand in Bethany's hair and yanked her head back viciously. Seeing Kane struggle to his feet, he tore open her gown to reveal the angry welt around her throat. "Don't get any idea about nobly saving your woman, cousin. The first cut was just enough to inflict pain. The next will slit her pretty throat."

"Spare her, Oswald."

At the sound of his cry, Oswald released her and walked toward his cousin. "Do I detect a note of anguish in your voice? Is the haughty Kane Preston actually ready to beg?"

Kane nodded. "Aye. I'll beg. I'll crawl like a dog, if it will save her life."

Oswald screeched with laughter. "The earl of Alsmeeth, the richest man in Cornwall, is begging? This is too good. What more can I ask? Perhaps you would renounce your title?"

"I do renounce it. And everything that goes with it. Just spare Bethany's life."

"Will you confess to the murder of your father? Will you return to Fleet?"

"Give me a parchment and I'll sign it. I'll swear to anything. But first, you must release her."

"And how am I to do that, here in the middle of the ocean?"

"Turn her loose in the skiff. Bethany is skilled in seafaring. She'll find her way home."

"You'd like that, wouldn't you, cousin?" He sauntered closer, holding the pistol against Kane's forehead. "Of course, if I were to do that, the girl would be a witness against me." His laughter grew. "Just for a moment there was hope in your eyes. I saw it. Just as I saw that look in your father's eyes when I told him I would spare his life if he would name me his heir. But he said you were a son to him in every way that mattered. He was still praising you when I fired my pistol. I would have shot again, but I heard footsteps and knew I'd be caught. So I grabbed his stickpin and tossed aside the pistol. And I very nearly succeeded in seeing you blamed for the murder. Too bad you were finally released from prison. A lifetime rotting in Fleet would have been sweet. But this—'' he pressed the pistol against Kane's flesh ''—this will be the sweetest revenge of all.''

Kane closed his eyes, prepared for what was to come.

He heard the roar of the pistol, and waited to feel the pain. Instead, his eyes opened to behold the most amazing sight. Bethany, feet still bound, had flung herself against Oswald, knocking him to the deck. The pistol had slipped free of his grasp, and the two rolled around, scrambling to retrieve it. Oswald got there first and filled it with gunpowder, then turned and aimed it at Bethany's head.

Though Kane's arm dangled uselessly, he got to his feet and kicked as hard as he could, sending Oswald crashing against the rail. When Oswald turned, the pistol was still in his hand. And his eyes were blazing with fury.

''Now you'll pay, cousin. I've decided I have no taste for your wildcat. Say goodbye to her.'' He aimed the pistol at Bethany and fired.

''Nay!'' Kane threw himself in front of her, taking the shot meant for her.

''Oh, Kane.'' Bethany dragged herself over his still form and watched as blood spilled from a gaping hole in his chest. Though she placed her hands over it, she was helpless to stem the flow.

She gathered his crumpled form up in her arms and began to rock him like a child, crooning to him not to leave her.

Oswald watched the scene without emotion. Then, stepping closer, he gave a crazed laugh. "Leave him. Now that we've passed through the treacherous shallows, I believe it's time to take my pleasure." He caught her arm and hauled her to her feet. "When I've finished with you below deck, I'll toss him overboard."

In a daze, Bethany felt herself being lifted and carried down the steps to the cabin. But though she knew what Oswald planned for her, she felt no fear. She was, in fact, beyond feeling. Her beloved Kane was gone. He'd exchanged his life for hers. Nothing mattered now. Nor would it ever again.

Chapter Sixteen

Bethany lay on the bunk in her father's old cabin, her feet still bound, her hands curled into tight fists. Kane dead. It didn't seem possible. But she had seen the wound. Had watched his lifeblood flow like a river and stain the deck beneath his still body. With a sense of detachment she watched as Oswald placed his pistol on the desk before kicking off his boots. As he began to remove his shirt, he plucked Kane's knife from his waist and placed it beside the pistol. Reaching for the fasteners at his waist, he turned and started toward the bunk.

"I hope you're a maiden. It will make this so much sweeter."

She seemed fixated on Kane's knife. She blinked and felt the blur of grief begin to slip away. In its place was raw, blinding fury. She was not about to simply lie here and allow herself to be brutalized by this monster. Not while she still had a breath in her lungs. "Nay. I gave my maidenhood to your cousin."

"Kane was your first?"

"My only."

"No longer." He reached for the bodice of her gown.

Her chin came up. "You will have a difficult time taking me without unbinding my legs."

"Quite right." He smiled as he turned away and retrieved the knife. With one quick slice he cut through the ropes that bound her. Then, tossing it on the desk, he reached for her, only to find that she had wriggled off the bunk and now stood facing him.

"So. You want to fight me? All the better, for it gets my blood hot." His hand snaked out, grabbing the front of her gown. But before he could drag her close, she pushed away, leaving him holding nothing but a scrap of torn cloth.

"I'd best warn you, woman." He struck out, sending her crashing against the wall of the cabin, where she stood, shaking her head to dispel the stars that danced. "I've been known to kill a few women after I took my pleasure with them." He stepped menacingly closer. "So if it's death you're craving, I'm happy to oblige." His hand swung out again, but this time she managed to duck and his fist slammed against the wall, causing him to let loose with a string of vicious oaths. "You'll pay for that."

He lumbered forward and Bethany backed away until she came up against the rough edge of the desk. She saw his fist close and knew that the next blow could knock her unconscious. But she couldn't step away until she found a weapon. With her hands behind her she frantically felt around the desktop until at last she felt the cold handle of the pistol.

Her heart was pounding as she held it in front of her and took aim. "Step back or I'll shoot."

Surprised, he stopped and stared at her. "Have you ever fired a pistol, my sweet?"

"Many times."

She expected him to lift his hands in surrender. Instead, he threw back his head and laughed.

Laughed?

"Then you must know that a pistol will only fire if it has been filled with fresh gunpowder."

She glanced down and realized that she'd made a terrible mistake. He'd already emptied this pistol of gunpowder when he'd shot Kane.

He advanced, his hands balled into fists. "I'm going to enjoy beating that beautiful face until it's unrecognizable even to your own family, my sweet. And then, when you're begging me to kill you, I'll take you like the wildcat you are."

She tensed, waiting for the blows.

Instead, the door was kicked in and Kane stood in the doorway.

"Kane." Bethany couldn't believe her eyes. "You're alive."

Oswald spun around and caught sight of Kane, holding tightly to the door. A slow smile spread across his face. "Look at you. So weak you can barely stand. Come to watch, have you? That's about all you're up to, cousin. Come in, then. You're just in time. I won't even finish you off until after I've taken my pleasure with the woman."

"What will you do with the rest of us?"

"Rest of—?"

Oswald's words died in his throat when Kane stepped aside to reveal Geoffrey and Newton, holding swords, Darcy with a knife glinting in her hand, and Miss Mellon and Mistress Coffey holding dueling pistols.

"I want him taken alive," Kane said hoarsely.

"Aye, yer lordship." While the others surrounded Oswald and held their weapons at the ready, old Newton stepped forward and began tying his hands and feet.

With a cry, Bethany rushed across the room just as Kane began to slip to the floor. With tears spilling down her cheeks she clutched him fiercely. "Oh, Kane, my love. Hold on. You can't die now. Please, Kane. Please stay with me."

"Missed your vitals. You're a lucky man, your lordship." Miss Mellon finished dressing Kane's wounds, while Bethany hovered beside the bunk, refusing to leave his side for even a moment.

"Thank you, Winnie." He looked up. "Do you mind if I call you that, Miss Mellon?"

"It's my name. And I'd say, now that I've seen you in this state of undress, we're on a first-name basis, your lordship."

He grinned despite the pain. "Then you'd better start calling me Kane."

"I couldn't do that. It wouldn't be proper." She turned away, missing his grin. She beckoned to Bethany. "Now let's look at your wounds, young lady."

Bethany waved a hand in dismissal. "They're nothing, Winnie."

"Nothing? I'll be the judge of that. Come over here."

She saw Kane's smile widen. Reluctantly she walked to the desk and stood hissing with pain as her cuts were washed and disinfected.

"You're making more noise over these little cuts than his lordship did over his."

"That's because you were gentler with him."

"His wounds were more serious."

"Tell me, Winnie. How did you and the others get here?"

"I'm ashamed to say that Newt stole a skiff from the village. But he promised to return it as soon as possible."

"Remind me to thank that old thief." Kane swung his feet to the floor and sat a moment, waiting for the dizziness to pass.

"What do you think you're doing?" Bethany demanded.

"I'm going up on deck."

"Then I'm going with you." She crossed to his side and put an arm around his waist.

As the two walked from the cabin, Winnie called, "Tell Mistress Coffey that I'll be up to relieve her in a few minutes."

"Relieve her?" Both Kane and Bethany paused.

The old woman gave them an innocent smile. "She agreed to keep watch over our prisoner while I saw to your wounds."

Kane shot a grin at Bethany as they climbed the steps. "You have a very interesting family, Miss Lambert."

"Aye, your lordship. Almost as interesting as yours."

"So Newt and I took turns rowing." Geoffrey stood at the wheel, bringing the *Undaunted* through the dangerous shallows.

Up in the rigging, Newton shouted warnings whenever he spotted another hazard.

"That was quite a feat, considering how high the waves are tonight."

"Not as difficult as yours, your lordship. I was quite a swimmer in my youth, but I doubt I could have managed to swim as hard or as far as you did this night."

"It's amazing what a person can do when the life of someone special hangs in the balance." Kane was leaning weakly against the railing, with Bethany still holding tightly to him.

He watched as the two old women held pistols aimed at Oswald, who'd been trussed with enough rope to hold ten men. "I doubt they need to stand watch. The prisoner has no chance of escaping all that rope."

"Leave them be," Geoffrey muttered. "The old girls are enjoying themselves. As a matter of fact, so am I." He glanced at his granddaughter and smiled. "I haven't had this much fun since our last adventure, lass."

"Fun?" Kane looked from Bethany to her grandfather. The two were sharing a knowing smile.

"Aye. It's a family tradition."

"Speaking of tradition..." Kane cleared his throat. "Bethany, would you mind going below deck while I speak with your grandfather?"

"Nay. I'd rather stay and hear—" She saw the sudden frown on her grandfather's face. "All right. But I don't see why I have to go."

"Indulge me," the old man said.

"Aye." She walked away. At the steps, she turned. Kane and her grandfather were already deep in conversation. Whatever Kane was saying, he seemed quite serious. Almost grave.

She felt a flutter around her heart. He would be a man who would first have to ask her grandfather's permission for her hand, before coming to her to speak directly. Duty and honor were important to him.

She wasn't a patient woman. But this one time she would hold her tongue and wait until Kane came to her. And then she would tell him all the things that were in her heart.

There had been no time for private conversation. Their return to shore brought a fresh flurry of activity. After beaching the little skiff, Newton loaded their prisoner into the back of the cart, then climbed into the seat and caught up the reins.

Kane pulled himself stiffly into the saddle of his stallion. "I'll ride along, Newt. The lord mayor's men are staying at the tavern. They'll be happy to see that the object of their search has finally been captured."

Bethany tugged on the reins. "Don't go, Kane. Your wounds have drained you. You need to rest."

He closed a hand over hers. "I have to do this, Bethany. Don't you see?"

"Aye. I understand that you're eager to clear your name. But I...worry about you."

"Don't." He softened the command with a smile. "I'll be fine."

"Will you come back to MaryCastle tonight?"

He shook his head. "This could take a very long time. You need your rest."

"I'll not rest until I'm with you."

"Don't say that. You need to take care of yourself. Promise me you'll rest." When she didn't respond he said fiercely, "Promise me, Bethany."

She nodded. "Very well. I promise. But hurry back."

As he rode alongside the cart, she remained where she was, watching until the darkness closed around him, obscuring the view. Then she turned and made her way to her home, fighting an uneasy feeling.

Bethany had told herself she wouldn't sleep until Kane returned. But after a hot bath, and a soothing cup of tea, she'd drifted off in a chaise by the fire. When she awoke the house was silent, and she knew the others had gone to their beds.

Where was Kane?

She stood stiffly and smoothed down the skirt of her simple shirtwaist before walking to the window. Dawn was just coloring the horizon. Her arm pained her, as did the cut at her throat. But neither caused as much distress as this uneasiness over Kane.

When she'd asked her grandfather what he and Kane had talked about, the old man had grumbled that he was too weary to discuss it until morning. Now she wondered if he was keeping something painful from her.

She heard the sound of a horse and cart and hurried to the door. Old Newton was just stepping down. In the gray light of dawn he looked old and defeated.

Bethany glanced around. "Where is Kane?"

"His lordship won't be coming, lass."

"What do you mean, won't be coming?"

"He said it will take hours for the lord mayor's men to record his testimony against his cousin. And then—" the old man looked away "—he said he would have a confession of his own to make."

"A confession?"

When Newton said nothing, she put her hands on her hips. "Does Grandpapa know about this, Newt?"

He stared at the ground. "I believe he does, lass."

She turned and flew up the stairs. At the door to her grandfather's bedchambers, she knocked, then stormed inside. "Grandpapa." She poked and prodded the figure in the bed.

He opened one eye. "What time is it lass?"

"Time for you to tell me what you and Kane talked about aboard the *Undaunted*."

He sat up, rubbing a hand over the white stubble of beard at his chin. "He told me he loved you, Bethany.

And because of his love, he felt he had to be completely honest, even though it would mean going back to Fleet.''

"Fleet?''

"That's where they send thieves and murderers. And he told me that he had long masqueraded as the Lord of the Night.''

"And you believed him?''

The old man caught her hand. "Kane Preston strikes me as an honest man. If he says it's so, it must be.''

"Do you hear yourself, Grandpapa? You consider him honest, and a thief?''

The old man grinned. "I guess that doesn't make much sense. But I believe what he told me.'' He looked up as she started out the door. "Where are you going, lass?''

"To Land's End. To stop Kane from making a terrible mistake.''

Bethany had never ridden so hard or so fast. She leaned low over Lacey's neck and pushed the little mare to the limits. When they arrived at the tavern, she tethered her horse and ran inside.

As always, there were clusters of sailors gathered around a wooden table in the public rooms. In one corner of the room were several men discussing the shooting by the outlaw. One man was bravely displaying fresh dressings, and Bethany thanked the fates for her good fortune. He was the very one she needed.

The tavern owner stood in the midst of the crowd, serving tankards. When she stepped into the room, the crowd fell silent.

"I'm looking for the representatives of the lord mayor of London.''

The tavern owner pointed. "They're in there. Meeting with the earl of Alsmeeth.''

"Thank you."

As she started in he shouted, "Here now, lass. You can't go in there."

She ignored him and stepped inside. Seconds later the owner stepped in behind her, his face flushed with embarrassment. "Forgive me, your lordship. I tried to stop the young woman, but she refused...."

"It's all right." Kane and three grim-faced men got to their feet.

The only one Bethany noticed was Kane. Blood was already beginning to soak through his dressings. His eyes looked red-rimmed and weary. But his jaw was clenched, and there was a look of determination that frightened her.

She turned to the three strangers. "I've come to report a crime."

"Indeed?" The men glanced at one another, then back at her.

One man, with steely eyes and a bushy beard, spoke with an air of authority. "It seems to be the night for such things. His lordship has already testified against his cousin." He pointed to Oswald, still bound and lying in a corner of the room. "His lordship tells us he is just now about to make a confession of his own."

She caught her breath. She had made it in time. He hadn't yet said the words that would send him back to Fleet.

"What is it, miss? What would you like to tell us?"

Her mind raced. She clutched her hands together, refusing to look at Kane. "I was abducted earlier this night by the Lord of the Night."

The men sat up straighter. "The dangerous outlaw?"

"Aye. Dangerous. He cut my arm." She held out her arm, and the men could see the fresh dressings. "He also nearly slit my throat." She unbuttoned the mother-ofpearl button at her throat and allowed them to see the wound. This brought gasps from all three.

She hesitated before saying, "I'm told there were others who were robbed of their gold by this monster this past night."

"Aye. They've talked of nothing else this night. One of the men was shot. He's lucky to be alive."

"Have they identified the thief?"

The three men looked at one another, then shook their heads. "Can you identify him?"

"I can." She pointed to Oswald, then shrank back, as though terrified. "There is the one. That man, dressed all in black, and riding a black stallion. He called himself the Lord of the Night. I'd know that face anywhere."

"Bethany—" Kane started to stand, but the one in charge lifted a hand to still his protests.

"Please, your lordship. This is most important." He went to the door and summoned the tavern owner. "Send in those men who were robbed."

When the tavern owner was gone, Kane started tapping a hand on the desk in agitation. Minutes later the three men entered the room.

The man in charge pointed toward Oswald. "Is this the man who robbed and shot you?"

The three men circled him, studying him carefully. Then all three men nodded and began shouting and even cursing.

"Aye. That's him. I'd know those eyes anywhere."

"Cruel, he was. With a high, shrill laugh that sent chills up my spine."

"A dangerous man. Just pointed his pistol at me and shot. Didn't care if he snuffed out my life and left my wife a widow and my children orphans."

"You're absolutely certain this is the man?"

The three men nodded vigorously.

"Thank you. I'll take your names for my report to the lord mayor." The one in charge turned to Oswald, who had spoken not a word. "I doubt you'll be spending much time in Fleet for your thefts. The charge of murder will likely cost you your head." He turned to Kane. "Now, your lordship. There is something you wanted to confess?"

Kane glanced at Bethany, then got slowly to his feet. But before he could say a word, he was forced to grip the edge of the table, as the room began to spin in dizzying circles. Before he could fall Bethany was beside him, her arm around his waist.

She shot an anxious look toward the tavern owner. "His lordship is in need of a bed, and quickly."

"Aye, miss." With the tavern owner leading the way, and two of the lord mayor's men offering their assistance, Kane was taken to a small room and helped into bed.

When they took their leave, Bethany pulled a chair alongside the bed and watched the steady rise and fall of his chest. It was, she thought, the most wondrous thing she'd ever seen.

Chapter Seventeen

Kane was in the grip of a nightmare, pacing the length of the tiny cell and back. The air was fetid with the odor of death and decay. The walls and floor were slick with blood and human waste. By day the prisoners shouted and cursed. By night they moaned and sobbed and railed against the inhumanity of this hellhole they called Fleet. He tried to breathe, to fill his lungs with fresh air, but it was impossible. The stench was all around him, eating away at his soul.

He lifted his head to catch a flash of light through the tiny window cut high in the stone wall. But it was impossible to tell if it was daylight or dark. And what did it matter? The days, the nights, were nothing but an endless chain of torture.

His hands fisted and he gave a hoarse cry. The sound woke him. His eyes opened. He saw the face of an angel looking at him.

"Beth—" His throat was dry, his lips parched. He moistened them and tried again. "Bethany, where are we?"

"In a room at the tavern."

"Ah." He looked around, wondering at the snowy linens. The window was open, allowing the fresh sea air from the harbor to billow the curtains and fill the room with its perfume. He breathed deeply. He felt something soft against his hand and looked over to see Storm lying in the bed beside him. The dog burrowed his nose into Kane's palm, needing to be petted. When he was, his tail wagged happily.

"You were having a bad dream."

Kane nodded.

"Are you in pain?"

Again the nod of his head.

"I have an opiate that should help." She poured water from a pitcher and returned to his side to lift his head.

He drank, then fell back weakly against the pillow. "What is the time?"

"Almost noon."

"Noon?" He sat up and waited for the room to stop spinning. "I must speak with the lord mayor's men before they leave for London."

"To confess?"

"Aye." He saw her quick frown and caught her hand. "Listen to me, Bethany. I need you to understand."

"I understand that you believe what Oswald said. That you are somehow undeserving of your wealth and title because you weren't born to them. And you intend to cast them aside with this confession."

"Oswald spoke the truth. I'm a bastard. A…mongrel." He glanced at the dog beside him, and Bethany understood their bond. "The earl of Alsmeeth and his wife couldn't have a child. And so they plucked me from the foundling home and lavished me with love and all the things I would have only dreamed of. I didn't know it, of course. I was just an infant. But when my father finally told me, it explained so much. This wild streak in me tells me that I can never be what they'd wanted. I'm not a gentleman. I went out at night, dressed like an outlaw, and relieved men of their valuables.''

''And returned them in such a way that they not only got back what was taken, but had an opportunity to see how others live, as well.''

He sighed. ''But I was a thief all the same. I have no right to claim the title of earl.''

''But don't you have yearnings? The desire to be free?''

''Aye, Bethany. I yearn to live as you do. To sail the seas. To ride about whenever, wherever I please. To live my life without pretense.''

''And so this makes you less of a gentleman?''

He nodded. ''Aye.''

''Oh, Kane. How can I make you see how wrong you are?''

He lifted a hand to her cheek. ''You can't, my love. So you mustn't try to stop me.'' He crossed the room and began to dress. ''I intend to tell the lord mayor's men everything. And if they insist that I accompany them back to London, so be it.''

As he picked up his waistcoat she crossed the room to touch a hand to his arm. ''The lord mayor's men left two days ago.''

''Two days? You said it was near noon.''

''Aye. But you didn't ask what day.''

''I've been asleep for that long?''

''Aye, my love.''

''And you've been with me the whole time?''

She nodded. ''Huntley came, and brought you fresh clothes. And, of course, Storm, who had been howling with misery ever since you left him. Mistress Dove sent the opiates and some broth, which I forced down your throat from time to time. And my family has come and gone, hoping with each hour you slept that you would awaken refreshed and renewed.''

Refreshed and renewed. He bowed his head for a moment, humbled by the love and affection of so many good people. He was undeserving of such loyalty. He lifted his head and came to a decision. He took Bethany's hands in his and looked deeply into her eyes, hoping to soften the blow. ''I must go to London.''

''Nay, Kane—''

''Hush, love. I know you mean well. But if I am ever to deserve this life of privilege I've been given, I must risk it all for the truth. Only then will I be free. Do you understand?''

Tears filled her eyes, then spilled over, coursing down her cheeks. ''Please don't go, Kane. If you do, I fear I'll never see you again.''

''Tell me you understand, love. I need to hear it.''

Her lips trembled. She nearly choked on the lump in her throat. But through a veil of tears she managed to whisper, ''I understand. And I love you for it. But I can't bear the thought of what lies ahead.''

''Shhh.'' He needed no reminder of that. The memory of Fleet was indelibly etched into his heart and soul. He pressed his mouth to hers and tasted the salt of her tears. ''Take care of Storm. Know always that I love you, Bethany.''

He dressed quickly, and then he was gone. Striding swiftly down the stairs of the tavern, and down to the wharf. Leaving Bethany at the window to watch as his ship prepared to depart for London. With the possibility that the man she loved could spend the rest of his life in Fleet Prison.

* * *

Kane's hands and feet were shackled as he was led before the magistrate. His chin and cheeks were covered with a dark growth of beard. His hair, untrimmed, fell over the collar of his filthy shirt.

His confession was the talk of London. Word of it had filtered all the way to Cornwall, where in the village of Land's End, nearly every citizen claimed to have been a victim of the gentleman bandit. Since learning that the earl of Alsmeeth was the Lord of the Night, their stories had changed considerably. Women old and young told of being stopped in the night and kissed by the handsome highwayman. Poor men told of being given coins by the outlaw, and rich men claimed to have received even more gold than had been taken from them. It was the stuff of legends, and everyone wanted to be a part of it.

The great hall was filled to overflowing with people eager to see this titled gentleman bandit. Outside on the streets there was a festive air as crowds gathered. Vendors sold pastries, and artists offered crude drawings of the handsome thief. Young women crowded around the doors and windows of the great hall, hoping for a glimpse of him. Some hearts fluttered, hoping even more fervently that he might notice them.

Through it all, Kane kept his head down, his gaze fixed on the floor. These three weeks spent in a cell had given him a taste of his bleak future. It was even worse than his nightmare.

"Kane Preston." The magistrate's stern measured tones broke through the chorus of voices, silencing the crowd.

The jailer gave a vicious jerk of the chains and Kane's head came up. His voice was rough, betraying his treatment at the hands of cruel jailers. "Aye, my lord."

The magistrate peered down from his lofty seat. "You

have confessed to being the highwayman who called himself the Lord of the Night. Is this so?''

"Aye, my lord."

"Do you understand that the punishment for such a crime is a lifetime in Fleet Prison?''

"I do, my lord."

"Have you anything to say in your own behalf?''

"Nothing, my lord."

The magistrate looked around the crowded hall. ''I understand there are many witnesses to this man's crimes. Let them come forth.''

There was a shuffle of feet, and the crowd began to murmur as wealthy, titled gentlemen from Cornwall stepped forward to tell of their experiences at the hands of the Lord of the Night. And to a man, they were forced to admit that they were treated in a most courteous fashion as they were relieved of gold and jewels. And when they claimed their valuables at the Mead Foundling Home, they were amazed to discover that every last coin had been returned to them.

"Are you saying that not a single one of you was mistreated by this man?'' The magistrate looked from the witnesses to the man in chains.

"Nay, my lord. He was always a gentleman.''

"But what about the man who was shot?''

The man stepped forward. ''It was not this man who shot me, but one who pretended to be the Lord of the Night. I have since learned that he was Oswald Preston, who was fleeing England because of his crimes.''

The magistrate dismissed the witnesses and folded his hands as he looked out over the crowd. ''Are there any others who wish to testify?''

There was a commotion as Deacon Welland and Jenna Pike stepped up, trailed by ten little children.

"This is Deacon Ian Welland, of Land's End, and Miss Jenna Pike, proprietor of the Mead Foundling Home. And these are the children who live with her."

The magistrate peered down at them. "Say your piece, Miss Pike."

"If it were not for the generosity of the earl of Alsmeeth, I would not be able to provide for the children under my protection. He has given us food and clothing, as well as a generous stipend of gold. Under the guise of the Lord of the Night, he left all the gold and jewelry that had been stolen, along with the names of those to whom they belonged."

"Why did he choose your foundling home, Miss Pike?"

"I didn't understand then. But I do now. I believe he wanted those fine people to see how we lived, so that they might be encouraged to lend a hand when we needed it."

"Do you agree with Miss Pike, Deacon?"

The young man nodded. "I do, my lord."

The magistrate glanced at the children. "Do any of you wish to speak?"

The children, awed by the size of the crowd, were rendered speechless. But gradually, one by one, they began to speak of the many kindnesses shown them by the earl. When all except Noah had spoken, the magistrate glanced at him, waiting to hear what he would say. Instead, the boy hung his head, refusing to look at Kane.

"Thank you, children." The magistrate looked around almost wearily. "Are there any others who wish to speak?"

Bethany and her family stepped forward.

Shame washed over Kane, and he wanted to look away. He hated having Bethany see him like this. But the truth was, he couldn't tear his gaze from her. She was so fresh and beautiful and dazzling. Like a ray of sunlight to a man who'd been living in total darkness. The need to touch her was so great, he had to clench his hands into fists.

"What say you?" the magistrate demanded.

Geoffrey Lambert cleared his throat. "This past year my son and grandson died aboard ship, in service to our king. I thought there would never be a man who could fill the void in my life. But since l have come to know this good man, I've begun to think of him as a son." He walked to Kane and clapped a hand on his shoulder, before taking his seat.

Old Newton walked toward the magistrate's high perch, his wooden peg sounding overloud in the silence of the room. "I'm not a man of words. And so I'll say only this. The earl is a fine man. If I had to choose a man to stand by my side in a fight, it'd be him. I'd trust him with my valuables and with my life."

He walked slowly back to his seat, leaving Bethany standing alone.

She looked up at the man who would decide Kane's fate. Her voice trembled with fear and emotion. "My lord, this man risked his own life to save mine. He threw himself in front of me and took the pistol shot meant for me, without regard to himself."

"Who fired this pistol?"

"His cousin, Oswald Preston."

"The man accused of murdering the late earl of Alsmeeth?"

"Aye, my lord."

The magistrate digested her words. "This was indeed a noble act. And I will consider it when I sentence this man. But I wonder if anything can atone for the fact that he is an admitted thief.'' When Bethany continued standing before him he said sternly, ''I'll ask you to take your seat while I state the punishment of this prisoner.''

Still Bethany remained. Suddenly, before the magistrate could order her removed, young Noah bolted to Kane's side and wrapped his arms around his waist. ''Don't put his lordship in prison, sir. He's...like a father to all of us. He makes us feel that we're special.''

''Thank you, lad. You may sit now.''

''There's more.'' Noah's eyes were round with fear, but he doggedly spoke the words that came from his heart. ''I never knew my own father. But I've always thought he would be just like his lordship. And I've prayed every night that he would take me into his home and make me his son.''

The crowd became animated.

The magistrate shot them a quelling look before leaning down to ask, ''Why, lad?''

''Because...he's so good and noble and fine.''

''He's a thief, lad.''

''Aye, sir. But there was another thief who was called the good thief. And on the day of his death, he was promised paradise by the one who died beside him.'' Overwhelmed, Noah began to cry. ''How can you do less than was done for the good thief?''

While the crowd murmured among themselves, the magistrate glowered at the boy. ''Did the deacon prompt you to say this?''

''Nay, sir. It's a story the earl of Alsmeeth told me when he discovered that I'd stolen. First he made me return the coin to its owner. And then, because I was ashamed, he told me the story of the good thief.''

''Did you ever steal again, lad?''

"Nay, sir. I wanted the earl to be proud of me, so that maybe one day he'd think me...worthy of him."

At that people pushed and shoved for a better glimpse of this extraordinary boy and man. A ripple of excitement raced through the crowd.

Above the sound, the magistrate shouted to the jailer, "Remove this child at once."

"Aye, my lord." The jailer tore Noah free of Kane, and handed him over to Deacon Welland, who had to forcefully carry the lad, who was openly weeping, through the crowd.

"If there's nothing else..." the magistrate began.

Before he could finish Bethany moved to stand beside Kane. "Please, my lord. I wish to say this. Kane Preston is the finest, most honest man I've ever known. He spent months in Fleet Prison for the murder of his father. A murder we now know was committed by his cousin, Oswald Preston. He has seen his name maligned, his family fortune stolen, his wife dead at her own hand and his beloved father murdered. And through it all, he has remained kind and generous. He could have taken his secret to the grave, and no one would have been the wiser. Instead, he chose to risk all for the sake of truth. I beg you, let him go free."

The magistrate turned a furious look on her. "Are you finished now, Miss Lambert?"

Unable to speak, she merely nodded as she swallowed back the tears that threatened.

"Very well, then. First, Kane Preston, I will tell you that I do not condone theft in any form. But, since everything has been returned to its rightful owners, what you did cannot actually be called theft. In fact, I know not what to call it. But this I know. I cannot order you to prison."

There was a roar of voices until he rapped furiously on his desk. The crowd settled down.

"Now, I wish to say that in all the years I have judged thieves and murderers, I have rarely seen the outpouring of love and respect that I see this day. I hope you will spend the rest of your life being worthy of it." He turned to the jailer. "Unshackle the earl of Alsmeeth. He is free to go."

Bethany covered her hand with her mouth to keep from shouting. Tears were already spilling from her eyes, but she no longer cared.

"A word of warning, your lordship." The magistrate's eyes narrowed. "Find some honest use for that...energy which drove you to behave as an outlaw."

"Aye, my lord."

"A use that falls within the law."

"Aye, my lord."

As his chains were removed, Bethany stepped closer to Kane and wrapped her arms around him, while the others rushed to their side, laughing and shouting.

Kane stiffened and pushed her away. "You mustn't touch me, Bethany. I'm filthy. I reek of prison."

"Nay, Kane. To me you smell of freedom."

"Freedom." He closed his eyes and breathed her in, knowing he had no right to touch her. "I wonder. Will I ever be free?" He looked at those clustered around him. "I don't deserve you. Any of you. But I thank you for your kindness."

"Kindness?" Geoffrey Lambert shook his head. "What you see here, my son, is love and respect."

"But I let all of you down."

"Nay, son. You told the truth, regardless of the consequences. In my eyes, that makes you a man of honor. A man I'd like to call my friend."

While the others nodded in agreement, Bethany took his hand. "It makes you a man I'd like to call my husband."

He lifted her chin with his finger and stared down into her eyes. In his own was the first glimmer of hope. "Are you proposing, my lady?"

"I am. I know it's bold of me. But then, I was never one to hold with convention. Are you willing to accept my proposal?"

Kane bit back the laughter that threatened. "I suppose I first ought to seek permission from your grandfather."

A voice beside them said, "It's about time. Permission granted."

As the others laughed and cheered, Kane lifted Bethany in his arms and swung her around, then covered her mouth with his.

"How soon will we be wed?" she asked against his lips.

"If the choice is mine, I'll ask the magistrate to say the words now."

"Oh, nay." Jenna Pike was shaking her head. "You must allow Ian to preside over a proper church wedding. It will be his first after his ordination as vicar."

Bethany saw Noah, standing alone, watching in silence, and motioned for him to come closer. "And we must petition for Noah to become ours, Kane."

"Aye." Kane turned to where the boy stood watching with naked hunger. "Would you truly like to be my son, Noah?"

"Do you mean it?" The little boy's eyes lit with such joy, it brought a lump in the throat of all who watched.

"Aye, Noah. On the same day I take a wife, I'll take a son, as well."

"A wedding. A family. Oh, and a lovely reception at

Penhollow Abbey,'' Mistress Coffey was saying. ''I'll get together with Mistress Dove as soon as we get back to Cornwall.''

''Oh, how lovely. I must begin making gowns for Ambrosia and Darcy. And all the little girls and boys, who will stand with Noah at the altar.'' Miss Mellon touched a hand to her heart.

While the others got caught up in the excitement of the coming celebration, Kane drew Bethany a little away and whispered fiercely, ''My love, I'll give you anything you desire. The biggest wedding ever. With receptions in Mead and Land's End and Penhollow Abbey, if you wish. We'll adopt every foundling in Cornwall, if you so desire. But for now, please take pity on me and find a way for us to be alone.''

Overhearing, old Newton whispered, ''The *Undaunted* is even now anchored on the Thames. It's but a short walk from here, and then a quick swim. Just enough to wash away the reminder of yer prison cell, yer lordship.''

When Kane and Bethany merely stared at him the old man winked. ''Don't worry, yer lordship. The lass is a fine swimmer.''

Bethany gave the old sailor a hug, then caught Kane's hand as she glanced at the others. ''The rest of them are so busy planning our wedding, they won't even miss us.''

''Do we dare risk it?''

Her eyes glinted with humor. ''Have you ever known either of us to refuse a challenge?''

Kane pulled her through an open doorway, then glanced back. For the moment nobody even noticed that they'd gone. With a laugh he caught her hand and the two of them danced down the steps and out into a day bright with sunlight and promise.

He pulled her close for a quick kiss. "My heart is so full, I fear it will burst at the seams."

"Aye. As is mine, my love. At last you're free. We're both free." She caught his hand and started pulling him toward the white sails billowing in the breeze.

While the others spun their dreams of a fine big wedding, Kane and Bethany slipped away to spin dreams of their own.

Epilogue

The old church in Land's End was quickly filling with guests. Everyone in the village had turned out for the wedding of one of their own, to the wealthiest man in Cornwall. Kane's unknown parentage had added a layer of mystery to the occasion, bringing many of the wealthy and titled from London out of curiosity. The fact that he'd admitted to being Lord of the Night only added to his allure. All the servants from both MaryCastle and Penhollow stepped into the church, pleased and honored to have been invited.

Miss Jenna Pike sat in the choir loft, cradling her harp to her chest. Her sweet voice, like that of an angel, charmed all who heard her. Her children, who wore their Sunday best, fidgeted in a front pew. They had been invited to be part of the wedding party, and would stand like cherubs around the happy couple.

Young and old, rich and poor, serving wenches and sailors, sat side by side, filling every space in the church.

In a small room in the back of the church Huntley helped Kane into his new black waistcoat. At Kane's feet lay the dog, who hadn't left its master's side since his return. When his manservant turned to leave Kane put out a hand to stop him. "Wait, Huntley."

The old man paused. "Aye, your lordship? Have I forgotten something?"

"Nay…aye…perhaps a glass of ale."

"Of course, your lordship." The old man filled a tumbler and handed it to him.

"Perhaps you'd share one with me, Huntley."

The butler arched a brow before he caught himself. Without a word he filled a second tumbler. The two men sipped in silence.

"I—" Kane swallowed "—I want you to know how much I appreciate all you've done for me through the years, Huntley."

"It was a privilege to serve you, your lordship."

"I was a bit of a handful when I was young. I know there must have been times when you would have liked to thrash me."

The old man showed no emotion as he took another sip of ale.

"And I'm sorry for my despicable behavior when I returned from Fleet."

"It was quite understandable, your lordship. You were in pain and grieving. I've heard it's a beastly place."

"It is. But that's no excuse for the way I treated you and the others at Penhollow Abbey. But I was…ashamed. Having learned from my father that I wasn't really his son…" He shrugged, afraid to say more.

The old man drained his glass, then very carefully set it on the silver tray before turning. "I've always known, your lordship."

"You…knew about the circumstances of my birth?"

The old man nodded. "Everyone at Penhollow Abbey grieved with your dear mother when she failed to conceive. And on the day your parents brought you home, we rejoiced that they had finally become a family. Your parentage was never in question. In a way, your lordship, we had all become family, as well. You brought your parents great joy in their lives. And if I may say so, you've grown into a man they would be proud of.''

''Thank you, Huntley.'' Deeply touched, Kane did something he'd never done before. He offered his hand. After a moment, the butler accepted his handshake, before stepping back a pace.

''Will you be needing anything more, your lordship?''

''Nothing, Huntley.'' When he was alone, Kane walked to the window and stared at the tranquil gardens of the old church. Was it his imagination, or had the sun grown even brighter? Didn't the flowers smell sweeter? Even the air seemed somehow cleaner. It had become the most extraordinary day. And he needed, this very minute, to see his bride-to-be.

''Oh. Oh. Just look at you.'' Ambrosia, tanned from her month at sea, fussed over her sister's veil before pausing to study her reflection in the looking glass. ''You've changed since I went away.''

''How?''

Ambrosia shook her head. ''I don't know. You just look…more like a woman than the sister I left.''

''She is a woman.'' Darcy finished fastening the last button of their mother's lacy wedding gown, which fit Bethany as if it had been made for her. The lace was so soft it could have been spun by angels. ''At least in Kane Preston's eyes.''

''Riordan knows Kane. He considers him a gentleman and a friend.''

''I'm so glad.'' Bethany hugged her two sisters. ''I want us to always be close. And it's easier if our husbands know and like each other.''

"Speaking of husbands—" Ambrosia turned to their youngest sister "—when is Gray's ship due back?"

"Any day now, I hope." Darcy dimpled. "I can't wait. It's been over a year."

"And she hasn't even so much as looked at another man," Bethany said with a laugh.

"Why should I? Gray's owned my heart since I was no more than a lass."

"And will forever." Ambrosia looked up as their grandfather and Miss Mellon paused in the doorway. "Have you come for a last kiss before our Bethany becomes a bride?"

"Aye." Geoffrey Lambert studied his middle granddaughter and had to swallow the lump in his throat as he crossed to her. "You're a beautiful bride, Bethany."

"Thank you, Grandpapa. And next to Kane, you're the handsomest man in the church." She pressed her cheek to his. "I'm so glad you're here to walk me up the aisle."

"Not half as glad as I am, lass."

She turned to her old nursemaid. "Are all the flowers in place, Winnie?"

"They are, indeed. The altar boasts more wildflowers than the fields around Land's End."

"And Winnie saw to it that they were arranged just so," Geoffrey said with a trace of pride.

The three sisters shared a smile. It was impossible to hide the fact that these two old people were enjoying more than simple friendship.

"Oh, my." Mistress Coffey paused in the doorway and wiped a tear from her eyes. "You're a vision, Bethany."

"Thanks to you, Mistress Coffey. I don't know how you've managed to keep Mama's wedding gown in such fine repair."

"It isn't just the gown. It's you, Bethany." The old

housekeeper walked close to brush a kiss over her cheek. "You're absolutely glowing."

"I said much the same, Mistress Coffey." Ambrosia linked arms with her younger sister. "I returned from my honeymoon to find that my sister has grown into this beautiful woman."

Seeing that all his women were getting close to tears, Geoffrey took charge. "I believe it's time we go out and greet our guests. Bethany needs a few minutes alone."

As they walked away old Newton paused in the doorway. "Well, just look at ye, lass."

"Newt." She hurried across the room and caught his hands. "I might say the same about you. Mistress Coffey's work, I'd say."

He flushed. "Aye. She even came to my room to inspect me, so's I wouldn't shame the family."

"You could never do that, Newt." Bethany brushed a kiss over his leathery cheek. "We're family, and family is never ashamed of one another."

He touched a finger to his cheek and smiled. "Aye. Ye and yer sisters have always been like my own. And now I'm losing ye to another. But his lordship's a fine man, lass. He'll be good for ye."

"I know he will. And I'll be good for him, Newt."

"Aye. That ye will." He lifted her hand to his lips. "I wish ye a lifetime of happiness, Bethany."

"Thank you, Newt."

As he left, a shadow fell over the doorway. For several moments Kane simply stood there, drinking in the sight of her.

Bethany felt her heart hitch at the look on his face. "Kane."

Before she could walk toward him he hurried across the room and took her hands. "Let me look at you."

She blushed under his fierce scrutiny.

"Bethany, you're so lovely." He drew her close and pressed his lips to her temple. "There are no words to tell you how I feel right now."

"Like you're about to plunge over a cliff?"

He nodded. "But instead of falling, I know I'll fly."

"Aye. Exactly." She laughed in delight. "You're the only man who feels as I feel."

"And you're the only woman who understands exactly what I feel."

At the first strains of the harp, Bethany walked to the little table and picked up her bouquet. Seeing it, Kane strode outside, then returned with Noah, who was carrying an armload of magnificent white roses. Beside him was Storm, wearing a white ribbon about his neck.

"I almost forgot. Noah and I picked these this morrow, from my mother's rose garden. We'd be honored if you would carry them."

"Oh, Kane and Noah. My two precious men." She buried her face in the blooms, and felt her eyes fill. "They're so beautiful."

"Not half as beautiful as the woman who is about to become my wife."

"Wife." She swallowed back her tears and smiled. "I like the sound of it."

"Good. For I intend it to last a hundred years or more."

"Will I still call you, Bethany?" Noah asked. "Or may I call you mother?"

"You'll call me whatever you feel in your heart." Bethany brushed a kiss over the boy's cheek and his smile bloomed.

"Then I shall call you mama and papa," he said as he walked from the room with his hand on the dog's head.

For a moment Kane and Bethany were too moved to speak. Swallowing the stone that was stuck in his throat,

Kane started out the door, then returned to press a kiss to her lips. "Hurry, love. I'm eager to begin our life together."

"Aye. As am I." She watched as he and Noah strode up the aisle to stand beside the newly ordained Vicar Ian Welland, and old Vicar Thatcher Goodwin, who had argued that it wasn't proper to allow a dog to be part of a wedding ceremony. But, as Bethany had pointed out, the Lambert family had rarely cared about tradition.

The children gathered around them, as colorful as butterflies.

Bethany paused at the back of the church and placed her hand on her grandfather's arm. "Ready, Grandpapa?"

"Aye, lass. And I can tell, by that gleam in your eye, that you're ready, too, Bethany."

"I am, Grandpapa."

Ready to make a life with the man she loved. Ready to become a family, with Noah at the core. Ready to savor every adventure. For she had a feeling that the one she was about to begin would be the greatest adventure of her life.

"Oh, Papa," she whispered as she sailed up the aisle. "Look at me. I'm finally flying."

* * * * *

If you enjoyed THE SEA NYMPH, be sure to look for Ruth Langan's new series for Silhouette Intimate Moments
THE SULLIVAN SISTERS.
Available in stores January 2001,
AWAKENING ALEX,
the story of a NYC cop running from his past who falls in love with the lovely owner of a rustic inn in New Hampshire.

PRESENTS

SIRENS OF THE SEA

The brand-new historical series
from bestselling author

Ruth Langan

Join the spirited Lambert sisters in their
search for adventure—and love!

THE SEA WITCH
When dashing Captain Riordan Spencer arrives in
Land's End, Ambrosia Lambert may have
met her perfect match!

On sale January 2001
THE SEA NYMPH
Middle sister Bethany must choose between a
scandalous highwayman and the very proper
Earl of Alsmeeth.

In June 2001
THE SEA SPRITE
Youngest sister Darcy loses the love of her life
in a shipwreck, only to fall for a man who
strongly resembles her lost lover.

HHSOTS2

AWARD-WINNING AUTHOR

GAYLE WILSON

presents her latest
Harlequin Historical novel

ANNE'S PERFECT HUSBAND

Book II in her brand-new series

The Sinclair Brides

When a dashing naval officer searches for the
perfect husband for his beautiful young ward,
he soon discovers he needn't search any
further than his own heart!

Look for it in bookstores in March 2001!

Available at your favorite retail outlet.

**Harlequin®
Historical**

Take a trip to the Old West with four handsome heroes from Harlequin Historicals.

ON SALE JANUARY 2001

MAGGIE'S BEAU
by Carolyn Davidson

Beau Jackson, former soldier/rancher

and

BRIDE ON THE RUN
by Elizabeth Lane

Malachi Stone, ferry owner

ON SALE FEBRUARY 2001

SWEET ANNIE
by Cheryl St.John

Luke Carpenter, horseman

and

THE RANGER'S BRIDE
by Laurie Grant

Rede Smith, Texas Ranger

CELEBRATE VALENTINE'S DAY WITH HARLEQUIN®'S LATEST TITLE—

Stolen Memories

Available in trade-size format, this collector's edition contains three full-length novels by *New York Times* bestselling authors Jayne Ann Krentz and Tess Gerritsen, along with national bestselling author Stella Cameron.

TEST OF TIME by Jayne Ann Krentz—
He married for the best reason.... She married for the only reason.... Did they stand a chance at making the only reason the real reason to share a lifetime?

THIEF OF HEARTS by Tess Gerritsen—
Their distrust of each other was only as strong as their desire. And Jordan began to fear that Diana was more than just a thief of hearts.

MOONTIDE by Stella Cameron—
For Andrew, Greer's return is a miracle. It had broken his heart to let her go. Now fate has brought them back together. And he won't lose her again...

Make this Valentine's Day one to remember!

Look for this exciting collector's edition on sale January 2001 at your favorite retail outlet.

HARLEQUIN®
Makes any time special ™

Visit us at www.eHarlequin.com

PHSM